Heather and the Highlander

ALSO BY ELIZABETH COLE

Honor & Roses

Choose the Sky

Raven's Rise

Peregrine's Call

A Heartless Design

A Reckless Soul

A Shameless Angel

The Lady Dauntless

Beneath Sleepless Stars

A Mad and Mindless Night

A Most Relentless Gentleman

Breathless in the Dark

Heather and the Highlander

ELIZABETH COLE

SKYSPARK BOOKS

PHILADELPHIA, PENNSYLVANIA

SkySpark Books
Philadelphia, Pennsylvania
skysparkbooks.com
inquiry@skysparkbooks.com

Publisher's Note: This is a work of fiction. Names, characters, places, and incidents are a product of the author's imagination. Locales and public names are sometimes used for atmospheric purposes. Any resemblance to actual people, living or dead, or to businesses, companies, events, institutions, or locales is completely coincidental.

Ordering Information:
Quantity sales. Special discounts are available on quantity purchases by corporations, associations, and others. For details, contact the "Special Sales Department" at the address above.

HEATHER AND THE HIGHLANDER / Cole, Elizabeth. – 1st ed.
ISBN-13: 978-1-942316-51-0

Prologue

LIGHTNING FLASHED, TURNING NIGHT INTO day for one brilliant second, and then thunder snapped its jaws into the returning darkness. Girls' voices rose in consternation. One choked back a sob and another stifled a scream.

Heather Hayes looked around the dormitory room of the Bloomfield Academy for Young Ladies of Quality, where every young lady of quality was hunched and shivering in her own bed. The ten-year-old (*almost* eleven-year-old) Heather liked to consider herself fearless, but even she had limits, and this storm was testing them.

Another bolt of lightning illuminated the room, highlighting pale faces and big, scared eyes. Heather could hear the sizzle in this one. The strange feeling of electric energy buzzed in the air—but thunder crashed so quickly after the lighting that there was no time to count. The storm must be right above them. The building that housed the school was called Wildwood Hall and Heather suddenly recalled that the corner tower was quite lofty…and undoubtedly a target for lightning.

"The lightning was so bright that time! It will start a fire!" a blonde girl named Daisy whispered.

"Or the rain will flood us out," her dark-haired friend Camellia grumbled. "I *hate* rain."

On the other side of the room, Rosalind asked, "Is something wrong? Should we not stay here?" Since Rose was blind, she had to rely on the others to report possible dangers, though she of course heard the thunder and knew it was far too close for comfort. Her cousin Poppy crawled out of bed and sat on the edge of Rose's, taking her hand.

Poppy said, "I'm sure we'll be fine. Wildwood Hall has stood for a few centuries. One more storm won't destroy it." But Poppy looked a lot more worried than she sounded, and she caught Heather's eye.

Heather nodded, understanding the implicit request. She climbed out of her own bed, her feet briefly chilled by the stone floor until she found her slippers.

"Why don't I just have a peek at the rest of the building?" she said, knowing that the others were too nervous to venture forth or (in Poppy's case) had to stay in the bedroom to maintain the calm.

Heather reached for her robe, which hung from a hook near the bed. It was rather too thin for the season, but she didn't much care at this point. If indeed the place was going to burn down, she'd be warm enough then, wouldn't she?

Meanwhile, Camellia had struggled to light a candle from the embers of the fire, and finally the flame caught. She offered the candle in its pewter holder to Heather.

"Be careful!" Camellia said. "Do you want company?"

"Rot!" Heather said, trying out a term she'd only heard servants use. It made her feel a little bolder. She *did* want company, but she wouldn't make her friends suffer. Only one person needed to look. "You all stay here. I'll be back in a few moments."

Once in the dark hallways, Heather's fear surged forth

again. Shadows leapt with every flicker of her candle flame, and the storm clawed at the windows like a great beast.

"Just a storm," she told herself. "Just wind and water. Nothing magic, nothing people haven't faced before."

Thunder growled in response, and Heather moved to the side of the hall that had no windows.

No one else seemed to be up. There were other dormitories (the school usually had around twenty girls as students), but they were located in other parts of the building. No adults roamed the halls either. How could anyone sleep in this storm? Or were even the teachers cowering under the covers?

Heather tried to picture it—the regal Mrs. Bloomfield or the fearsome Mrs. Cannon pulling a blanket over her head—but simply couldn't imagine such a thing.

She reached the main foyer from the upper hallway and felt a breeze on her cheeks. Odd. The candle guttered, and Heather cupped her hand around the flame to protect it. Rounding a corner, she found the double doors to the main study hall blown outward, with the wind rushing through. Had a window broken in the storm?

She got closer, puzzling about a glow coming from the room. The strange glow flickered, but not as a lamp flickers. It was almost like… "Fire!" Heather whispered.

She rushed in to confront a blaze centered near the fireplace. The wind must have pushed down the chimney and blown the embers onto the floor.

"Fire!" she screamed out. "Everyone, wake up! There's a fire in the study hall!" She cast about for a way to extinguish the flames. She ran to a window nearer the fire and opened it. But the rain that pelted her didn't hit the fire…it angled the wrong way!

She needed water *now*. There was a teapot left on a

desk. She hefted it and found it was full. She flung the cold tea on the fire, which steamed and sizzled where the liquid struck, but otherwise roared on.

Heather realized that defeating the blaze would not be an easy feat. Still yelling to warn the others, she pulled away the furniture, clearing the area around the fire to deny it fuel. But the smoke was already pluming up, making it difficult to breathe.

Then Heather remembered Mrs. Bloomfield saying that fire was like a living thing—it also breathed. It wanted air, and if smothered, it would eventually suffocate.

She pulled hard at the rug near her feet and with a sudden strength borne of fear she yanked the whole heavy rug free and flung it onto the flames, then hurled herself atop it, forcing it to settle over the fire.

Heat overwhelmed her skin and she cried out as the discomfort grew into pain. Then a strong arm pulled her upwards by the shoulder and voices surrounded her. Grown-up voices, reassuring in their authority.

"Throw the water there, and there! You, toss that sand at the edge." It was Mrs. Cannon, marshaling her forces like a general.

"Heather, are you all right?" That was Mrs. Bloomfield's voice, and Heather was folded into the embrace of the headmistress. She sagged against the adult body, relieved to be out of the fray.

"Are you hurt?" her teacher asked.

"I don't think so," Heather said. She felt very tired, and rather overheated, but when she glanced at the fire, the teachers and servants had gained control, and now only a few flames sputtered defiantly against their efforts. Then the huge figure of Mr. Barlow (Cook's husband) took the half-charred rug and mashed out the remaining flames.

"Got you!" he boomed out.

"I tried to smother it myself," Heather said, blinking the smoke out of her eyes.

"So we saw," said Mrs. Bloomfield. "Thank goodness you had the presence of mind to call for help, though. One small girl is not an adequate fire brigade. What were you even doing out of bed at this hour?"

"The storm woke us all up. I volunteered to go through the house to ensure all was well, so we could get back to sleep."

"Heather, you're the bravest!" Daisy said, pushing her way to Heather. She put a cool hand on Heather's cheek. "You saved everyone."

"That was very dangerous, Heather," Mrs. Bloomfield said. "You could have been hurt. Or worse. Not to mention that you girls are supposed to remain in your room at night!"

"But Mrs. Bloomfield, if I'd chosen to stay in the room and not explored, no one would have seen the danger. And after all, it would be a shame if Wildwood Hall burned down. Where would the school go then?"

Mrs. Bloomfield shook her head, but smiled. "All the same, it would delight me if you considered your options a bit more carefully before rushing in. Look before you leap into the flames, one might say."

"I'll do my best, Mrs. Bloomfield."

"See that you do, Miss Hayes." Her teacher hugged her tightly, negating any censure in her words. "My sweet Heather. You *are* very brave. And that is more important than anything I could teach you."

Chapter 1

DEAREST HEATHER,

I am now settled in at my new home. It was so lovely to have all of my friends at the wedding, but I scarcely got to speak with anyone. Won't you consider a visit to London in advance of the Season? We've heard not a peep from you all summer long, though I suspect the mail may be delayed due to the poor weather. It seems every week brought news of more storms. Happily, it sounds as if my husband's (so strange to say!) estates were spared the worst, and of course London is a storm all its own. I plan to host several musical events this autumn and I would so adore for you to attend one. I need hardly say that you are welcome to stay here. Poppy has moved back with her mother and stepfather, and it is a little lonely without her, though my lord never lets me grow melancholy. Truly, he is a most attentive husband....

"Husband!" Heather Hayes snarled. She didn't want to think of husbands just now. She refolded the much-read letter from her friend Rose and turned to regard the wedding dress occupying the corner of the room.

In Heather's opinion, there were a few small problems with the dress. The first was that it was horribly out-of-date, stuffy and old-fashioned. Her grandmother might have worn such a dress. It was silk, featuring a stiff stomacher decorated with taffeta ribbons, and huge heavy skirts meant to be supported underneath by the wooden panniers contraption that sat nearby. It resembled nothing so much as a cage, and Heather hated it on sight.

The second problem was simple aesthetics. The silk had been dyed *puce*. Had this color once been fashionable? Yes. Did it cause the bile to rise in Heather's throat? Also, yes.

The third problem was even more simple: Heather did not want to get married. She certainly did not want to get married to a man she despised, who was at minimum thirty years older than her, who only wanted her because she was young and pretty, and who was a friend to her uncle.

"This is not going to happen," Heather whispered to the dress.

Heather hadn't always been in such dire straits. Growing up, she'd been a very normal little girl with a cat and a dog. She attended boarding school to educate her and prepare her for the future, enjoying life at home with her parents when not at school. But then came the fatal day when she learned that her parents' ship was lost at sea. In one moment, Heather lost two pillars in her life, and without her friends to support her, she wasn't sure how she would survive.

Naturally, the young, orphaned Heather had been provided for. Her uncle Cyril Hayes stepped in as her appointed guardian and life went on. She still went to school, and she returned home during the holidays, though "home" felt different with Uncle Cyril as lord of the manor.

And then, about a year ago, things began to get very bad indeed.

A knock at the door broke her out of her thoughts. A key scraped in the lock, and an older woman walked in, closing the door firmly behind her. The woman's name was Lydia. Heather and she did not get along.

"Let's get you ready for your wedding," Lydia announced, with a certain amount of glee.

"Over my dead body!" Heather snapped back. "That…*thing*…is hideous. And the wedding is hideous. And the groom is hideous. And my uncle is hideous!"

Lydia's eyes narrowed. "How dare you speak so of your family and guardian. What an ungrateful chit. Now come here and stand still so I can dress you. You want to impress your bridegroom, don't you?"

The wheedling suggestion did not sway Heather, who said, "He probably picked it out because he's so old this looks fashionable to him!"

"You're in need of discipline," Lydia told her. "Luckily, Mr. Webb is a believer in the rod, and you will soon be biddable. Now get over here to be dressed."

"I'll do it myself. I certainly don't need your help."

"You've never worn such a gown before. The panniers alone will confound you."

"Oh, my goodness," Heather said, widening her eyes with false concern. "Would that delay the wedding ceremony? Quelle tragique. Now leave me! I'm not stripping down just to amuse you as you wrap that shroud over me. Get out!"

Lydia at first stiffened listening to Heather's tirade, but by the end, she just smirked. "Very well. One ought to indulge a bride, I suppose. You have a half hour. I'll come back then to fix the tangle you'll be in. Lord, it will be a pleasure to see you married off!"

"It will be a pleasure to never see you again!" Heather shouted to the closing door. The key jabbed into the lock again, and Heather was a prisoner once more.

She'd been a prisoner for three days, once her uncle revealed his diabolical plan to marry her off to his crony Mr. Webb, who would then get control of her meager inheritance. Webb had agreed to split the money with Cyril right down the middle, provided he got Heather all to himself. The very idea of Mr. Webb touching her with his clammy hands made Heather quake with disgust.

And she was going to be married to him in an hour!

"Over my dead body," she repeated. She walked to the window, looking down at the ground far below.

Her uncle was not a fool, and he'd secured Heather in a room at the very top of the house, a literal tower room with two windows, both frighteningly high. A jump from either one would ensure that Heather would not get married, or take another breath on this earth.

A last resort, to be sure. Heather much preferred to live. But how could she possibly get free of this prison? She'd already tried to knock down the door (impossible, as it was a heavy oak that was probably harvested in Cromwell's day). She tried to pick the lock (also a failure, as she had no tools and didn't know the mechanics of locks). She screamed. She cried. She once knocked Lydia over in an attempt to take the key. Her uncle then hit her in the face, sending her to the floor.

There was nothing in the room to help her escape. Only a bed with a heavy brocade coverlet that smelled of mildew, a pitcher and bowl for washing, and a chamber pot that had been emptied only once so far.

And now there was the wedding gown.

Heather stared at it, wondering if somehow this abomination could be used to escape in some way. Dress as a ghost? No, her uncle wasn't superstitious. Break the framing of the panniers to use as a weapon? Her uncle owned a gun, so that wouldn't be a fair fight.

What was left? The layers and layers of puce-colored silk.

Heather suddenly smiled.

Previously, she'd tried to tear the brocade of her bedding, but it was far too thick, and anyway it would never have reached the ground. But the silk was thin and light.

Heather grabbed the hem of the dress and brought it to her mouth, biting down to snare the silk on her teeth. After the first puncture, the fabric ripped easily. Heather tore the skirts into strips, and then tied them together to make a long rope, which she secured to the bedpost. Praying that the length of fabric would reach low enough to allow her to drop to the ground safely, Heather allowed it to tumble over the windowsill. She peered over, seeing the breeze play with the puce rope. Fifteen feet of space, perhaps, between the end of the rope and the hard earth. It would have to do. Heather ran to the bed and gathered up the heavy coverlet, throwing it to the ground below. She hoped it would soften her final fall.

With a deep breath and a prayer, Heather climbed onto the sill and took hold of the rope, intending to climb down hand over hand.

Instead, she could barely hold on. She slid down the silken rope, pausing only when her hands hit one of the big knots every few feet.

"Ow," Heather grunted each time.

She'd reached the midway point when she heard a ripping sound from above.

"Oh, no, please." Scared, she gripped tighter for a second, then quickly slid down the rest of the way.

Dangling from the bottom of the makeshift rope, Heather closed her eyes. Could she really just let go? The ground seemed much more than fifteen feet down. Before she could jump, another ripping sound came from above, and Heather fell in a heap.

She groaned in pain, having missed the dubious comfort of the mildewed blanket, which lay beside her. She rose to her feet. At least nothing was broken. And she could walk.

Heather hobbled away from the bulk of the house, knowing that she had only minutes, at best, to get some distance between her and her jailers. As soon as Lydia opened the door to the tower room, she'd know what happened. And then they'd pursue Heather, like hunting dogs running down a fox.

Just then, Heather heard an enraged cry from above. Lydia.

Heather inhaled to fill her lungs with precious air, and ran.

Chapter 2

MR. MACNAIR,

We regret that the bank cannot advance any more funds against the collateral offered. If you would consider the value of your family properties, then perhaps something may be done...

Niall re-read the beginning of the letter for the hundredth time, and then crumpled it up in disgust, hurling it out the open window of the coach.

If Niall MacNair could make a deal with the devil to make the coach go ten times faster, he'd have done it in a heartbeat. His business in London had been depressing and inconclusive, leaving a foul taste in his mouth (or was that the inferior whisky he'd been drinking?). He cursed all bankers and lawyers. He cursed bookmakers, moneylenders, and gamblers. He cursed London, all Englishmen, and men in general, just to make sure he wasn't missing anyone.

He couldn't wait to get back home to Carregness in the highlands. The air was purer, the people kinder, the world more peaceful. He wouldn't be constantly worrying about the precarious state of the family's wealth, at least not for a while. He had plenty of coin with him now, thanks to selling off some jewels that made the buyer's eyes gleam.

Niall fidgeted with the ring in his pocket. It was set with a sapphire, and he had intended to sell it with the others. But when the moment came, he couldn't bear to part with it. It had been his mother's.

He pulled the ring out and looked at it for the thousandth time. It was gold, etched with a design of leaves, and in the middle, like a flower emerging from a bud, the deep blue sapphire glowed with an inner light. Niall put it on—it fit only on his pinky finger, and then only to the knuckle. He smiled to himself, thinking how small a woman his mother had been, and yet such a force to be reckoned with.

Niall cautiously stretched his legs, using all the available floor space in the coach to do so. Not that the coach was full—in fact, he was the only one in it. But Niall was a big, lumbering ox of a man, and he had a track record of bumping and breaking things unless he was very careful. His childhood and adolescence were marked by a string of clumsy accidents. His mother had rolled her eyes with every new report of a ripped seam, or broken vessel, or dented wood.

He cherished those eye rolls now. Yes, he needed money, but he refused to sell his memories. Not yet.

"Niall my lad, you're growing so fast you don't know where you end and the world begins," she'd say. "Will you only take a look before you leap, darling?"

He promised that he would. And he tried. He truly did. But young boys are not the most temperate of beings, and he continued to leave destruction in his wake.

He'd improved over the years. But it was still difficult, being the bull in the china shop of life. Niall looked out the window at the passing English landscape. Green and lush, the very end of summer, when the long, lazy days turned to the earliest bustle of the harvest. He saw a few more buildings than before, and hoped that it heralded a town along the road.

"If the next village has a decent inn, stop there," he called to his driver, who nodded. Niall leaned back and sighed. It would be good to stretch his stupidly long legs, even if it meant delaying his return by a few more moments.

Soon they rode into a little crossroads town, with a smattering of buildings to cater to the needs of locals and travelers alike. The coach pulled up into the courtyard of a posting inn with a sign of two swans hanging above the door. Niall stepped out, grateful for the open air.

"See to the horses, Tavish, and grab a quick meal for yourself and more food for the coach. After we get back on the road, I don't want to stop till nightfall. Now I need a walk. Won't be more than a quarter hour."

"Aye, sir. I want to look at that front wheel, anyway. It's wobbly and I don't like it," Tavish said, accepting the coins Niall handed him to cover the costs.

Then Niall passed through the courtyard entry and headed down the high street. He walked fast, swinging his arms as much as he could. Not exactly the picture of a gentleman, but no one knew him here. Who would care? He was just another traveler.

The town wasn't very big. Just as Niall was about to turn and head back to the posting inn, he glanced down a side street and saw something odd. A group of men surrounded a woman whose stance was like a cornered cat. Her dress was shabby, dated, and fit badly. Perhaps it wasn't her dress at all. Was she some sort of escapee from a local asylum? He took in her unbound blonde hair and bare feet. More than that, he caught the animal fear in her face.

His blood heated and his muscles tensed, reacting to that primal emotion. No one should ever have to be stalked like prey, least of all a young woman who obviously needed help in the first place.

"Get away from me!" the woman warned the circle of men, her voice rising clear through the air all the way to Niall's ears. She raised her arms, her hands curled into fists, as if a butterfly decided to turn prizefighter. She looked commendably fierce, but one girl against a gang of men? Not exactly a fair fight.

This is no good, Niall thought, sensing the anger and jumpiness in the mob. Any second now, things would turn violent. Unless he could stop it.

"Ah, there ye are, my girl!" he called out, surprising everyone—including the girl, whose wide brown eyes locked on him.

"Where've you got off to, lass?" he continued, easily pushing past the spectators as he made his way toward the center of commotion. "I've been looking everywhere for you. Come on, we've got to go. Spent enough time on your account. Come *on*," he repeated, taking her by the elbow.

She gasped in indignation, but didn't actually get any words out, perhaps too flummoxed to reply to his nonsense.

However, one of the men who'd been taunting her stepped up to Niall.

"You know this woman?" he asked, his breath fogged with the smell of gin. "You ought to keep a better eye on her. She's been wandering up and down the high street begging for a ride from any man she sees, and all the while dressed like a wh—"

Quicker than thought, Niall lashed out with one arm,

grabbing the man's shirt in his hand and pulling him toward Niall.

"Best not say that word in front of me," he warned in a cold tone. "Or her."

"Then you'd best take her out of this town. We got standards here."

Niall sneered at the man. "I can see the sort of standards here, ye radge. Stinking drunk before noon, harassing young women who can't fight you off."

Just then, he sensed the girl move, trying to slip away while his back was turned. He reached out and took her by the hand without looking.

"Right you are, lass," he said, ignoring the girl's struggle to extricate herself from his grip. "We'd best be on our way."

Niall pivoted and stepped close to her, both to shield her from the other men and to ensure that she wouldn't bolt.

"Who the blazes are you?" she said in a tone that was very nearly a growl. "I don't know you. Did Uncle Cyril send more men—no, it's too fast…"

He didn't know what she was going on about, so he said, "Never mind who I am, lass. Just think of me as the guard dog you need to keep those lads from getting ideas. I promise I've got no ill intent."

She glanced at him, the fear in her eyes changing to curiosity. "In that case, would you mind walking me as far as the posting inn? The Double Swan?"

"As it happens, that's where I'm headed myself."

"You're traveling through here?" she asked, with hope in her voice.

"Aye, back to Scotland."

"Oh." She sounded more subdued. Disappointed, even. Wherever she was hoping to go, Scotland wasn't on the list.

"My name is Niall MacNair," he said, remembering his manners. "Are you all right?"

"I am in one piece, sir. Thank you."

"That's not what I asked." He also noticed that she avoided offering her own name.

"I'm…all right. For the time being."

"That doesn't sound promising," He saw a purpling shadow on her face. "Did someone strike you? One of those diddies?"

"No."

Looking closer, he reevaluated the wound. "No, that bruise is a few days old, isn't it. Who was responsible?"

"It doesn't hurt anymore," she replied, again avoiding the direct question.

"Who did it?" he pressed. He had the urge to go find the man and challenge him to a duel, or simply teach him a lesson. He did not like men who hit women.

"Please, it's not important," she demurred. "I just need to get away from here as soon as possible. Someone is after me."

Niall raised an eyebrow. "Well, now you're definitely going to have to tell me a bit more."

Chapter 3

IN THE DINING ROOM OF the Double Swan, Heather watched the man in the seat across the table from her. He was impossible to ignore, for he seemed to fill the whole space. He had to be nearly six and half feet, and at least fifteen stone. His limbs were long, but not at all lanky. Muscled arms strained under the cloth of his jacket. An anatomist would have a field day with him.

Whereas most men would sport a white cravat, he wore a loosely tied length of plaid fabric in blues and greens. The colors complemented his bluey-greeny eyes, she thought, then wondered why she cared about the color of his eyes. They tended to shift in the light, now deep blue, now a little green and gold, then blue again…

Lord, she must be starving to be so addle-brained, gaping at a stranger.

Just then, a serving girl slid two plates heaped with food onto the table. Heather inhaled, the smell of roast beef and potatoes nearly making her faint.

"Did we request food?" she asked, not remembering any such conversation. She had no money to pay for a meal!

"I did, when we came in. You looked in need of a few

bites." He paused, watching her internal battle between hunger and propriety. "It's on my bill. Consider it part of the rescue."

"That's very kind of you."

"Not particularly. You're going to pay me back with a true story while we dine."

"A true story?" Heather put down the cider she'd just picked up.

"Aye. That's only fair."

"So what do you want to know?" she asked.

"Let's begin with why you're running away," he said.

"Running away?" Heather asked indignantly (*very* indignantly, considering that she had, in fact, run away). "No, not at all! I'm, uh, going to the city to work as a seamstress."

"Oy, are you a bad liar." He caught one of her hands in his own, examining it with a critical eye—and a caressing touch. "You never worked for a living before. You were raised as a lady." Heather wanted to take her hand back… or did she? It was actually quite nice to be held like that.

He went on, "By your speech and your manners, you're gentry. And gently born ladies don't simply become seamstresses on a whim. Which means you're running away." Finally, he released her hand. "Eat. Your beef's getting cold."

Heather picked up her fork and took a bite, chewing rapturously. When she swallowed, she said, "I don't know why you're so interested. It's my own problem, and I'll solve it."

"When your problem resulted in you getting hounded by a gang of country bampots, I became interested. What's the matter? Is it something scandalous?" His leer was too comical to be insulting.

Heather laughed in spite of herself. She sobered as she

remembered why she left. "It's merely…oh, I can't explain…you would call me silly for even attempting it."

"How will you know what I'd call you unless you tell me?" Niall pressed gently.

"But we're strangers," Heather protested.

Niall said, "All the more reason to spill out your story. I'm a clean slate, an unbiased listener."

Heather stared at him for a moment. He looked sincere.

So she said, "I *am* gentry. My name is Heather Hayes, and until yesterday I lived with my uncle, who is my legal guardian."

"The one who hit you." Niall guessed, gesturing to the bruise on her face.

"He was angry at me for opposing his choice of husband."

"So you're running away. Why have you not got further already? The Double Swan is a posting inn, so you can surely get a ride with any passing coach to your destination. Or did your odd attire prevent any coach drivers from accepting your money? As far as I know, they'll let anyone ride if they can pay."

"I…do not have any money with me," she admitted. "I left in rather a rush."

"Ah." There was a world of understanding in that one syllable.

Heather went on, "My attire was one more way of his to make leaving more difficult. So you see, I just need to be able to stay in one place for a bit. Then I can write to a friend and request a small loan. I'm very good friends with the Duchess of Lyon."

"Are you," he said, skepticism now creeping into his voice. "Can she lend you a pair of shoes too? You're in need."

"Our feet are different sizes!" Heather retorted, realizing he didn't believe her. She went on, "Or I could go to Wildwood Hall, that's where I went to school."

"With the duchess, no doubt."

"As a matter of fact, yes." Heather glared at him. "Or London, I have a friend in London."

"Another duchess?"

"A viscountess, actually."

"Of course she is. However, I'm afraid London is very far from here," he noted, his expression both sympathetic and cautioning.

She knew why. A woman with no money and no protection would never reach any destination she was interested in. She'd be assaulted or worse long before she ever got close.

He tapped the table. "Look, finish eating before we discuss anything further. Food always helps me think."

It was solid advice, and Heather took it to heart, diving into the meal with all the gusto one got from not eating for a full day.

Just as Heather was sopping up the last of her sauce with a piece of bread, a man's voice boomed out from the hall that separated the dining room from the other half of the inn. He bellowed for the proprietor, and the tone of the voice was unmistakable.

Heather's stomach dropped, the food sitting in it like a brick. "Oh, no. I know that voice. They're here," she whispered.

"Your uncle?"

"Well, maybe not my uncle. But Brom is," she clarified, picturing the brute her uncle employed. "That's his man. My Uncle Cyril will be following. Brom is always in the vanguard." Heather's hand tightened around the handle of the table knife, as if that would be a sufficient weapon against Brom, who could pick her up and toss her into a cart without breathing hard…or caring if he broke her back.

Niall's gaze lingered on her white-knuckled grip. Then he abruptly gestured to the serving girl, who hurried over.

"Yes, sir?" she asked.

"That man who's yelling in the next room…he needs to be kept occupied for a few moments." He handed the girl a silver coin. "Ask him what he's looking for and then spin him a tale that will send him in a different direction, preferably south."

"Please," Heather added, her expression tight. "He's after me."

The maid looked at her, and then suddenly nodded with comprehension. She took the coin and said, "One of those, eh? I'll tell him I saw a young lady beg a ride from a man heading south toward London. He'll be off like a…"

But it was too late, for they all heard a man responding to Brom's demands, saying, "Oh, aye, there's a girl like that here now. Just this way, sir…"

"Go out that back door," the maid told Heather, helping her out of the booth. "Take a left and you can get round the stables from the back way. Ask for Stephen, he'll help you get saddled and out of here. *Go.*"

Heather moved as fast as she could. The smell of the stables was strong and Heather needed no guidance to reach it. She nearly bumped into a stablehand leading a sweating roan to a stall.

"That's Brom's horse," she said to Niall, who was following closely. "He must have ridden like the devil."

"Help you, sir, miss?" the stablehand asked, uncertain of this conversation.

Niall took over. "If you're Stephen, then yes. The man

who rode the roan is after this girl, and we'd rather he not find her."

"If he treats people as poorly as his animals, I can see why you'd avoid him," Stephen said. "So you need to leave, eh?"

"Where's your coach and driver?" Heather asked Niall anxiously.

"Can't take the coach. Tavish is tending to a shifty wheel, and we need to move fast." He looked over the horses, then nodded to Stephen. "That black stallion is one of mine. He's been fed, eh?"

"Yes, sir. He'll be ready to ride." Stephen moved to the stall and began to saddle the massive black stallion.

"You're leaving your coach and man behind?" Heather asked in surprise.

"He's a smart one. He'll catch up. Come now."

Niall mounted the horse in an instant, and then held out an arm to assist her. With a whoosh she was sitting more or less on his lap, her legs dangling over his right thigh.

He slipped his arms around her to take the reins. "Comfortable?" he asked.

"Hardly."

He glanced at the stable doors, front and back. Then he dropped a few coins to Stephen. "Any way to block the main entrance after we leave?"

"I'll think of something, sir," Stephen said with a nasty grin.

Niall rode out of the stable and then past the courtyard entrance at a steady trot.

"Can't we hurry?" she whispered.

"That would attract attention," he returned. "Lean into me."

"What?"

"You'll be less visible. Quickly, Miss Hayes."

She leaned against him, ducking her head to his chest, using his shoulders as a shield. Heather realized he'd angled himself and the horse to make Heather very hard to see from the dining room's sightlines. Whatever else this man was, he was clever.

They'd turned onto the main road and Heather was breathing a sigh of relief when she heard the enraged voice of Brom.

"Oy, Heather, you chit! You get back here or I'll tan your hide when I reach you."

"*Now* can we hurry?" Heather gasped, pressing closer to Niall.

He answered by muttering to the horse and pressing his heels to its flanks. The black stallion shot off down the road like a bullet.

They left the village behind a moment later, the astonished faces of the people in the street blurred and indistinct. Heather gave an involuntary squeak of alarm. She'd never gone this fast on a horse in her whole life, and the streaks of green trees and grey rocks and earth-brown road made her dizzy. Surely she was riding to her death. Either Niall MacNair was insane and he was going to get them both thrown, or Brom would catch up and snag her right from the saddle. To prevent that second event from happening, Heather clung to the massive body, her right hand curled tight around Niall's shoulder, the left clutching the lapel of his jacket.

Niall rode fast but well, controlling the horse with the confidence of someone born to it. His arms held her firmly even while he was concentrating on riding, and Heather relaxed a little, since it seemed she wasn't going to be thrown to the ground.

When another track intersected the road, Niall took it,

turning left.

"Where are we going?" she gasped.

"Anywhere off the main road. Don't worry, I never get lost."

That was the least of her worries right now. In fact, Heather wouldn't mind being lost to the world. That way, her uncle couldn't find her.

Niall rode for some time, turning from one path to another to another, seemingly at random. After a while, he slowed the horse's pace, conserving energy. Niall's arms dropped a bit, the reins now held only loosely in his right hand. His left came to rest on her shoulder, cradling her to his chest.

"You holding up?" he asked.

She nodded, then realized that his chest was heaving in the aftermath of the chase, and his body was hot against hers. She breathed in the scents of horse and leather and sweaty human male, the last being totally foreign to her.

Salt. Musk. Something else. Her nostrils flared, trying to identify it. Not unpleasant, exactly. Intriguing…

"Where are we?" she asked, it being the most pertinent question (and a distraction from his more physical presence).

"Who knows," he replied.

"You said you never get lost!"

"I don't. But that doesn't mean I always know where I am."

She pulled away—or rather, she tried to, but there were limits when one is on a horse, encircled in the arms of a strong man with bluey-greeny eyes. "I have no patience for riddles, sir. I think it would be best if you put me down, now, and I will trouble you no longer." Then she added hastily, "Though it was very kind of you to help me get away from Brom. I do appreciate your efforts, especially as they must come at considerable inconvenience to your own plans."

His lip twitched in amusement. "You *are* a proper miss, aren't you? But then, you must know that the one thing I can't do is to leave you on the side of a track in some unknown corner of the country. It would be like leaving you to the wolves."

Heather frowned. "Then what will you do?"

"I'll continue on until we reach a suitable spot. With luck, my driver Tavish may even meet us soon."

"But we're lost."

"Not at all. Tavish and I have a method should we be separated. Two lefts, one right. Follow that pattern every time you come to a place in the road where there's a crossing or fork, and you'll never get lost."

"Oh, that's clever. Wait. Why have you ever devised such a method in the first place?"

"Nothing wrong with being prepared," he replied (rather evasively, in Heather's opinion).

While this discussion was going on, the horse continued to trot, and then Niall pointed to a right fork. "See? This is our right turn. The following two will be left. Understand?"

"Perfectly, since I'm not an idiot," Heather replied in a frosty tone. She felt something about this situation ought to be cool, since she was still conscious of the heat between them.

"Never said you were. But now that we've some leisure to chat, I think a few more details about your... adventure...are in order," he said.

Fair enough. He did gallop through seemingly half the shire on Heather's account.

She sighed, and said, "The crux of the matter is what I told you before. In particular, my uncle wants to marry me off to a friend of his, who's about thirty years older than I. You think I'm exaggerating," Heather accused him, when she saw his wry smile again.

"You truly had no admirers to your taste?" he asked, intently.

"None," Heather said. "For most of my life, I didn't think about courtship or marriage at all. I knew that I was due a modest inheritance when I turn twenty-one, so I thought I'd be able to wait to receive that, and then decide about a husband. But my life has been very sheltered since my school days…and only recently did I come to consider just how much my uncle has proscribed my social contacts. I thought it was because he wished to protect me, but…" She shrugged.

"And he has a particular suitor in mind for you."

"One of his cronies. Not a close friend, but close enough, I suppose, that he's willing to marry me off to the man."

"When is your birthday?"

"I'll be twenty-one in six weeks. First week of October."

"Hence the hurry."

"If I hadn't ripped the wedding dress to strips and got out the window, I'd be a bride already."

He leaned back. "What did you say? A window?"

"I'd been locked in a room on the highest level of the house," she explained. "I tried to leave through the front door earlier last week, but I was caught."

"You're like a princess in a tower!" he said in astonishment. "Does that make me a knight errant? What century are we in?"

"The nineteenth, sir. But it may as well be the thirteenth, for all the difference it makes to a woman."

"It can't be as bad as all that. Soon you'll be able to

claim your little inheritance and be a rabble-rousing suffragette or whatever it is you're hoping for."

"Schoolteacher, most likely," Heather replied. "Anyway, the money wasn't important, not compared to…" She struggled for the right word.

"Saorsa," Niall supplied. "Er, that's liberty…more or less."

"Liberty, then," Heather agreed. "I just don't know how long I can survive on my own. Six weeks feels like a lifetime." She felt a sense of despair rising in her chest. "I am sorry to heap this story on you."

"I did ask," he said slowly, as if thinking.

"Yes, but you were surely hoping for a story more amusing, and less tiresome."

"On the contrary, I haven't been this entertained in weeks."

"Oh, well. I am glad that I have entertained you," she replied tartly.

"Miss Hayes, you are too sweet for sarcasm. It doesn't suit you."

"Excuse me? How would you know what suits me? We are, as I said before, strangers."

Niall did not reply to that, but the fact that she was essentially sitting in his lap, albeit astride a horse, didn't exactly help her argument.

Just then, as if to make things worse, thunder rumbled.

Chapter 4

NIALL SAW HEATHER'S DISMAY AS she cast a look at the sky. He hadn't noticed the change in the weather (being rather distracted by the fugitive bride in his arms), but now he saw that the clouds were gathering quickly.

"Maybe we can avoid it," he said. "Looks like that storm is tracking east. It might blow past before we're in its path. I need to slow down anyway. This horse needs a rest."

"Oh, no. We're going to be stranded out in the woods during a storm, I just know it."

"Unlikely. England is packed to the gills—can't throw a rock without hitting an inn."

Heather looked skeptical, and in truth, the north of England was far less densely populated than the south of the country. But Niall had confidence that they'd reach shelter soon enough. In the meantime, he had to pace their travel more carefully. The mad dash from the last town took a toll on the horse.

So Niall rode the stallion down the track at a steady, measured trot. He kept a keen eye on the clouds, gratified to see that the heavy, grey-bottomed masses were moving directly west to east. The thunder grumbled occasionally, but didn't grow louder.

In front of him, Heather slumped a bit, and he realized she was dozing. He nudged her. "You all right?"

"What?" she asked, snapping back to awareness. "Oh, yes! Just a little…" She yawned, raising one hand to hide her open mouth. "Excuse me!"

"You are excused. Did you not sleep well since you escaped from your enchanted castle?"

"Not a wink. I walked through the night to get more distance from my uncle."

Her inflection was matter-of-fact, and she wasn't fishing for sympathy. Nevertheless, Niall felt a wrench in his gut at the image of Heather trudging barefoot through the forest, looking over her shoulder to see if anyone was coming after her.

"We'll have to find you some shoes," he said. *What an inadequate response*, he thought. Here was a woman on the run, with no allies and no means of support. Shoes wouldn't save her. Sooner or later, she'd be located and taken back by her legal guardian, to be dealt with as he wished. Niall was all too aware of the power of the law, and how impossible it was for a single person to change it.

"I can work…for shoes…" Heather replied, her voice muffled because her head nodded into his chest.

"What work can a young lady like you do?" he asked. She'd mentioned becoming a schoolteacher, but surely such a job took considerable effort to find.

He got no answer. Heather's eyes had slid closed once again, and he knew that this time, she wouldn't rouse herself. The girl had had a *very* long day.

So he settled her against his body. She murmured but didn't awaken. Her head nestled on his shoulder, and he inhaled something sweet and fresh. Possibly lavender, if that's what she used to wash her face and hair. He liked it.

And he liked the weight of her, the softness of her curves pressing against him. Her strawberry blonde hair had got even more unruly, sending curls down her neck and around her face, softening the hunted look she'd worn since they met.

He wasn't entirely sure the girl wasn't mad. But then again, the man who came after her in the inn—Brom?—was real enough, and he didn't seem to have her best interests at heart.

Niall should have left her at the Double Swan. She was not his problem.

But she had a fire in her that he respected, and he admitted to curiosity about her. Who wouldn't want to know where her path took her?

He kept one arm around her shoulders, riding at a steady pace. When a spattering of rain hit for a few minutes, he opened his coat to tuck Heather under it, keeping her dry. He was rewarded with a direct downward view of her breasts, thanks to the gaping neckline of the ill-fitting gown. He quickly pulled the coat around her and tried not to think of her body…which was impossible when her body was glued to his. He quickened pace, and hoped that his torture would end.

About an hour later, he heard the lowing of cattle in the distance.

"A farm," Heather said then. She had woken without him realizing it. "We must be getting close to somewhere."

She was correct, and within a quarter-hour they could see a cluster of buildings in the distance. Good thing too, because more clouds were gathering in the western sky, and they looked nastier than the first brigade.

They approached the small village at a walking pace.

A local who was walking along the main path directed Niall to a white-plastered building at the west end of the street. Niall was glad to find the inn, really just a private home with a few rooms to let and an expanded dining room for travelers and locals who didn't or couldn't cook for themselves.

"Here's our shelter in case that rain finds us," he said. He dismounted, then helped her down to the ground. He took off his coat to wrap it around her. "Just till we find you something to wear," he murmured. "Folks would take note otherwise."

Heather nodded, trying to run her fingers through her messy hair. "Do I look like a ragamuffin?"

"You look like a traveler in need of a quiet room," he replied diplomatically. "Let's go in and see what they've got."

He was frankly relieved to have Heather no longer perched on his lap, because he was trying very hard to be a gentleman about the whole encounter, and well, certain things were just getting very hard, full stop.

Something about the feel of a woman's bottom across his legs, her hip pressing into his crotch to match the rhythm of the horse's stride…it was maddening. He wanted to carry Heather to the nearest bed and make her feel the way he'd been feeling for half that ride.

It was damn tempting to pull her closer and kiss her as prelude to other negotiations, except that she wasn't the sort of woman who'd welcome that. In fact, despite her tattered dress and bare feet, there was an unmistakable sense of gentility about her. And a wounded dignity that got to him—Niall's dignity had been wounded often enough that he recognized the look.

He'd help Miss Heather Hayes out, like a gentleman. And he'd keep his impulses to himself. There were other women in the world, after all.

But did other women have Heather's spirit? Or those sweetly pink lips?

As they stepped into a plain but tidy foyer, the proprietor of the inn hurried in. "How can I help you, sir?"

"We'll take two rooms," he told the innkeeper.

The innkeeper looked chagrined. "I can offer only one, sir."

"One?" Heather echoed, glancing at Niall, clearly wondering what he would do. What could he do? Demand someone else give theirs up? Offer a bribe?

"We'll take that one, then," he agreed.

"Very good, sir. Fine room, one of our biggest. Your luggage?" the man asked, looking puzzled.

"No luggage, I'm afraid."

"Oh, well, if you'll follow Maisie up then…"

A maid had appeared in the foyer as well. She bobbed a curtsy. "This way, sir, ma'am."

No one questioned Niall's and Heather's presence. No one asked what he was doing with a poorly dressed woman without any accouterments.

Everyone assumed they were husband and wife, he realized.

Maisie opened the door to a room at the end of the short hallway. "Fire is laid," she said. "Will you take dinner downstairs, or would you prefer it to be brought up?"

"Brought up!" Niall and Heather said simultaneously.

"Aye then. About an hour, it will be." Maisie scooted out of the room.

Left alone, Niall looked around the room, peering in corners, examining the window. "Looks quite acceptable," he said. "You should be able to sleep secure in the knowledge that neither your uncle nor his man will come crawling in to take you back."

Heather swallowed. "Um, about sleeping...."

Niall looked over, one eyebrow raised. "What about it?"

"It's just that...there's just this room. And one bed. And two people."

He just stared at her for a moment, not comprehending the problem. Then he realized all at once what she thought he meant to do. "I'm not *staying*," he said, offended. "What do you take me for?"

"I don't know you," she returned in a level tone.

His eyes narrowed, but then he saw her side of things. "You don't know me, that's true enough. This room is yours, Miss Hayes. I'll sleep elsewhere."

"Thank...thank you," she replied, her expression softening. Those big brown eyes were locked onto him, and he had to look away. So Niall walked to the door and leaned out into the hall. As he'd hoped, the maid was still nearby, coming out of another room with an empty pail.

"Maisie, is it?" he asked. "Come here."

"Sir?" she asked, polite but wary.

"A small task, I hope. If you can find a gown and shoes that will fit the lady, bring them to this room as soon as possible, I will pay their cost, and more for your trouble."

"Ain't got nothing suitable for a proper lady in this place," the maid said doubtfully. "Only such as women like me wear."

"That will be perfectly suitable. She doesn't need to impress the King, she just needs to be warm."

"Very well, sir. Let me see what I can find."

He handed her some coins to help her quest, and she hurried off.

* * * *

Inside the room, Heather looked over at Niall after he returned from his conference with the maid. "What was that about?" She asked, thinking that the maid was *very* pretty.

"Making arrangements," he said shortly. "Speaking of which, I need to step out for a few minutes. I'll ask the innkeeper to send up some paper and ink. You can write your letters to your various duchesses and viscountesses before dinner and they'll go on the next coach toward London. With luck, you'll have an answer from your friends in a few days."

After receiving the supplies, she wrote to her friend Daisy first, deciding that she would be best placed to tell Heather what to do.

Dear Daisy,

I am writing to you from a small village in the north of England, but by the time you receive this, I will no longer be here, and indeed I am uncertain of my final destination. Tonight, I write mostly to inform you that I have left my own home and do not intend to return. Uncle Cyril attempted to force me to marry one of his friends, and I ran away before the event could occur. You will think me rash (and you will be correct), but I assure you that I saw no other option.

However, as of this writing, I am safe and well. After leaving home, I encountered a gentleman by the name of Niall MacNair. He took it upon himself to see me fed and escorted to an inn, where I now write to you. He has been very kind.

Heather paused in her writing, reading over the last part. Her description of events was woefully restrained. *Encountered a gentleman?* He shielded her from a gang of ruffians and personally rode her out of town! And *very kind*? Those two words might be technically true, but hardly conveyed any real sense of the man.

And now she was practically sharing a room with him, though he had promised to make other arrangements for later. Heather suspected that the maid figured into those plans, hence his conversation with her a little while ago. Maisie was a full-figured woman, and Heather knew how men behaved whenever they could get away with it. (Well, she knew how her uncle and his friends behaved, and extrapolated that to the general populace.)

Heather frowned. She was out of her depth, she knew. She should not be here with Mr. MacNair. It was only the anonymity of the country inn that allowed them to put a gloss of legitimacy on their encounter. Before Heather could continue her letter, there was a knock at the door. She got up and opened it to find Maisie.

"Oh, I'm the only one here," Heather said, surprised to see her. "If you're looking for—"

"No, no, ma'am. The gentleman requested some clothing for you. Here." Maisie held out a stack of nearly folded fabric. "A gown that should suit, a shift, and stockings. And shoes that may fit."

"Why, thank you. But I don't have any money."

"Your husband paid already," Maisie explained. "Let me know if you need anything else." She gave a little curtsy and hurried off.

Heather locked the door and went to change. The blue gown had been taken in and mended several times, but it was sturdy, warm wool. The shift was cream-colored cotton (also mended and patched in a few places). Once dressed in fresh attire, Heather felt immensely better. She could have conquered the world.

Sitting back down, she finished her letter to Daisy on an optimistic note, promising more information the moment she had it. Folding the letter, she used the wax from the nearby candle to seal it.

She walked to the door, thinking to take the letter downstairs with a request for the innkeeper to add it to the pile destined for the post. But the moment she opened the door, she jumped at the huge figure of a man standing right there.

Instinctively, Heather whipped the letter at his face.

"Ow!" Niall turned his head, clapping a hand to his cheek, where the edge of the paper had struck him.

"Oh, sorry!" Heather gasped. "I didn't know it was you!"

"Who else? Ach, am I bleeding?" He pulled his hand away.

"No, it's just red. I really am sorry."

Niall stooped to pick up the fallen letter. "An unexpected weapon."

"If I'd had a moment, I'd have grabbed the fireplace poker," she said.

"I'll keep that in mind. Should I post this for you?"

"Er, yes, thank you."

Niall retreated. When he came back, the innkeeper was on his heels, bearing a tray laden with food. Maisie followed, carrying a steaming tankard in each hand.

"Here we are, sir and madam. Beef roast just off the fire. Nice hot food to chase the chill of that rainstorm."

"Ale for you, sir." Maisie handed Niall a tankard with a wink. She turned to Heather and offered a mug of cider. "Madam." At Heather's thanks, she bobbed a curtsy and followed the innkeeper out, not without another meaningful glance at Niall.

"Well, a toast to escape," he said, holding up his tankard.

Heather raised an eyebrow as she took a sip of her

own beverage. It was delicious. "It may only be a momentary escape. I can't stay hidden forever. He'll look for me no matter where I go."

"Maybe not," Niall said. He sat back and regarded her, his expression speculative.

"If I got to America or Canada, I'd probably be safe," she joked.

"What about Scotland?" he asked, not laughing.

"You mean…travel with you?"

"We've got this far, haven't we? And I expect Tavish will catch up to us tomorrow, so we'll have a carriage and driver once again. There are plenty of towns along the way to Carregness—that's where I live. When you find one you like, I'll drop you off there. You can either stay there till your birthday, or travel to a place you like better. I could give you enough money to last a few weeks, in a modest way."

"I can't take your money! Not when you've already gone so far out of your way."

"Not that far. As long as I'm heading north, it's on the way." He took a sip of his ale, looking pleased with himself.

"It's not a terrible idea," she said slowly. "Though I'm not certain I can evade Brom for six weeks. Sooner or later he'd track me down. And let's face it, I'd stick out like a sore thumb, being female, single, and English all at once."

She stood up, pacing near the fireplace, where a blaze crackled away merrily. She was so intent on thinking about the hiding-in-a-small-Scottish-town plan that she didn't immediately notice MacNair surveying her with an amused, interested expression.

"What is it?" Heather asked nervously.

"You know that's your only dress," he pointed out.

"And?"

"You're getting sparks on the hem."

"Oh!" Heather jumped away from the fire, angry that she hadn't noticed. "Bother."

"Are you quite sure you'll survive a night on your own?" he asked, almost beside himself with amusement. "Or will I come back in the morning to find only ashes?"

"I can manage. And by the way, where do you intend to sleep?" she inquired, still thinking of Maisie.

"The stables. There's always a loft above where the stable boys sleep. It's good enough for them, it will be good enough for me."

But even as he spoke, the weather outside finally caught up with them. Heather hurried to the window, staring at the scene in the last light of the day. Rain lashed down, turning the inn's courtyard into a muddy pond within minutes.

"You can't sleep outside now," Heather said.

"It's not outside, it's a stable," he replied cheerfully, though he looked a bit concerned when hail began to patter against the window.

"You'll get cold and wet and die from a fever and it would be all my fault," she said.

"You tend to assume the worst, don't you?"

"It saves time," Heather muttered. "But look at this storm! Even the stable boys will be sleeping in the kitchen tonight, I'd expect."

"You may be right," Niall agreed, joining her at the window.

Two lanterns burned on either side of the courtyard door to the inn, just visible from the window. The pools of light illuminated tiny daggers of rain racing down, hitting the ground with little splatters that shimmered and then went dark.

A gust of wind blew one lantern out. "It will be a bad night," she murmured. Brom was probably out in the weather right now, getting soaked to the skin, and perhaps freezing to death. Heather smiled, thinking that the storm was not *all* bad.

She turned abruptly to Niall, finding him nearer than she thought, since he'd been leaning over to look out the window next to her. Before she lost her nerve, she announced, "You should stay in this room."

"We've discussed that," he said, shaking his head firmly.

"That was before the deluge. Look, no one knows who we are, and I've never been overly concerned for my reputation because I'm probably never getting married. I'm going to travel the world before I settle down somewhere and live with a dozen cats."

"No dogs?"

"If one wanders by and needs a home, I'll be happy to take it in," she said. "You know, you could have the room, and I could go sleep in the kitchen."

"Where anyone could walk in and grab you? Absolutely not," he declared. He reached into his boot and withdrew a knife. "Here's a solution."

Heather stepped back, more puzzled than alarmed. "Excuse me?"

"To protect yourself. I'll sleep on the floor, but you'll feel better if you're armed. Right?"

"A knife?" She'd likely cut herself in her sleep!

"Or you could write another letter," he suggested. "They do seem to be a good weapon for you."

Heather laughed, but he offered the knife again, hilt toward her. "Take it. Keep it with you tonight. And if I— or anyone else—tries anything improper, use it."

She reached out and took it. Her fingers touched his as

she accepted the weapon. "It's not a cursed blade, is it? I don't want to wander the hills of northern England as a shade. A shade with a blade."

"What sort of books do you read?" he asked, smiling. "I promise it's an ordinary knife. Absolutely not anything stolen from the fairies, or a graveyard, or the object of a blood oath gone wrong. But it is sharp. So be careful."

"It's a very nice knife," Heather said, looking it over. It was lightweight and carved with an intricate design along the blade. The hilt was ivory-colored and felt comfortable in her hand. "Not that I have much expertise in the matter."

"Well, I'll do my best to ensure that you won't need to practice using it tonight."

Heather hoped so. She didn't want to stab him in the chest…but she would if she had to.

Chapter 5

THEY TALKED A LITTLE MORE, but Heather started yawning again. The room was warm and dry and dim, and she was so comfortable that it was difficult to keep her eyes open. Niall announced that he would go downstairs for a half hour, allowing her to wash up and prepare for bed in privacy.

"I'll knock three times before I open the door," he said. "If it's any other number of knocks, you've got the knife."

"Indeed I do."

He left. Heather was amused by how conscientious he was. She honestly couldn't have asked for a better rescuer. It was a shame that their lives were so far apart. She would have liked him for a friend.

She washed her face in the basin, appreciating the pitcher of hot water that Maisie had brought up after dinner. Then she removed her gown and folded it carefully—it was her only outfit for six weeks. Ugh, it was so frustrating that she couldn't touch her own money until she was twenty-one. It wasn't as if she was going to be frivolous with it. Heather knew well that she couldn't afford to be. She'd manage whatever income she got very carefully so she could travel and live as she wished. On her own terms.

"No more Uncle Cyril telling me what to do," she whispered out loud. "*No* one will tell me how to live my own life!"

But not until her birthday. Sighing, Heather slipped into the bed. The sheets were soft and the blanket thick enough that she felt quite sheltered in her little nest. She left the candle burning on the table, and then realized that she'd left the knife on the table as well. She was just about to get out of bed to retrieve it when three soft knocks sounded.

Heather pulled the covers up a little higher for modesty. "Come in!" she called.

The door opened a crack, and Niall stuck his head in, looking around. The sight of his disembodied head made her laugh out loud.

"*All* of you can come in," she clarified.

"I just wanted to be sure I wasn't, er, interrupting."

"Interrupting what?"

"I don't know. Who knows what eldritch rituals women perform to prepare for bed, or to stay beautiful?"

"Eldritch rituals has quite a nice sound to it," Heather said, secretly wondering if his words meant that he thought *she* was beautiful. "I'll have to learn some."

"You can brew potions while living with your dozen cats. I believe there's a term for that sort of woman."

"Entrepreneur?"

He covered a laugh, shaking his head. Then he pointed to the table. "You forgot your knife."

"I noticed just as you knocked. Please bring it to me?"

"So long as you promise not to cast a spell on me for daring to approach."

"You have my word."

Niall walked over and handed her the knife, which

Heather tucked under the pillow. "Thank you."

He nodded, and there was a moment of charged silence. Once again, the impossibility of this situation struck Heather. She was alone in a room with a man she'd only met that morning.

"I'm, um, going to try to sleep now," Heather said awkwardly.

"Yes. Of course." He stepped away from the bed. "I'll just…do you mind if I keep the light burning for a bit? I'm not tired yet."

"Oh, please do." The excessive politeness between them nearly made her laugh again. Was she nearing hysteria? Or just extreme sleepiness?

She lay her head on the pillow and closed her eyes.

Quiet descended, save for the rain and wind that still battered the building.

Heather slitted her eyes open when she heard Niall get up and move across the room. He didn't go near the bed, though. He went to the fireplace, and tossed another log onto the embers to fend off the night chill. Then he sat down, staring into the flames.

Heather relaxed, slowly drifting toward sleep. She heard Niall shift in his chair from time to time, and the sounds were rather comforting.

A while later, he got up, and she opened her eyes by instinct. He poured water into the basin, and dropped a square of cloth in to soak. Then he stepped back and pulled off his shirt.

Heather swallowed at the sight of him, hulking and half-naked in the candlelight. She had thought him muscular before, but now it was evident that she had severely underestimated his physique. He was *only* muscle, and taut skin across it. His skin looked coppery in the light from the fire and the candle flame. She could see the ridges and dips of his body when he turned to the side, and the wiry hairs on that massive chest. She wondered what it felt like to touch.

He took the cloth and washed his face, running a hand over the stubble on his chin. He reached out for something and stopped halfway.

No razor, she guessed. All of Niall's possessions had been left behind when he carried her out of town.

He sighed softly in annoyance, cast about, and then glanced over toward Heather. She shut her eyes, feigning sleep.

Niall walked toward her—how was it possible that he could make no sound when he was the size of a bear?—and knelt by her bedside.

Heather felt the slight shift in the balance of the bed as he slipped his hand under her pillow, searching for the knife. He must have seen her slide it under when she went to bed. She was too nervous to breathe.

After a moment, he retrieved the knife and moved away. Heather exhaled very slowly. What was he up to?

Then she realized. He was merely borrowing the knife to shave. Soap, scrape, splash. The little sounds repeated, mundane and yet foreign to her. There was something terribly intimate about listening to him go through this particularly male ritual.

Eldritch ritual, she thought sleepily, enjoying the sounds in the phrase.

Afterward, Niall approached the bed again. This time he smelled of soap. She heard his breathing as he slid the knife back under her pillow, almost exactly where it had been before, and then the shuffle of his footsteps as he retreated.

That could have gone very *differently,* Heather thought.

She opened her eyes a little, watching him arrange a blanket on the floor near the fire. Then he blew out the candle, leaving only the low fire to illuminate the room. He lay down and rolled onto his side.

Moments later, his breath came slow and even. He was asleep…unless he was pretending just long enough to trick her into sleeping and then he was going to take advantage of her…which he could have done already, and he hadn't. Instead he'd taken care to return the knife she could use to stab him if she chose to. Really, he was putting a lot of trust in her. She could be a madwoman, luring handsome men into "rescuing" her so she could murder them in their sleep later!

What books have *I been reading?* she asked herself. Too many gothic novels, that was certain. In any case, Niall was safe from her.

Heather's eyes slid closed again, and this time she fell asleep for the rest of the night.

* * * *

In the morning, Niall was up and about when Heather woke. He had demolished a simple breakfast on a tray, and she saw a similar (undemolished) meal on a second tray.

"Oh, good, I'm starving," Heather said, moving to a sitting position.

Niall looked over at her with a sunny smile, but then he froze for a second, and Heather remembered that she only wore the thin shift.

He stood up abruptly. "Er, I'll just step out for a moment, shall I? Not that you're not a fine sight to a man first thing in the morning," Niall added in a lower voice, hastily walking to the door.

Heather leapt out of bed and pulled on her dress. *A fine sight?* Lord, she was getting far too comfortable with him.

She washed her face and ran her fingers through her hair, getting out the worst of the tangles. When she got dressed and looked more or less presentable, she opened the door to the main passageway. Niall was leaning against a wall, one leg bent with his foot tapping against the plaster.

"You can return to the room," she announced grandly, and then spun on her heel to walk back to the table, where she sat down in front of the tray.

Her breakfast consisted of warm bacon, crusty bread, and stewed apples. A small brown, clay teapot stood at one corner, and Heather poured herself a cup.

"May I?" Niall asked, indicating the other chair.

Heather nodded assent while trying not to scald her tongue. When she could speak again, she said, "I hope your sleep was not too uncomfortable."

"Oh, I've had worse, believe me. It was better than getting soaked in the stable."

Heather smiled as she buttered her bread.

"By the way," he said, "thank you for not killing me in my sleep last night."

"Well, you didn't give me a reason."

"You could have just murdered me and stolen the money I had, then gone on your way."

"That sounds both morally wrong and *very* impolite. Mrs. Bloomfield would not approve."

"Who?"

"My old headmistress. She believes girls benefit from studying ethics, if only to realize how few people have them. I should write to her once I actually know where I'll be staying." Heather moved to the bacon, saving the apples for last. She loved anything sweet.

Then, there was a loud knock on the door.

"MacNair, sir?" a voice called.

Niall straightened up in his chair. "Tavish, that you? Get in here."

The door opened, and Niall's driver from the day before walked in. He sighed in relief on seeing his employer.

"Had a hell of a time finding you, sir."

"The system worked, didn't it? You did find me. Us, that is."

Tavish looked at Heather in astonishment, then back to Niall. "The madwoman from the village, sir?"

"I'm not mad," Heather said, crossing her arms and frowning at Tavish. "I'm strong-minded."

"Aye, that she is," Niall agreed.

"A word, sir?" Tavish tilted his head, clearly hoping to speak without Heather overhearing.

Thankfully, Niall didn't indulge him. "Just spit it out, Tavish. She's not going to reveal any deep dark secrets you share."

"Well, I suppose it doesn't matter since it's about her. The man after your little friend there, he's still on the trail."

"He is?" Heather asked, alarmed.

"Aye, miss. He rode around all the inns and villages to ask about you. I'm lucky I got far enough ahead of him this morning. But he'll be here soon enough."

Niall stood up. "All right, time for us to be on our way then. Heather, got all your things? I suppose that's not a tall order."

Heather laughed, for she was wearing all her things. "I'm ready to go."

"You're keeping her?" Tavish asked, then quailed at Niall's glower. "I mean, aye of course you'd keep her with you…why not….”

"We've discussed it, and she'll hop off when she finds a town she likes the look of. Provided we can evade this radge following her." He stretched out one arm in invitation. "Come, Heather. No time to waste."

She put her own hand in his gigantic one, and allowed him to lead on.

* * * *

In the carriage, traveling at a frankly dangerous speed, Heather looked out the back window nervously every few minutes.

"This is never going to work," she said at last. "Whenever I stop anywhere, Brom will scoop me up a moment later. And you can't keep dragging me around with you like an extra traveling trunk. What am I going to do? Brom will take me back to Uncle Cyril, and I'm going to be married off before I know it."

Niall said, "I've actually been thinking about that. The solution to your problem is simple."

"It is?" Heather asked warily, looking over at him.

"You won't have to marry that man you despise. Instead, you will marry me."

Heather stared, wondering if he'd hit his head when she wasn't looking. "Are you mad?"

"Are you game?" he countered, smiling at her enticingly.

"Did you just propose to me? We've only known each other for a day!"

He shrugged. "Sometimes when you're outmaneuvered, you have to make a dramatic move to stay in the game."

"Life isn't a game."

"Of course it is, and right now, you're about to lose—unless you change the rules. So what do you say? Marry me, and watch your uncle's face crumble? Or give in to his strategy, and regret it for the rest of your days?"

Heather slowly shook her head. "You're joking. And it's not kind of you."

"It's no joke, Heather. Unusual, I grant you. But you have a problem that I can solve. Why not let me?"

"Perhaps because I don't trust you. Marriage to a woman with no assets to speak of...what would possess you to do such a thing? And even if this plot succeeded, and I was able to take control of any inheritance I do possess...we would both be shackled to a stranger for the rest of our lives."

"You haven't heard the whole plan." He leaned forward. "We're already heading north, and we're close to the border. We can have a little marriage ceremony at Gretna Green. It's right on the way to my home, in fact, and there you'll be as safe as a queen in a castle. But we'll remain married only until your birthday, and you will be able to pick and choose your own husband. When you're safe, we'll have the marriage annulled. Simple."

"Is an annulment simple?" Heather frowned. "I have heard that it is a difficult and expensive sort of transaction."

Niall shook his head, waving it off. "Shouldn't be. Annulments only become expensive if one partner fights it. We won't be doing that, since it is in our plans all along. I promise you, this will work."

"You still haven't told me why. *Why* would you do this?"

Niall smiled slowly. "Let's just say that marrying you, if only for a few weeks, would make a few other people scream in frustration. And that will make this little scheme completely worth it to me. And if I can also perform a genuine favor to a damsel in distress—that's you, by the way—I can practically call it altruism."

"I suppose," Heather said doubtfully. "Are you sure this would work?"

"Come, Heather. It will be an adventure. We'll take this game and turn it on its head. What do you say?" He held out a hand across the space between them, just as though they were conducting a business deal.

Hesitantly, she put out her own hand and shook his. "Very well."

"Excellent. Let the game begin!"

Chapter 6

AFTER HEATHER AGREED TO THE proposal, Niall leaned out the window of the carriage and yelled to Tavish, "Drive fast as you safely can! Take the road through Gretna Green."

"Yes, milord!" Tavish howled back.

Heather thought the driver was already going at his top speed, but the moment when Niall pulled his head back in, there was a jolt and they sped up.

"God save me," she muttered. "We're going to crash."

"Tavish is very adept," Niall reassured her. "I chose him especially for my journey down to London."

"Wouldn't a ship have been faster?"

"I hate ships. I love watching the sea, but the moment I'm on it, I beg for dry land."

Heather nodded in understanding. "Hence the carriage."

"Hence the carriage."

"And did you accomplish what you set out to do? In London, that is?" she asked, thinking that she knew next to nothing about him.

Niall frowned, shook his head, then nodded, then closed his eyes. "Not to my satisfaction."

"Will you have to return?"

"Lord have mercy, I hope not. If I never see that cesspool again, it'll be too soon. I can't wait to get back home."

"Tell me about your home. Please. I mean, I know I'll only be, er, visiting, but I should like to know."

"Would you?" He looked surprised, and more than a little pleased that she'd asked. "Well, it's beautiful, to begin."

"A good beginning." She smiled. "How is it beautiful?"

"Ach, well, it's in the Highlands, and Carregness lies in a glen at the east end of Loch Oban, which is the loveliest of any loch in the country, surrounded by mountains. And the land falls to the west, so that from the top of Carregness, one can view the sea. There's no better place in the world."

"It sounds wonderful. And who lives there, apart from you?"

"Who doesn't?" he responded, as if it were a silly question. "My father, of course. My brothers and my sister Maeve. Fionnuala—she's the youngest—married last year, so she's with her husband's people now."

"Your mother lives there as well?"

"My mother passed when I was young," he said, and a shadow darkened his expression. He put his hand to his waistcoat pocket, a gesture she'd noticed before.

"Oh, I'm sorry. It would have been nice to meet her."

"She'd have liked you," Niall said, with a soft, musing tone. "Probably would have rescued you herself, if she'd been riding by."

Heather said, "You mentioned making some people miserable with the announcement of this so-called marriage. Who, exactly?"

He looked out the window. "Remember when you ran away to avoid a wedding? Well, my journey to London was something similar."

"Hold a moment!" Heather said, alarmed. "You're already *engaged*?"

"No! That is, not exactly. I mean, my father got in his head that Brenna is my match, just because our families have been aligned for such a long time. He and her father hatched the plan over whisky one night about twenty years ago. But I just don't think of her that way, and when we're in the same place we tend to fight a lot. I don't know why."

"But your father still insists?"

"Yes, but your arrival should finally get his mind off the notion, and by the time we're done being married, no one will want anything to do with me, least of all Brenna, and I can gain my freedom as well."

"I wish I'd known these details," Heather murmured, though she was angry with herself more than Niall for not being more careful. How did the saying go? Marry in haste...

"I suppose I could have explained a bit better, but—"

Just then, the carriage lurched.

"Sir!" Tavish yelled. "Look behind!"

Niall leaned out one window, while Heather chose the other.

She peered out past the clouds of dust kicked up by the hooves and wheels, and saw a shape emerge out of it.

"It's Brom!" she said in dismay.

"Damn the man. He's more persistent than a flea." Then Niall called up to Tavish, "Can you go faster?"

"Aye, if you want us all to die!"

"Never mind!" Niall returned to his seat and pulled Heather in as well. He asked, "This man Brom, is he greedy?"

"Well, he works for my uncle, who's greedy. So Brom probably shares that trait. How will that help us, though?"

"We need to slow him down." Niall dug into a bag he'd been carrying and then threw a handful of coins out the window. Heather caught a glimpse of shining silver spots before the carriage left them behind.

"How much money did you just throw away? I hope that was worth it," she told him.

"It's not the worst way I've wasted money," Niall said. "If he's like most men, he'll stop to pick up every coin he can find."

Heather twisted around again and peered out. Brom was bearing down on them, but then he did slow and stop, looking to the ground. He glared at the speeding carriage suspiciously, and started to urge his horse on. Then he stopped again, and dismounted.

"My word, he's doing it. He's going to hunt down each and every coin!" Heather sat back down. "But that only buys us a few minutes at most."

"Maybe. He might feel the urge to spend his new-found wealth immediately. Men behave oddly when they've got a sudden windfall."

"How would you know that?"

"Because I got a sudden windfall, and on the way home, I rescued a woman I didn't even know." He smiled at her.

"Is that why you've been so free with your coin since I met you?"

"Perhaps. I really should be more miserly with it," he admitted.

"What was the windfall from?"

Niall only shook his head. "I'd rather not discuss it."

"Excuse me, but as your fake fiancée, I think I have a

right to know."

He shrugged. "It's not a very interesting tale. The MacNairs have fallen on hard times, and the road to better times is an expensive one. I went to London to attempt to raise a loan, or at minimum, secure some more ready cash so we can do what needs to be done on the estate. I was only marginally successful. Not many banks look at impoverished Scotsmen as a great investment opportunity. And while certain other…businessmen, let's say…would have been happy to lend me money, I don't particularly care for the terms, which include me losing limbs if I can't pay."

"So what did you do?"

"Sold some heirlooms," he said. "Fortunately, I don't wear diamonds or pearls, so it wasn't as if I was giving much up."

Heather could tell he was making light of it. "You had to sell your mother's jewels?"

"Some were hers. She would have approved, if she were alive. The family comes first."

Heather had not found that to be true in her own situation, so she said nothing, instead looking out the window at the blur of trees as Tavish raced along the byways at an alarming pace.

And then, the carriage came to a halt.

"Now what?" Heather asked, fearing the worst.

Niall looked out. "Ah, we're here. Gretna Green."

Nervousness blossomed in Heather. "Are you sure this will turn out all right? I mean…marriage…"

"Only a little marriage," he reminded her. "And then we'll both be free again."

Niall ushered her out of the carriage and over to the nearest building, which happened to be a blacksmith.

"Horseshoeing or wedding?" the burly man asked,

winking at Heather.

"Wedding," Niall replied.

"Oh, aye. One moment." The smith put aside the tools he'd been working with and walked out into the sunshine, brushing his hands on his heavy leather apron.

"So. A wedding. Oh, right, I need the book." He popped back into the smithy and returned with a ledger, which he placed on a table that was ready for any impromptu wedding that might occur.

Heather smoothed out the wrinkles in her hand-me-down dress. Unlike many girls, she never dreamed of a perfect wedding day. But she definitely never thought she'd be married in a secondhand dress while on the run.

"Don't worry," he whispered out the side of his mouth. "A pretty face suits the dish-cloth."

"What?"

"That is…it doesn't matter what you're wearing, because you're fair of face, ye ken?" Niall assured her. His accent seemed to thicken when he was jumpy.

And no man was jumpier than one at his own wedding.

"Name?" the blacksmith asked, pen poised above the book.

"Niall MacNair," he replied. "Of Carregness."

The blacksmith raised an eyebrow. "Proper Scotsman," he murmured, writing it down. "What's a man like you need to come to Gretna Green for?"

"It's complicated," Niall said. "But the important thing is that we both want to be married. And we are in a bit of a hurry."

"You want to marry this gentleman?" the blacksmith asked, turning to her.

"Oh, yes, very much." Heather said quickly. Much more than she wanted to marry Mr. Webb!

"And your name, lass?"

"Miss Heather Hayes, of Lancashire."

"Hmm. Scottish groom, English bride. So that's why the rush. Well, let's get to it."

"Wait!" Niall said.

Heather thought he was backing out, but he instead pulled a ring from his pocket.

"You had a ring at the ready?" she asked, more confused than ever.

"My mother's," said Niall. "One of the heirlooms I couldn't bear to part with down in London. Let's put it to better use now."

The blacksmith conducted the ceremony with the confidence of someone who'd done this many, many times before. Niall and Heather agreed to love and respect and honor each other till the end of their days. At the blacksmith's instruction, Niall slid the ring on her finger. Heather blinked at the quality of the sapphire. This was no mere trinket.

And then it was over. They were married.

"Eh, aren't ye going to kiss the lass?" the blacksmith asked Niall.

"What? Oh. Yes."

Niall bent his head and kissed Heather on the cheek.

The blacksmith snorted in derision. "Got to do better than *that*, man."

Niall frowned at him, then without any warning swept Heather into his arms and kissed her directly on the mouth.

Heather gasped in surprise, and then again in shock because this kiss completely surrounded her, inside and outside, stirring up a maelstrom in her belly and leaving her breathless. Who knew kisses could do this? Who knew kisses involved Niall's tongue teasing hers, his teeth tugging on her lower lip, his chin with a trace of beard growth rubbing against her cheek in a way that made her all warm and liquid inside?

Then it was over, Niall pulling away as he asked the blacksmith, "Acceptable?"

"A sight better than the first one, m'lord." Grinning, the blacksmith tapped his book. "There ye are, sir, all witnessed and signed. People may rant, but this marriage is as binding as any in a church."

"Oh, is it really?" asked Heather, worriedly.

"Thank you," Niall interposed, pulling out his money and counting out the cost of the service, and a generous gratuity as well. "We'll be on our way."

"Whose family gets the pleasure of learning about ye first, then?"

"Mine," he said firmly.

"And I hope mine *never* does," Heather muttered under her breath. She was still reeling from the kiss.

Her wish was almost immediately dashed. A horse thundered up to the smithy, and she recognized the rider.

"Oh, Lord," she muttered. "Why could his horse not have thrown him?"

"I'll handle it," Niall told her.

Brom dismounted and strode toward them. "Everyone stop what you're doing. There will be no marriage. I'm taking the girl back to her uncle."

"Too late," Niall said, his voice mild, but with a gleam in his eyes. He pointed to the book the smith had so recently updated.

Brom frowned, looking between Niall and the blacksmith.

"Too late?" he asked, apparently not believing it possible.

"Just conducted the ceremony," the smith replied, his

own voice calm as well. He'd probably had many encounters with aggrieved parties. "You are the first to know, if that's any consolation."

"Cancel it!" Brom yelled at the smith.

"Cancel…what?"

"The wedding, you idiot!"

The smith gave him a pitying look. "That's not how wedding ceremonies work, my friend. I already conducted it. It can't be unconducted. More or less defeats the purpose, you see."

"I said cancel it! Undo it! Stop it!"

"Again, not within my writ, sir. However, if you've got a horse that needs re-shoeing…"

Furious, Brom advanced on the smith, who picked up an iron bar from the forge and held it up in a warning gesture.

But before Brom got anywhere near the smith, Niall blocked his path.

"Your quarrel isn't with him," Niall said. "If you insist on fighting about it, you fight me."

Heather didn't like where this was going at all. "Niall, please don't do this! Brom won't fight fair." Her uncle's lackey was known for ruthlessness. And she couldn't stand the idea of Niall getting hurt on her behalf. How had this become so complicated?

"He won't fight at all," Niall said confidently. "Now be a good little wife and get in the carriage, please. Tavish can cover you."

"Cover…?" As Heather took a step back toward the carriage, she looked over and saw that Tavish had drawn a pistol, probably kept for protection against highwaymen. Now, Tavish leveled it toward Brom.

"Just by the carriage door, miss…er, ma'am," Tavish said. "Apologies if I can't help you in."

Heather scooted toward the carriage door, and remembered that she still had the knife Niall gave her last night. She drew it from its sheath, just in case.

Brom considered the odds. The calculations did not come out in his favor. There was the hulking Niall, armed with a gun and knife he clearly knew how to use. The blacksmith, now holding a red-tipped bar and a heavy hammer. Tavish the driver, aiming like a sniper. Heather breathed out cautiously, keeping her own knife up.

Brom met her gaze, his eyes full of malice. "You stupid, stupid girl."

"Don't call her that," Niall warned.

Brom ignored him, keeping his attention on Heather. "Mr. Hayes will hear of this," he spat at her.

"Good," she retorted. "Tell him that I'm safely married now, to someone *I* chose, not he. And tell him that he was a most unsuitable guardian!"

"You're going to regret stealing from Mr. Hayes," Brom warned Niall, even as he continued backing away.

Niall frowned. "Stealing? She's his niece, not his slave."

"You know what I'm talking about. And don't think Hayes gives up easily!" Brom remounted and wheeled his horse about, riding south at a breakneck pace.

"Good riddance," she muttered.

Niall helped her into the carriage, then sat beside her, noting, "After all, we're married now."

"I need a moment," she said, her stomach still churning from the near-fight, and the kiss, and oh yes, the wedding. She twisted the ring on her finger.

He laughed quietly. "Understandable."

"Oh, Niall, I hope this will work. It's not a real marriage. I mean, it is. But it isn't."

"We just have to convince people it's real for a while.

Six weeks, Mrs. MacNair," he assured her. "And on your birthday, we'll announce that it was all a big mistake and get it annulled. And we'll both be on our way."

Heather smiled at him. "You really are being a good sport about all this."

"It's the most fun I've had in ages. By the way, what did that mean? When Brom said I should know what he's talking about? I assure you, I don't have a clue."

Heather shrugged, equally mystified. "Brom isn't an intellectual bastion at the best of times. He was probably too angry to make sense when he yelled that at you."

"Well, who cares. I trust we've seen the last of him," Niall said.

"Me too," she agreed. But she was wrong.

Chapter 7

ONCE NORTH OF THE BORDER, they traveled on the main road, no longer concerned about pursuit. Still, Tavish put in as many miles each day as he could, and Niall explained that both men hoped to return home as soon as possible.

"Is there some urgent reason?" she asked, realizing once more how little she knew of this man or his life.

"Oh, not in the way you mean," he said. "It's just that my business in London kept us away for a long time. A couple of months, when I thought it would be a couple of weeks. Very frustrating."

Every mile northward seemed to make both men happier, more at ease. Heather also relaxed as she put more distance between herself and her uncle's threats. The last year of her life began to seem like a bad dream.

It was also notable to her that the further north they rode, the more Niall and Tavish's accents broadened, as if the Scottish air itself was having an effect. They said *very*, but it came out as *verra*. Sometimes Tavish's brogue was so thick, and filled with words she didn't even know, that it was like another language altogether. She had to keep asking Niall for explanations, and learned more about the

Scots as people than she ever expected.

"What's canny?" she asked at one point.

"Clever, quick minded. You're canny, ye ken," he added.

"Ken?"

"Know. If you don't know, you'd say I dinnae ken."

"I dinnae ken if I can manage all this," she said. "I did not expect to be learning another language this week! I was just trying to not marry a nasty old man."

"Dinnae fash yeself, Heather. Whit's fur ye'll no go past ye."

She narrowed her eyes at him, hiding a laugh. Heather realized with a start that she had great fun with Niall. He had already become so easy and comfortable to be around, almost like her dearest friends from school. Other than the wee fact that he was a man…and a distractingly large and handsome one too. That is, he wasn't exactly handsome. (Now *Rose's* husband was handsome, with the sort of face and form that had women fainting in his wake. It was ironic, really, that he'd ultimately fallen for a woman who was blind, and thus he couldn't rely on his looks, but rather had to prove himself a good person to catch her attention.)

So Niall wasn't the sort of man to swoon over… though he was ridiculously tall and strong, with a broad chest and shoulders and arms that looked as if he still swung a broadsword every day like his ancestors must have done. No one would accuse him of having brooding good looks. Ginger-haired men with sparking bluey-greeny eyes were not natural brooders.

What Niall did have was a sense of humor. He loved jokes and wordplay and he seemed to always be ready to be amused by life. Heather had rarely laughed so much as on this trip north. Of course, she'd had very little to laugh about over the past months. Perhaps she was just giddy.

* * * *

It took several more days to reach Niall's home. Each night, Niall went out of his way to locate lodgings where Heather had her own room, or shared with other female travelers. While they were in public, he never said a word about being married, and (if anyone asked) he often gave the impression that she was a sister or cousin of some sort, without actually lying outright. He also purchased not one but two pairs of shoes for her as a wedding present, which made the both of them laugh hysterically for some reason.

She appreciated his discretion, but did rather wonder if she'd ever experience another kiss like the one he gave her at the blacksmith's.

The roads got narrower and rougher, and the land grew wilder. They were in the Highlands at last, passing by mountains Niall called the Cairngorms, and then west and north and west again, to a country that seemed to be all mountains and woods and hidden rivers, and sudden, tantalizing glimpses of the sea.

After noon on the final day, Niall was peeking anxiously out the window every other moment. He pointed to random houses, explaining who lived there (as if Heather could ever remember). Or he gestured to mountain tops or little lakes, giving names that were usually in Gaelic. Every time, he had a story to go with the name. And he kept pointing out that, spectacular as all these sights were, they paled in comparison to his home.

Like a little boy awaiting his birthday, she thought. Niall was sometimes just an overgrown puppy, clumsy but sweetly sincere in his excitement.

Heather was recalling the names of his siblings once again, determined to get the names correct when she met them. As a pretend wife, she ought to show interest in the family…otherwise they'd get suspicious. It was Ian, Maeve, Robert, and Fionnuala…

Just then, Niall took her hand as he pointed out the window to the right.

"Look, Heather, there it is! Carregness. Isn't it bonny?"

She looked, and saw a structure that rose up and up at the end of the long, narrow lake (*loch*, she reminded herself). Its grey weathered stone was broken only by narrow windows, and slender towers flanked each corner. Shocked, she whispered, "Niall! This is a castle!"

"Aye, so it is," he agreed. "Quite impressive to look at, but don't think for a moment it would do the job it was built for. It was designed to withstand sieges of a year or more. But gunpowder would level this place in a day."

"Not once did you say you lived in a castle!"

"A castle is just a croft with towers in the corners," he said, waving the matter away.

"Tell that to those living in the crofts."

"So it's a bit bigger. But honestly, it's not much grander." He sighed. "Must be a disappointment to the ancestors floating around the halls."

"Ancestors? Who are you?"

He looked over, caught her eye, and grinned. "I'm Niall MacNair, of Clan MacNair. There's a lot of Mac-Nairs, but my father is laird—meaning the MacNair. So was his father before him, and so on and so on."

"Is a laird the same as a lord? What is his rank?"

"He's the MacNair," Niall repeated, seemingly puzzled by the question. "Oh, you mean does he have a rank in the English sense? Well, he's also Earl of Carregness.

But laird means more than lord…around here, anyway."

"He's an earl?" Heather asked, more alarmed than before. "Who is to be the next earl? One of your brothers? You said Ian is the eldest."

Niall looked a tad sheepish now. "Well, he's the oldest…after me."

"You're the *heir*?"

"You sound so upset, Heather. I thought lasses were impressed by such things."

"I am upset! This marriage is meant to be a convenience to thwart my uncle's plans. But you failed to tell me that I'd be annoying an earl in the bargain. You said your father wishes you to marry another."

"Aye, but he can't dictate everything that goes on here. You'll be a breath of fresh air, Heather."

"Why do I get the feeling that not everyone will feel as you do?"

"Give it an hour, then. Who couldn't love you?" He smiled at her, and she wished she had his confidence.

The carriage rushed onward. At the gaping maw of the keep's front door, Tavish brought the carriage to a halt. Several people stood outside, most dressed as servants or in common clothes, but one was clearly a lady.

Niall leaned over to Heather, his breath stirring her hair and tickling her ear. "The one in front, that's Maeve," he explained. "My little sister."

As soon as they got out of the carriage, the tall woman with long auburn hair stepped up to Niall, scolding him even while putting out her hands to take his own. "Can you not ever learn to use a pen? We had no idea when you'd return."

"I rushed the whole way," he replied, embracing her. "What was the point of writing when I knew I'd beat my own letters back?"

"You will never change," she chided affectionately. Then she gave Heather a polite but intensely curious glance. "And this is?"

"My darling Maeve, please meet Heather. We got married a few days ago," he added, in an offhand way.

She blinked. "*What?*"

"Married. It's a sort of ceremony. Usually in a church, though we had ours in front of the smithy at Gretna Green."

"You got married?" his sister gasped. "At Gretna Green? And to an *English* lass?"

Niall patted her shoulder, grinning like he just told the best joke in the world. "Aye. That I did and I don't regret it for a moment."

"Sweet Lord, she's wearing Mam's ring," Maeve said, regarding Heather's hand in shock.

"Oh, yes I am," Heather said quickly. "Niall gave it to me…as part of the wedding. Um, how do you do? I'm Heather Hayes…well, Heather MacNair, that is."

Maeve just continued to gaze at her, rendered speechless.

"Well," Niall said with false heartiness. "Let's go in, shall we? Heather, wouldn't you like to see your new home?"

"I truly don't know," Heather murmured.

They entered, Niall shepherding Heather along as she tried to take in the surroundings. Mostly she got the impression of massive, medieval stone and heavy shadows. Though it wasn't gloomy—it was far too populated to be gloomy.

Housemaids moved to and fro, and footmen traipsed about on various errands. A giant of a man bearing a long rifle strode by. He stopped to greet Niall respectfully, and offered a bow to Heather. Of all the people so far, he was the first to take the news of "Mrs. MacNair" in stride.

"Ach, welcome to Carregness, ma'am. I'll have to bring back something special for your first feast here. Do ye like venison?"

"I think so," Heather replied. "Though in truth I can't remember the last time I had it." The last few years under her uncle's guardianship were not exactly times of extravagance—she usually ate mutton or fish. And at Wildwood Hall the fare was plain, though plentiful. Mrs. Bloomfield believed that girls didn't benefit from exotic foods. They required fresh, filling meals to keep them growing and happy. "Are you gameskeeper here?"

He chuckled. "Aye, ma'am. I bring the forest to the table...and keep the poachers at bay."

"We don't have poachers," Niall objected.

"Aye, sir, because you have me!"

It was clearly a long-running joke between them. Niall wished him good hunting and they continued inside. Heather was heartened by the encounter, but once they reached the great hall—a massive space with clerestory windows, heavy roof beams, and an army's worth of weaponry on the walls—Heather got nervous again.

A man who looked nearly the twin of Niall stood up from where he'd been sitting at a table near a dark-haired lady.

"Ian!" Niall called. "I'm back."

"And he's brought a bride." That came from Maeve, who'd caught up with them.

The brother looked more astonished than upset. "Did I hear that correctly? Bride?"

"Is your heid made of stone?" Maeve said. "Aye, *bride*!"

The man bowed to Heather. "Ian MacNair at your service! So you snagged Niall, did you? That's a feat. Years of lasses flinging themselves at his feet, and he comes back from London with a brand-new wife in tow. Where'd you meet, and what did you do that floored him so?"

"It's a long story," said Heather (though in fact it was not a long story—just a madcap one).

"Later, Ian," Niall muttered. "Heather hasn't even been able to sit down yet, and she's not here to be interrogated."

"Oh, she'll get used to us, won't she?" Ian grinned. "After all, she's family now."

"Shut your mouth, Ian." Niall gave his brother a slight shove, more to add to his point than as physical intimidation.

"What's wrong?" Ian asked, suddenly shooting a look at his older brother. "Why are you looking all peely-wally?"

"It's not the time to talk about it," Niall looked over to the woman who sat stiffly at the table. "Um, Heather. This is Miss Brenna McGlashen. She's…ah…a friend of the family."

Heather bit her lip, remembering Niall saying *He thinks Brenna is my match.* So this was the woman that Niall said he had no interest in marrying? Brenna was one of the most beautiful women Heather had ever seen in her life. She had long raven locks and glittering blue eyes, and high, regal cheekbones.

And when she looked at Heather, it was rather like being examined by a queen…and then found irrelevant.

After a brief nod to Heather, Brenna looked over at Niall. "Niall, I think we should speak when you have a moment."

"Er, of course," he said. "Ian, where's Rob? He should meet Heather as well—"

Just then a cold wind seemed to blow through the hall, and the light dimmed. Yes, it was probably a cloud passing in front of the sun, but in retrospect, Heather would always connect that moment with evil portent.

A creaky, crotchety voice screeched out, "What's all this?"

Niall stiffened, and despite his incredible height and sheer presence, now he seemed to shrink a little.

An old man using a walking stick hobbled up to the group, glaring at everyone but reserving special enmity for Heather, the stranger.

"Father, I'd like to discuss a few things…" Niall began to say.

"Hush up, boy, I asked a question. Everyone's chattering like magpies around here. What's happening? Who's this girl?" The old man poked at her feet with his stick. Heather thought about stomping down on it, but restrained herself.

Niall put a protective arm around her shoulders. "This is my wife, Heather."

"Your wife's been chosen for you years ago, and it's not this chit. Get her out of here."

"No."

"What, boy?"

Niall frowned. "I said no. Heather is my *wife*, for God's sake. She's not going anywhere, and you can grouse about it if you like, but you can't change what happened."

The laird's eyes flared open and he wheezed in a breath. He then pinned his gaze on Heather, who wanted to hide behind Niall. (Not that she did. Girls raised at Wildwood Hall never hid…unless it was during a game of hide and seek.) Instead, she offered a polite curtsy

"How do you do, my lord," she said, deciding to refer

to his rank of earl rather than his clannish lairdship, whatever that was.

"I'd do a sight better if my own house wasn't overrun by English vermin," he snapped back, then coughed

Unsurprisingly, Heather didn't have a polite reply.

Niall's brother stepped up. "Ach, father. One little lass is hardly an invasion, and I don't think she looks a bit like vermin."

"Shut up, Ian!" the laird snapped. "I'm going to my room. When I come out for supper, I expect this mess to be cleaned up. And the vermin gone!"

He stalked off, his twisted walking stick adding an angry third beat to his paces.

"Sorry," Niall said. "I hoped to prepare you a little better, though I didn't expect him to be *that* rude."

"Why not? Since when has our father ever been gracious?" Ian asked. He looked over to Brenna, and added, "Seems like the engagement's off then?"

Brenna just shook her head. "Let's assume nothing." She looked at Heather with narrowed eyes.

"Niall, where shall I be staying?" Heather asked then, trying to diffuse the awkwardness.

"This way," he said. "Follow me."

Niall led Heather to a room on the upper floor. "It's not very big," he apologized. "There used to be one long room, but we broke it into several over the years. Centuries, that is. More practical, since it's less fashionable now to sleep with the whole household, not to mention the pigs and chickens."

"It's very pretty, thank you." Heather could barely put two words together. She was woefully unprepared to be here. What a total naïf she'd been to think that this fake marriage could ever work. The family would kick her out before nightfall.

On the other hand, Carregness was definitely *defensible*. When running away and hiding from one's uncle, it's a benefit to have a castle to hide in.

She looked out the window to the green blanket of forest and then the rise of one of the mountain ridges. She walked to a door and opened it, finding not a closet or passageway, but a whole other bedchamber. Aside from a massive bed that looked like it would never leave the room in one piece, there was little else in it, and yet the appearance was distinctly masculine.

"Er, that's my room." Niall said, crossing to where she stood. He closed the door hurriedly. "Don't worry, there's a lock. I mean, I think the lock works. It's never been used, since it's assumed…"

Heather bit her lip. Of course. Everyone thought they were married, so of course she'd be put in an adjoining room to the heir apparent. Suddenly Heather wondered what they'd have done if Niall didn't live in a castle with dozens of rooms. Most married couples shared a chamber. To think that she might have been expected to sleep in the same bed with Niall for six weeks.…

The idea failed to repel her. In fact, it stirred a rebellious little flare of interest. Ever since he'd kissed her at the blacksmith's, Heather was aware of something under the surface, something in her body that woke up and refused to go back to sleep.

But it remained that the two of them had to put on the appearance of a marriage until her birthday, and that meant they'd be together more often than not.

"Niall," she began, and then realized she had no idea what she wanted to say. "Niall…I'll do my best." The words came out in a rush.

"I will as well," he returned. "It occurs to me that this all might have been a bit hasty."

"Oh, do you think?" Heather laughed despite her concern.

"It will work out through," he assured her. "We want the same thing, after all."

She nodded, and watched him go. Did they want the same thing? It was a difficult question to answer, considering she barely knew Niall at all.

Chapter 8

NIALL LEFT HEATHER TO GET settled in her room, but before he got twenty steps, Maeve bore down on him and grabbed him by the arm.

"Come and talk to me," she muttered, dragging him down the hall toward her own room. A chambermaid dashed out of the way as they passed, cowed by Maeve's angry expression.

Maeve's bedchamber was small and obsessively tidy (she used to share with Fionnuala, who'd been a sight messier).

"Niall, nothing about this makes sense," Maeve said. "Who is this woman? Where did you find her? Why doesn't she have any *luggage*?"

"Well, as to that last part, it's complicated. I don't suppose you could lend her some clothing until her things arrive?" Which would be never, but Niall didn't want to get into that.

"Certainly I can, but it doesn't explain why the lass is here at all. Niall, is this a prank?"

"A prank? No, of course not." *Not exactly.* Niall took Maeve's hands in his, appealing to her natural desire to care for anyone and everything in her sight. "Listen, Maevey-doll. I know it's confusing, but I promise that I will reveal all the details in due time. But for now, can I ask you to be a sister to Heather and help her navigate Carregness until she's got her feet under her? As a favor to me?"

"Niall, I'll move mountains if you ask me too, but I will need answers."

"Soon, sister. You have my word."

"When is soon?"

"Er, let's say a month or so." On Heather's birthday, he'd be happy to tell the world what had happened, but until then, he had to maintain the secret.

Her eyes went wide. "A month!"

"Or so. It's for a very good cause."

"Where are you off to now?" Maeve asked.

Niall grimaced. "I must present myself before the laird and give an accounting of my deeds. Like Judgement Day, but we get to experience it every day."

His sister rolled her eyes. "Good luck to you. His temper is worse than ever. He's been demanding news of your return practically since you left."

"Ach, now you know why I didn't write," he joked. "That's the only way I could deny him what he wanted."

Leaving Maeve, Niall made his way to his father's chambers. He always hated going there. He associated the room with reprimand and regular beatings, and always his father's cruel judgements.

Thus it was almost a relief when Ian met him in the hallway, clearly hoping to talk.

"I'm supposed to speak to Father," Niall said.

"He's waited weeks, he'll wait a few minutes more. Niall, are you truly married?"

Niall wanted to laugh. How many people were going to ask him that question over the next five weeks? And would he ever get the answer right? "I had a wedding at Gretna Green, and I've got a wife in this very castle. What else do you want me to say?"

Ian frowned. "You gave Brenna the shock of her life, you know."

"Aye, I expect I did, and I'm sorry for it. I wouldn't ever want to hurt Brenna, and if I could have given her some notice, I would have. But the wedding was…well, let's say we took advantage of opportunity."

"This lass of yours," Ian asked, curiosity burning in his expression. "Did you find her in London? Is that why you gave us no word the whole time? You were too busy with some whirlwind courtship? My God, man, you can only have known the lass for a month at most!"

"Try a week at most." Niall couldn't resist revealing that gem, knowing how Ian would take it.

His brother's reaction was gold, almost worth all the discomfort that this false marriage would engender later on. Ian's eyes bulged out, and his jaw dropped. "A week? Did you say a week? It takes a week to get from here down to York!"

"Then I must have met her a bit north of York."

"Did ye fall for her the moment ye laid eyes on her?" Ian demanded. (Niall always suspected his little brother of being romantic.)

"Not exactly, though we found ourselves rather attached to each other quite quickly. Heather's an unusual girl."

"She'd have to be, to want you."

"Ach, look who's talking, with yer ugly face!" Niall shoved him playfully, and Ian ducked and faked a punch.

Ian laughed, but then sobered. "He's not going to deal well with this, you know. And what will McGlashen say?"

"McGlashen can be dealt with. And Brenna's not going to suffer a broken heart over it."

"Aye, that part's true enough," Ian murmured. "But

you'll have to soothe the old man's ire, and that won't be easy. Unless you secured a loan that will save the family?"

"Do I look so rich?" Niall asked, with a shrug.

"We'll think of something. MacNairs do have a knack for survival. All the same, I'm glad you're the one who has to deal with *him* today."

"Aye, and what a treat it will be."

Niall continued on to his father's chambers. He was a grown man now, but still he felt like a child in the vast, cold room. The place never seemed to change. When Niall entered, his father was sitting in a high backed chair facing the fireplace, which was blazing. Though the area around the fireplace must be uncomfortably warm, MacNair was bundled up in woolens and had a fur pulled over his knees.

The old man looked over, his eyes beady and bloodshot. "Niall. Get over here. Stand in the light, don't skulk in the shadows."

"Shadows, eh?" Niall strode over to the window and yanked the curtain fully to the side, allowing the sunlight to stream in.

"Not that much light!" his father growled, then coughed.

"What are you, a vampire? The sun will do you good."

"It hurts my eyes."

Niall didn't give a damn about his eyes. "What do you want to discuss, father?"

"How did the London business go?"

Niall rolled his eyes. "As badly as we expected. No bank will offer a loan without putting up property as collateral."

"The MacNair lands stay with the MacNair!" his father practically shouted. "We do not carve bits off like a roast lamb. The land is our blood."

Niall had heard all this before (and in fact believed it. It was probably the one thing he and his father agreed on). He explained, "I did sell the bulk of the jewels and the gold. It took a long time to find buyers willing to pay a reasonable price. If I'd gone to the first pawnbroker, I could have completed the business in half a day. But got only one twentieth the value."

"How much did you get?"

"Eighteen hundred pounds, more or less. It will sustain the household until spring, barring some new disaster."

"Huh. You should have got more." He coughed again, sounding as if a cold had settled in his lungs. "You didn't sell the sapphire. Already gave it to that little whore?"

Niall's hand clenched into fists. "Call her that again, and I will turn around and leave here, with the money, and the ring, and my wife. You can enjoy your triumph while slowly starving to death."

MacNair sneered. "Touchy about her, are you?"

"I'm not touchy about her, I'm merely suggesting that you don't refer to your own daughter-in-law in a bad light, if only to preserve the family's name." Niall knew that his father hated even the littlest smirch on the Mac-Nair reputation.

"Bringing an English chit back with our sapphire on her finger..."

"Mama's sapphire."

"My sapphire. Everything in this castle is mine. Your mother merely wore the ring."

"Yet she paid the price for it." Niall remembered seeing his mother black-eyed too often, or walking softly to hide a limp. "The women of this family haven't fared well under your rule, have they?" His own mother, his aunt, even his sister Maeve now, who was slowly losing her light as caring for their father ground her down.

"Watch your mouth, son. You're under my roof."

"And I got the funds to patch the roof. You're welcome, by the way."

"As if I'd be grateful for your wandering, especially when you drag a wife back."

"Does that bother you, Father?" Niall asked, suddenly grinning. After all, this was what the whole charade was about. Needling his father, putting him in his place, reminding the elder MacNair that he wasn't the omnipotent master he imagined he was. "My pretty, blonde, very English wife? Does that vex you?"

"God damn you, you know it does! What the hell were you thinking, boy?"

Niall thought back to the moment he'd first seen Heather, hounded by strangers, and later when she revealed her story, showing her true spirit. "Truly, Father, you wouldn't understand if I did tell you."

"Ach, I don't need details. Short-sighted, always in the moment, never thinking ahead. No strategy, Niall. You should have taken what you wanted from her and then left her to her own devices. Once they're soiled, women have no more use, save one."

"Is that what you told Aunt Morag?"

His father inhaled sharply, the enraged breath ending in a choked sound. "Don't say her name! You know nothing about that."

"I know she was a good woman. She was kind to us after Mama died. And she fell in love with Simeon Farquhar, one of our most loyal men. I remember how he'd come to the keep to give his reports on the farming, and that he always said hello to Ian and Maeve and Fionnuala and me, even though we were children. And Aunt Morag would come over, and she'd smile like the sun came up whenever she saw him. You didn't like it though, that she cared for a common farmer. Then all of a sudden he was gone, and she was gone."

"So she left! What of it? She made her choice."

"You drove her out."

"This is *my* house."

"This was her house too. But you forced her to fend for herself when you knew she couldn't. And a few months later, when she turned to selling herself—"

"*Silence!*" his father spat. "You were what, twelve? You didn't know a thing about it!"

"She came back one night. I was awake, I heard her. And I heard you. You refused to give her any money. You told her she was a whore who wasn't fit to step on Mac-Nair land. And I know that two months after that, she was dead."

"Don't speak of her ever again."

"Why not? Because she had to prostitute herself, a MacNair woman? And yet you called Heather a whore. She's also a MacNair woman." For now.

"Get the hell out of my room!"

"Gladly." As Niall turned on his heel, MacNair broke into a fit of coughing, a wet hacking sound that must have been painful. Niall didn't allow himself more than a shred of sympathy. The old man caused others plenty of pain. Now it was his turn.

Chapter 9

DEAR POPPY,

I hope this letter finds its way to London without too much delay, for I imagine you may have already heard from Daisy and worry for me. But I assure you, there is nothing to worry about. I'm at a place called Carregness in the highlands of Scotland. It's owned by the MacNair family, who have taken me in as a guest. I expect to remain here until my birthday in October, when I intend to go to London by either ship or coach. Then I'll settle all the details of my majority and my inheritance. After that, I will go abroad, beginning with the Continent.

As soon as I arrive in London, I will call on you and give you the full story of why I am in Scotland, and what has transpired since. Also, should my uncle or his associates contact you, do not tell them anything. It is my keen wish to never encounter Uncle Cyril again. When I tell you the story, you will understand...

Finding pen and paper in her bedroom had been a delight for Heather. As soon as she could close the door, she immediately sat down to write to her friends. She'd written letters to Poppy and then her other friends, regretting that she couldn't pour out the whole saga immediately.

But it would take more paper than the castle could hold, and Heather had to be circumspect in case her uncle tried to squeeze information out of her schoolmates. That was the sort of thing he'd do.

Funny how she was once again in an upper room of a huge stone building…but at least she wasn't locked in this time! She got up and stretched, assessing the angle of the sun in the sky. It was getting to be later in the afternoon. Time to think about facing the music.

Heather resolved to look her best for the evening meal, to counter the very odd impression she made upon her arrival. Partly it was circumstances. After all, she arrived with only the clothes on her back.

Thankfully, a little while before (between letters) the maid had brought in a few gowns sent by Maeve, so her wardrobe now numbered four outfits. Of the new items, there was a day dress of green wool, a slightly finer evening gown in a deeper green, and a dress and jacket that would be suitable for riding, along with riding boots that were nicer than any she'd owned before. She looked over the collection of additional items, hoping to make some improvement in her appearance. There was a pair of gloves, some stockings, a few handkerchiefs, several ribbons for her hair, and a lacy fichu that looked so fragile Heather was afraid to touch it.

She picked up a roll of cloth in the MacNair tartan pattern, which she recognized from Niall's own clothing, the pattern on the carriage seats, and nearly everywhere else she looked at Carregness. She unrolled it, discovering it was a shawl or wrap.

Against a white background, broad stripes of blues and greens mixed with a little grey. A narrow stripe of bright gold stood out from the more muted, wider stripes. The pattern mimicked a bright sky, brilliant waters, and green leaves. She liked it.

"Can I wear this, Susan?" she asked the maid, who'd come in to help her dress for dinner. "I mean, is it proper to do so?"

The maid nodded vehemently. "Why, you're a Mac-Nair now, milady. You should wear it! Miss Maeve would not have given it to you otherwise."

"Good, then I shall." The addition of the shawl ought to make her outfit more interesting, or at least different. Heather was never obsessed with fashion the way some women were, but evidently she had found her lower limit of tolerance. Perhaps she could ask Maeve for advice as to where or how to acquire more clothing. She'd need it after her birthday…when she left Carregness.

Oddly enough, Maeve entered the room at that exact moment, carrying a small tray. "Ah, I see you can make use of the clothing. Oh that reminds me. Susan, will you go fetch the heavy blanket from the linen press for our guest. Just in case it gets cold. Scottish weather is notoriously changeable," she added, for Heather's benefit.

The maid nodded and hurried out.

"It's very kind of you to consider me," Heather said.

"Niall requested I make you comfortable," Maeve replied. "What *did* happen to your luggage?"

What was Heather supposed to say to that? She didn't like the idea of lying to Niall's family. Particularly on top of the huge lie about the marriage. "Ah…it got lost."

Maeve raised an eyebrow, but then just put the tray down. It held a bottle and two glasses. She poured and offered one to Heather.

"Welcome to Carregness," she said, in a toast.

Heather took a sip, and found the drink to be both sweet and a little spicy. "What is this? A kind of wine?"

"Mead, made on MacNair lands. Our hills produce

some of the finest honey in the Highlands," she added proudly.

Heather took another sip. She wasn't sure if she liked it or not, but it was interesting.

"Mead is an acquired taste," Maeve said, smiling. "But the only way to acquire the taste is to drink."

"Is it strong?" Heather couldn't tell due to the unfamiliar flavors.

"Oh, no, it's like wine," Maeve assured her. "There will be more at the supper table, of course. The evening meal is served at seven."

"I'll be ready," Heather said, drinking again.

Maeve regarded her for a moment, then said, "I have some matters to attend to, but perhaps we can chat after the meal. I imagine you have so many questions about Carregness before you take over as chatelaine."

Heather nearly choked on her drink. "Chatelaine?"

"Well, of course. I have been serving in that role for years, but Niall is the heir, so you'll naturally take on the responsibility. After all, you'll be a countess."

Oh, no she wouldn't! Heather would never attain that title, because she'd be long gone. But she could hardly say that to Maeve. She had to think of a plausible excuse. "I'm afraid I don't know enough to accept the keys anytime soon. Perhaps a month or so?"

"A month." Maeve repeated that word in a soft voice. Her expression was suddenly suspicious.

To cover, Heather took another sip, and said hurriedly, "Anyway, I'd love to talk with you later. There is so much I want to know."

"Likewise," Maeve agreed.

Then Susan returned, bearing a heavy blanket to add to Heather's bed. Maeve left, reminding Heather that supper would be served in less than an hour.

The maid braided her thick blonde hair, trying a green ribbon at the end, which fell to the center of her back. Heather draped the tartan around her shoulders like a shawl, liking the way the pattern complemented the green of her dress.

"Is it all right to wear it this way?" she asked Susan.

"Yes, milady. You've got the touch," she added, sounding surprised.

Thus garbed and feeling the warmth in her belly from the drink, Heather walked downstairs and into the great, drafty dining hall.

"Good evening," she said to everyone.

The men all stood, as was proper, but this time they remained standing, staring at her.

"My soul, but she looks like a proper highland lass now!" Ian declared in wonderment.

"This is the new MacNair lady?" another man asked. He was obviously the youngest brother, Robert. While Niall and Ian practically looked like twins, Robert was a little shorter and slighter, with a shock of dark brown hair instead of the ginger of his brothers. "Niall, you've done better than I ever expected."

Brenna also looked surprised at Heather's appearance but gave her a little begrudging nod.

Niall was smiling broadly. "The MacNair colors suit you, wife."

Heather smiled back, feeling a little thrill when he called her wife. *Don't get used to it*, she warned herself. The marriage was just a temporary solution.

The evening meal looked to be an enjoyable one, until the patriarch stomped in and took his place at the head of the table. Everyone went quiet. MacNair glared around the table, and narrowed his rheumy eyes at Heather.

"Who gave you our colors to wear?" he growled, taking in the shawl.

"Your family," she replied, taken aback. "But judging by your tone, I think it's best not to tell you the specific person."

"I wouldn't want to know," he snarled. "Just have to disown them, and I've got enough to worry about."

The meal was served, and the talk around the table resumed, as the family members were in general too spirited to remain silent for long.

Robert asked Heather if she rode, and she replied that she did. "I learned at school. Mrs. Bloomfield—that's the headmistress—felt very strongly that girls needed plenty of exercise, and riding is excellent for that."

"School?" MacNair said suddenly. "What's the point of sending a girl to school? Is that what the English do now? Soft! We should launch an invasion next week. We'll sweep the whole island under our rule, if the English are spending good time and money educating girls."

She stifled a laugh, imagining him attempting to besiege Wildwood Hall. Mrs. Bloomfield would likely have him tarred and feathered by sundown.

Maeve also chuckled. "I went to school, Father."

"To learn your letters so you could run the house. A girl needs only to read a ledger and figure the household expenses. All else is a waste."

"I shall inform Mrs. Bloomfield of your opinion in my next letter to her, sir," Heather replied. "She certainly will give it all the consideration it is due."

Niall covered a snort of laughter behind a cough.

MacNair slammed his fork down. "Food is cold."

Behind the table, a maid scurried forward, intending to take the dish from him.

"Leave it! It is not cold," Heather said, before the maid could take the plate. "I can see steam rising from the bowl."

"Don't tell me what's true in my own home, girl."

"True is true, no matter what. That food is fine, it's your attitude that needs warming."

"You insult me."

"You invite it." Heather gave him a tight smile. Spar with a Wildwood girl? He'd learn to regret it.

"This is intolerable!" He got up and stormed out.

"My goodness, does your father drink vinegar before breakfast?" Heather burst out the moment his hunched form disappeared through the door.

There was a moment of silence, then the whole table rippled with laughter.

Ian said, "I always thought he started with whisky, but vinegar would explain it."

As everyone turned to their meal and began to talk normally again, Niall leaned over to her. "No one's *ever* spoken to my father that way."

"That's because everyone else wants something from him," she murmured back. "I don't care. In a few weeks, I'll never see him again."

"I don't want anything from him," said Niall.

"Of course you do. He's your father. You want his approval."

He snorted. "I assure you I don't. There's no love lost between us. And anyway, he's always seen me as a failure."

"You seem successful to me."

Chapter 10

SUCCESSFUL? WAS HE?

Niall leaned in toward Heather, interested in her assessment of his relationship with his father, which she couldn't know anything about. She also didn't know the MacNair, though she'd certainly managed to needle him in the most painful way at the dinner table. Niall couldn't get over how her lovely brown eyes sparkled when the old man got up and left the table. *Round One goes to the English contender*, he thought.

"Why do you say—" he began to ask.

He was interrupted by the banging of forks against the pewter cups.

"Kiss your wife! Kiss your wife!"

The call went up, largely driven by Ian and Rob, but happily taken up by the others in the room.

Niall groaned inwardly. He'd forgotten about this, all the teasing that newlyweds went through for the first few weeks, all the toasts and calls to kiss the bride at dinners and whatnot.

Now, Heather was looking up at him with a slightly alarmed expression. "I think we have to kiss," she whispered, putting her drink down.

"Aye, I'm afraid so." He leaned over and kissed her lightly on the mouth, knowing that a mere peck on the cheek wouldn't assuage his annoying family.

Heather accepted the kiss. Her mouth was the sweetest thing in the world, her lips deliciously smooth and yielding. Was that the mead? Or was there something else, possibly the way those same lips could snap out lines that sent the MacNair—the old man himself!—fleeing for the safety of his lair.

Niall loved the way she stood up for herself, the way she fit right in at Carregness. She was perfect, perfect in his arms, her mouth perfectly molded to his...

Wolf whistles and cheers echoed around the hall. As he pulled away, all Niall saw was Heather's wide, stunned eyes.

He hadn't meant the kiss to last as long as it did. But his body had several other ideas once his mouth touched hers, and in truth, she'd responded in a way that made him think she liked the kiss too.

Dinner resumed, and the chatter increased. Heather remained beside him, still smiling and laughing at the various comments around the table, though he was on edge now, recalling the feel of her lips against his.

Heather giggled at one of Robert's stupid comments (not a particularly funny one either). Niall noted how she placed her glass carefully—too carefully—down on the table. Had the mead got to her already? She couldn't have had more than two servings.

"Heather," he said.

She whipped her head around to meet his eyes, and yes, the signs were there. Heightened color in her cheeks, that slightly unfocused expression in the deep brown eyes. If he didn't get her out of there, she might make a scene, and that would not be something she'd live down easily.

He stood up. "I think it's time to retire."

Ian looked over, confused. "But it's early…"

Rob threw a roll at him. "You eejit."

Maeve began to push away from the table. "Why don't I walk Heather upstairs? The castle must still be confusing for you, dear…"

But Niall was already helping Heather up, disguising her unusual clumsiness with his own exaggerated actions, making the display funny.

"The eager bridegroom," Brenna noted, with cool amusement. "We must not begrudge our newlyweds their evening."

"Suppose not," Ian agreed, now with a wink.

Niall got Heather on her feet. She was steady enough, and he decided that no one else had noticed anything odd about her behavior.

"Do we have to leave? I was having fun," Heather whispered to him as he escorted her out of the great hall.

"I'm glad, but yes, it's time to leave. You may have had a little too much fun…if you take me meaning."

"I don't take your anything," she protested. "And certainly not your meaning, because you're not mean."

"You're not making sense, Heather," he said as she steered her up the stairs. She stumbled slightly, and he decided it would be easier to carry her. He scooped her up in his arms, and she gave a little squeak of surprise when she found herself parallel to the floor.

"Niall," she said breathlessly, her face suddenly very close to his. "What are you doing?"

"Taking you to your room."

"Oh, my goodness, is that wise?"

Very probably not, but what could he do?

When he reached her door, he carried her through it. The room was lit by a low fire and a single candle on the desk.

"Niall, Niall, Niall," she said, half-singing his name. "Things are quite confusing, Niall."

"I know, I'm sorry." He helped her to the edge of the bed, encouraging her to sit.

She leaned her head on his chest. "We know the truth, but they don't know the truth, but they think they know the truth, and the truth is…I don't know what I was saying."

"You need to rest, Heather," he told her. "I think you didn't quite know how strong that mead was."

"Maeve said it was no worse than wine. She gave me a bottle before dinner, see?" Heather gestured wildly, but when Niall looked around, he did see an empty bottle and a glass on a small table. "A whole bottle?" It was on its side now, clearly empty. No wonder Heather was tipsy.

"The room is spinning," she told him.

"Lay back. You'll feel less dizzy soon."

He helped lower her down, grabbing a pillow for her.

"That's better." Heather closed her eyes and sighed.

She was still wearing her shoes, so he picked up one foot to unlace the shoe and tug it off, then did the same to the other. Heather's feet felt small in his hands. He started to rub them without thinking too much about it.

Then Heather let out a *mmmm*ing sound that was so raw and sensual that he nearly dropped her foot. He hadn't meant to arouse her…or himself. And yet, here he was, on her bed with her body in his hands, craving more.

"That feels so nice," Heather murmured.

"I should let you sleep," he said, somehow not moving away at all. God, but she looked tempting, her hair spread across the bed and her gown in disarray. He could take it off for her…

No. They were only pretending at the marriage. And

the longer he stayed in this room, the more likely it was that he would make a terrible mistake.

Niall gently put her foot back onto the bed, and moved to stand up. "Good night, Heather."

"No goodnight kiss?" she asked, her eyes still closed but her lips curved into a smile. Then she opened her eyes, pinning him with her gaze. "Or do you only kiss me when people are watching?"

"That was the general idea," he managed to say. His body, however, loved the idea of kissing her now, when no one was watching.

"I might start to think you don't really like me," she said, with a little pout. The mead was definitely bringing out a new side of her personality, one that was far too interesting for his peace of mind.

"I like you," he assured her. "Rather too much."

"Then kiss me," she implored, holding her arms out.

Niall stepped closer, even as he said, "You're not feeling like yourself, Heather. You've had more to drink than you ought to..."

He never finished, because all the time he'd been talking, he'd also been staring at her mouth in fascination, and then he'd leaned over to kiss her.

Heather kissed him back with an attention and focus that had him reeling. When she sucked on his lower lip, he had to push her away or risk violating every promise he'd made.

She lay back, her breathing quick and her eyes shining. "Now was that so bad?"

Not bad at all. And that was the problem.

"You need to sleep, sweetheart," he told her. Clenching his jaw, he worked the gown's ties and buttons loose, allowing Heather to breathe freely. She smiled at him, looking so sweet and happy that it almost broke his heart.

"I wish you'd stay," she said.

"Heather, I have to leave. You understand that, don't you? If you want to be free for the rest of your life, it means I can't stay here with you tonight. Or ever," he added hastily.

He walked to the connecting door, but the knob only rattled. That's right, earlier he'd locked it out of a sense of chivalry. Now he'd have to go back out into the hallway. Well, hopefully no one would be there.

But the moment he stepped out, two men who worked as retainers walked past. One gave him a knowing nod. Niall groaned inwardly. Now all the servants would know within the hour that he'd walked his wife to her room and emerged later, alone and with his clothes disheveled.

The conclusion would be obvious.

Then again, for the next few weeks, did it matter? He wanted people to think him well married. Then Brenna could move back home and resume her life, rather than waiting for a wedding that would never happen. And his father would perhaps stop grousing about Niall making a decision he didn't personally approve of ahead of time.

Niall turned to go to his own room, only a short way down the hall. But then he saw Maeve coming up the stairs, and quickly changed his objective.

His sister saw him approaching and waited, her expression outwardly pleasant, though he could sense some apprehension there. And she *should* feel apprehensive, because Niall was not pleased with her.

"What the hell was that about?" he demanded when he reached her. "I know what you did before dinner. Trying to embarrass Heather by getting her drunk, hoping she'll make a fool of herself?"

"I did not!"

"She told me who offered her the mead I found in her

room."

"Niall, I didn't want to embarrass her. I only wanted to…soften her up."

"So you could interrogate her? Maeve, you're ruthless."

"Well, you're maddening! There's something very odd going on and I'll be damned if I let it catch me by surprise! Do you think it's been easy to manage the household and manage Father at the same time?"

"You've done brilliantly."

"But I'd rather just be done," she said. "And yet your little wife refused to take the keys from me. Says she's not ready to be chatelaine and she needs time. About a month."

"Sounds fair."

"Sounds fishy! Both you and her mentioned a month. What happens then? My God, are you waiting to find out if she's with child?"

"What? No!"

"Well, how was I to know? That's why I wanted to take her back to her room tonight, so I could have a little chat with her. But then you stepped in, and I couldn't very well tell a husband not to walk his wife upstairs."

"Little sister, you are not to pry or wheedle anything out of Heather. I forbid it. Do you understand?"

"Aye," she said grudgingly. "But if she wishes to talk, I'll be there to listen, and you can't stop that, Niall Mac-Nair."

"No, no one can stop Heather from doing what she wants," he said.

And that would probably be his undoing.

Chapter 11

THE NEXT MORNING, HEATHER WOKE with a dull headache and a dry mouth. Getting out of bed seemed too great a task to manage, so she curled up on her side, reliving every moment of the previous night, most especially the final kiss, and Niall leaving her. God, she'd been a clown.

At the knock on the door, Heather called for whoever it was to enter. She expected the maid, but it was Maeve who walked in, bearing a tray.

"I thought you might not feel up to taking breakfast downstairs," she said, placing the tray down.

"You thought correctly," Heather groaned.

"Our drinks seem to be stronger than you're used to," said Maeve, fussing with the breakfast tray, and not looking at Heather. "But I've made some tea that will go far to restoring your good humor. And it will knock any pain out of your head, I promise."

"Then by all means, bring it to me."

Maeve offered her a cup of tea. "I hoped we could get to know each other. Your arrival was surprising to say the least. But that's Niall, never thinking more than a few moments ahead. He's always been driven by impulse."

As someone driven by impulse the night before,

Heather could sympathize. Aloud, she said, "I'm afraid I took advantage of that, because I never should have allowed him to get involved in my life."

"Well, he's a major part of your life now. What will your parents say when they find out you married at Gretna Green?"

Heather put down the tea. "My parents are dead. Their ship was lost at sea years ago, and that's when my Uncle Cyril took me on as his ward. He probably knows about the marriage by now, and *he'll* be furious."

Heather took her time sipping a dark, robust brew that required milk to take the edge off. She liked it. A bowl of oat porridge followed, and eventually Heather felt well enough to get out of bed and dress for the day.

Maeve had provided yet another dress, explaining that she'd found one of her sister's last night. This one was a yellowy-gold wool. It was plain in the best way, and the shawl in the MacNair colors went well over it.

"Perhaps I should call on the seamstress to come soon," Maeve offered. "The wife of the heir does need to look the part. Or will you send for your own things from home?"

Heather shook her head. "There's not much that would suit. Uncle Cyril didn't like to waste money on outfitting a girl who wasn't allowed out."

"Not allowed?" Maeve echoed.

"Oh! I just meant…I was rather isolated. Didn't have much opportunity for social calls." Heather didn't want to explain that she'd been stupid and short-sighted enough to get locked in, in her very own home.

"I take it you didn't get on with your uncle," Maeve ventured, not realizing how much of an understatement that was.

"It was well enough at first, but the last year or so…

let's just say we disagreed on the direction my life should take."

"How so?"

"He wants me to obey him. I want to obey myself."

Maeve sipped her tea slowly, and then smiled. "Carregness has been waiting for a woman like you."

Heather didn't know what to say, especially because she wouldn't be at Carregness for long.

Then the maid Susan opened the door, and looked to Heather. "Excuse me, ma'am, but the MacNair wishes to see you."

"I suppose that means I have to go? What if I refuse?"

Maeve coughed in surprise, and the maid's eyes went wide.

"I won't refuse," Heather said, putting a hand on Susan's arm. "I'm not as cruel as all that."

Maeve stood up. "Shall I accompany you?"

"No need," Heather said. "I will have to endure his comments, but why should you sour your own morning? In any case, I don't expect the interview will last very long. My English accent probably turns his stomach."

Heather followed the maid to a room at the opposite side of the keep. It was the largest space besides the great hall and served as MacNair's bedchamber, but also as his de facto throne room. Heather sensed that he liked to make people come to him, to be overawed by the heavy tapestries, and the iron candelabra lit even during the day, and the huge carved chair he sat upon.

But in fact, MacNair didn't cut an impressive figure. He was old and thin, and coughed into a handkerchief every time he finished speaking. His clothing was well-made, but cut for a larger man, indicating just how much MacNair must have wasted away since the outfit was made for him.

The MacNair gestured to her. "Come closer, girl. I won't bite."

Heather had her doubts about that, but she straightened her spine and walked toward the old man. "You wanted to see me, my lord."

"Of course I want to see the English girl who seduced my son into marriage in a matter of hours. What's your name? Where are you from?"

"I was born Heather Hayes, and I'm from Lancashire. My father owned land there, before he passed. My mother was from Bermuda. That's where they were sailing to when their ship went down in a storm."

"Orphan, are you? Thus no parents to keep you in line, I see. Just a wild thing running about the countryside, laying in wait for fool Scotsmen." He coughed loudly.

"I wasn't laying *or* in wait when I encountered your son, sir."

"Well, you must have been doing something you oughtn't," he said with a leer. "I see he put the family sapphire upon your scrawny sassenach finger. Funny, you don't look like a temptress."

"Because I'm not," Heather replied, keeping her voice even. "I did not tempt or seduce Niall. In fact, he intervened when he saw me in danger on a village street, and then he took pity on me and helped keep me safe later. I did not plan any of this, I assure you."

"Ach, so you just happened to cross paths with the heir to an earldom! Don't know what your game is, lass, but I know you'll lose. Think you could marry him for money and title? Ha! He's not got much money, and as for title, I'll disown him. Then you can both scrape for your living. See how you like your fine lord then."

"I didn't marry him for money," Heather said. "And to be honest, I didn't know he was going to be a lord till well after he proposed to me."

MacNair stamped his foot in frustration. Evidently he wasn't used to someone countering every line he spoke. "Then why did you do it?"

"Because he offered and I accepted. I don't see why you need to know any more than that."

"Evasive. Just as I expected."

Heather got more annoyed the more he talked. "In fact, I have already told Maeve some of the same details, because she asked nicely and seemed to have a genuine interest in knowing. Whereas you only wish to insult me."

"He was meant to marry Brenna!" MacNair said, coughing. "It would have bound the MacNairs and McGlashens closer, broadened the lands we need for grazing, giving us another harbor for fishing. What do you bring, as an English woman of no account, no breeding, and no name?"

"I'll have about a thousand a year, and I make very decent shortbread."

"We don't need an English bitch to make shortbread!" He coughed harder, bending over as he held the handkerchief to his face. "Damn it all, you'll be the death of me."

Heather glimpsed the dark red spots on the handkerchief as he bunched it up. She caught her own breath, shocked into realization. "Sir, your death is already assured. You have consumption, don't you?"

"So the girl is a doctor too, eh? Aye, that's what I'm told. But I'll live long enough to see you discarded and Niall married proper, mark my words!"

"You may indeed," she said, thinking that he might endure till October. If he was a more pleasant man, she would have told him exactly what the plan was, just to reassure him. But he was a mean-spirited old fart, and she was quite done with older men deciding her fate.

"You're hiding something," he declared. "Don't think you'll keep hiding it. I've broken stronger men than you."

"Perhaps, sir. But have you broken stronger women?" Heather spun about and strode out of the room.

She needed a breath of fresh air after that. Heather walked downstairs. Maeve had mentioned that Carregness had several gardens surrounding the keep. Heather thought it would be relaxing to visit them.

However, she went to the great hall first—it was the heart of Carregness, where most of life was lived. Meals seemed to largely be communal, with the family and guests at the high table, and all others partaking of food wherever they could squeeze in at the benches. In between mealtimes, the room served as a gathering spot, a workroom for any number of indoor tasks, and a council chamber.

And yes, there was Niall now, speaking with a group of men around the table, discussing something that riled them up. One man kept gesturing to a paper on the table. Heather felt her cheeks burning. She'd acted like a wanton last night. Niall probably thought less of her for it.

Still, she couldn't run away from her behavior. She had to own up to it. She walked over to him, nodding a polite hello. He nodded back and dismissed the men, who left to go about their daily tasks.

"What were you talking about with those men?" she asked, mostly to open the conversation.

"Some cattle and sheep have gone missing. We were talking about the best way to retrieve what was lost."

"By lost, do you mean stolen?"

"Possibly," he said, his expression grim. "We can't afford to lose any more before the cold sets in."

"I'm sure you'll find out who is behind it. Niall, may we talk privately?" she asked, keeping her eyes lowered.

He nodded and escorted her over to a corner of the room near a window. "What is it?"

"I behaved very badly last night. I apologize."

He was already shaking his head. "It wasn't your fault. Surely, just a mistake on Maeve's part—she overestimated your capacity. *You* did nothing wrong." He still seemed annoyed though, in Heather's view.

"You're being kind again," she told him. "I was drunk…but not so drunk that I don't remember what I said and did. I never should have asked you to kiss me last night."

"And I shouldn't have listened to your request. But I did. And I didn't have the excuse of being drunk."

"Then why did you do it?" she asked, curious.

"Ah, let's just say…it was a tempting scene."

She blushed. "I'll avoid getting us into such a scene again."

"You're dressed to go outside," he noted, clearly wanting to change the subject.

"Yes, Maeve mentioned some gardens."

"Let me show you," Niall said.

They walked outside, following the walls of the keep. Niall led her down a narrow path that suddenly turned around the northwestern corner of the building, where the original outer wall had been lowered to allow those in the garden to have an uninterrupted view to the west.

The garden itself was lovely, with a collection of roses and many more flowers in carefully marked beds, separated by white gravel paths.

However, the vista commanded the most attention. The land behind the keep dropped away precipitously, rolling away to the west to a distant ocean horizon, just visible behind a shoreline of hills and islands.

"Oh, it's beautiful!" Heather said.

"Aye, that it is. MacNair land all the way to the sea," he noted.

"You're very proud of your heritage."

"Well, it's about all we have left," Niall admitted. "I think one of the reasons I was hesitant to tell you about my family and the title coming to me is that, to be honest, there's not much to any of it. If you'd seemed to be the sort of woman who'd be impressed by a title, I might have. But if you were, I somehow doubt I would have found you standing in a village street with no shoes."

"True," Heather agreed with a laugh. "I never set my sights on marrying for a title, and Uncle Cyril never hinted that he'd care about it either. Though I wonder now if that could have been a way to evade his plans. If I'd said I was hellbent on becoming Lady Something or Other, would he have put aside his own goal of pawning me off on his friend?"

"The aristocratic marriage mart can be expensive," Niall said. "And you mentioned that your uncle was a miser."

"True again. I guess I'll never know. And it doesn't matter anyway. What's done is done…until it's undone." She smiled at him. "Our little deception is going to surprise a lot of people once it's revealed, you know. I can't imagine what your father will say when we tell him that we've annulled the marriage. I saw him this morning, and he all but called me whore. And swore up and down that he'd find a way to end the marriage. Out of spite, I refrained from telling him that all he had to do was wait."

Niall nodded. "He told me essentially the same thing last night. He's still trying to make Brenna the next Lady MacNair. I thought that he'd have an apoplexy over it."

"Speaking of that," Heather said, "You should have told me your father was so ill."

"What do you mean? He's not ill," Niall protested. "I mean, he's under the weather now with some ague. But it will pass. It always does."

"It's consumption," Heather said bluntly. "He admitted it to me."

Niall looked offended now. "Why would he tell you that?"

"He only confirmed it when I guessed. He's coughing up blood, Niall. When that happens, the cause is consumption."

"You're exaggerating."

"Do I seem like someone who exaggerates?"

Niall frowned at her. "No. But this is serious. I think we ought to talk to Maeve. She'll have been the one who was with the doctor most often. And if you're in this house, you'll need to know how the laird's health fares."

They returned inside and Niall asked where Maeve could be found. The answer, it seemed, was anywhere. Maeve was an indefatigable worker and patrolled nearly every corner of Carregness while she checked on the various servants and verified supplies and asked for reports.

They finally found her in the kitchen, discussing the week's meals with the cook. Heather asked Maeve if she could spare a moment, and the three of them stepped into the hallway.

"Now what?" Maeve asked. "If you two are having your first lovers' spat, I'm not the one to solve it!"

"Nothing like that," Heather assured her. "It's about your father."

"Heather said he has consumption," Niall said abruptly. "That's nonsense."

That way Maeve looked at Niall, that long moment of silence, nearly broke Heather.

"It's not true, is it?" Niall asked his sister.

"I'm sorry, Niall." Maeve reached for him, but he stepped away.

"Did you not think to *tell* me?" he burst out.

Maeve sighed. "I didn't know until after you'd left for London. We'd all thought it was just a cold that lingered, but it got worse after you left. The doctor came, and…he was the one to tell us."

"But no one told me?"

"I believe my arrival distracted everyone," Heather said, feeling guilty, though she could hardly have known the issue.

"What did the doctor say? How long does he have?"

"Nothing is certain," said Maeve. "But he can measure his time left in months, not years."

"He'll never die," Niall said, moving away from them both. "He's too contrary to die."

"Everyone dies, Niall," Heather said.

"Well, he can't. Not now." Niall suddenly turned to Heather. "Do you understand how bad things could get if he dies now?"

Chapter 12

On reading your letter, my first thought was that you were joking, just like that time when you convinced Mrs. Cannon that you saw a ghost at school by inventing all the details of her filmy dress and her big sad eyes and her silvery hair. You are so quick on your feet when it comes to things like that. I almost believed you, and I KNOW that ghosts are not real! But then I noticed that the letter was posted from Scotland. Unless you are devoting considerable effort to play a prank on all your friends, I have to assume that you are indeed living in Scotland with a family I have never heard of.

I burn for more information about your situation, so much so that I am inclined to persuade Daisy, Rose, and Poppy to mount an expedition into the wilds of the north to retrieve you. Unfortunately, Daisy and Rose are rather preoccupied with their marriages, and Poppy has devoted herself to her family's business. Alas, I am somewhat confined here myself. My mother is unwell again, and she prefers me to stay close when that happens. So I must appeal to your good nature...I beg you to write again, using no less than five sheets of paper, and cross-write if you must. I will read every word no matter how long it takes. If you need anyone to rescue you, simply include the phrase "the lackluster pear tart" in some sentence, and I will organize a party to invade.

Camellia

Heather smiled while reading her friend's letter, which had arrived that morning. For all the distance between London and Carregness, the mail coaches ensured that written communication moved swiftly. It was marvelous, really, that one could pass word from one end of the island to the other within a matter of a few days, so long as a person could afford the stamp.

By now, she was sure that all her friends at least knew where she was, and that she was safe. But she'd have to confide in someone about the actual facts of the matter, most specifically the hasty marriage and what she intended to do after the annulment.

Over the past several days, life at Carregness had settled into a fairly normal routine for Heather. Normal, that is, for a woman who was participating in a facade of a marriage for the sake of evading her uncle's plans, while simultaneously helping her husband-for-now evade his own father's plans.

It involved a lot of Heather and Niall riding out together in the afternoons, mostly to reassure the residents of Carregness that they were newlyweds simply mad about each other, so much so that they simply had to spend time in the woods all alone. From the knowing glances and smiles Heather got from the various women, from Maeve down to the undercook, Heather knew exactly what everyone *thought* was happening.

In reality, Niall gave Heather a full tour of all the MacNair lands (which took a number of days, for the area was large, and the land itself rocky and wild). While they traveled, he told her stories about his childhood, growing up with Ian and Robert and Maeve and Fionnuala, running through the woods and fields as a sort of miniature army.

They rode to the nearest town one day when the weather precluded a longer excursion. Niall explained all the major points of interest.

"That inn is the Cat & Mouse. It's the biggest one in the area, and Brodie brews his own ale. There's the church where my parents married," he said when they got to the stone building with its lichen-encrusted bell tower. "That's where my own wedding was expected to be," he added. "The locals might be annoyed about that, being done out of a wedding party and a day off."

"You can still host a party for them, but it will be to celebrate your annulment," Heather suggested. "Though the priest might not approve."

"Father Ross would see the humor," Niall mused.

The people in the village all seemed to recognize Niall, and greeted him respectfully when he passed. Heather smiled and nodded to them, but felt odd about introducing herself as "Mrs. MacNair" when in a few short weeks, she would be gone.

"We could ride to the harbor, if you like," he said, after they chatted with a local magistrate. "It's mostly for fishing boats, but there's a little trade, so you never know if a ship from an interesting locale has come in."

"Oh, we'd better head back home," Heather decided, after glancing at the sky, which had grown steadily cloudier by the hour. "I think we've done well so far to avoid rain. Let's not tempt fate."

"Aye, homeward we go." Niall grinned at her. "Race you!"

He was off at a gallop before Heather could even reply. "Oh, you sneak," she muttered.

She nudged Sterling, the horse she'd been riding each day, and he was quite aware that he was in second place at the moment. Sterling bounded forward and galloped hard to catch up. Heather gave the horse as much freedom as she could, only watching for rocks and lowered branches that would endanger them both. In truth, she had very little idea why Sterling took the route he did. They had Niall in view most of the time, but once when he turned right around a hillock, Sterling plunged to the left.

Heather was surprised to see Carregness rising ahead of her as she rode at a breakneck pace toward the walls. She was even more surprised to hear a shout from behind her—Niall had emerged from the trees well after she did.

Heather slowed and wheeled about at the gates, laughing as Niall rode up. "I won!"

"How did you do that?" he asked, looking astonished. "I had a head start."

"So I noticed. Let that be a lesson to you, sir. Though you used deceit to gain the advantage, I was clearly destined to win."

"I think you took a shortcut," he said, narrowing his eyes.

"What a thing to say! I'm the newcomer here, how could I even know a shortcut."

"Then you've got quite an understanding with Sterling."

"Horses know their way home," she told him, petting the horse's neck. "You have to trust them."

At night, Niall always walked Heather to her own room, and then went to his. But everyone assumed that he then opened the connecting door between the rooms and all the usual newlywed activities ensued.

Heather was still ignorant of *exactly* what those activities were, though every time Niall happened to brush against her, or help her onto her horse, or when one his vile brothers teased them into a kiss at the dinner table… well, she was getting very curious about what she was missing. She was, however, careful to not drink more than a single glass of anything again, lest her curiosity lead her to make Niall another offer, one he might accept.

But thus far, her resolve held. She had a world to travel, and upon her birthday she'd be free to do it.

One day, she rounded a corner while walking down the halls of Carregness, almost running headlong into Brenna.

"Oh!" Heather yelped. "I didn't expect you there."

"Clearly not," Brenna said. "Though to be fair, no one here expected *you*."

"We've never really had a chance to speak," Heather said, well aware that not everyone was overjoyed by Niall's so-called marriage. "I'm sorry for…confusing things."

"Are you?" Brenna asked coolly.

"Niall had mentioned that his family was expecting him to marry another woman, but he didn't say that you were actually at Carregness."

"Well, I am. Not that I seem to have a purpose in being here any longer." She frowned, evidently rather perturbed by her change in status.

"Oh, stay," Heather said in a rush. "Please!"

Brenna blinked in confusion. "Why?"

"Because…" Heather couldn't tell her the truth, could she? That the marriage was a sham, designed only to protect her for a little while. "Because you just never know."

"I know that I can't stay on here as Niall's fiancèe. Half the family is wondering why I've not started packing. And the other half…"

"Do you love Niall?" Heather asked. She had wondered every time she saw the other woman, just as she wondered if it were possible that Niall didn't love Brenna. She was so beautiful and lively, who wouldn't fall for her?

Brenna stiffened, and looked away. "I don't want to discuss who I may love or not love. Certainly not with you."

"I do understand," Heather said, inspired. "But listen, I'll tell you a secret."

"Please don't," Brenna said, taking a step back. "We are not friends."

"It may help you."

"How?" she asked, curiosity taking over.

And so Heather explained the truth. Perhaps if Brenna *did* care for Niall, she could persuade him that marrying her didn't have to just be to appease their parents, but because Brenna truly loved him. It pained Heather to think of the two of them together (why, she wasn't sure, because of course Niall was just a friend). But it seemed just as cruel to lie to Brenna, who'd been pushed aside through no fault of her own.

At the end of the explanation, Brenna simply stared at her in wonderment, and a good dose of disbelief. "You are telling me that both you and Niall entered into a marriage thinking that it would last only a few weeks?"

"Six weeks. But less than four left now. On my birthday, which is the sixth of October, Niall will publicly explain that it's all been a mistake. We'll get an annulment and I'll go back to England. You'll never need to see me again."

"Six weeks with a MacNair, and then you'll walk away?"

"That is my goal."

"But I thought you and Niall…um…" Brenna suddenly flushed in embarrassment.

"Oh! No, we haven't! I mean, I suppose if anyone wanted us to remain married, they could point to me being compromised in theory. We were alone…a lot, actually. But the marriage is not consummated and never will be."

Brenna shook her head, as if trying to clear it. "I cannot believe that any of this happened. Is Niall truly agreeing to this?"

"He's the one who proposed it…so to speak. Also, please don't tell the earl. The laird, I mean."

"As if I'd tell the MacNair that his son is duping him solely to get out of a marriage contract with me! I'd rather die of shame."

"It's not that Niall doesn't care for you, you know," Heather said. "He's always spoken of you highly. As a sister."

Brenna raised an eyebrow. "He told you that? Aye, that's how it's always been between Niall and me. It's funny, really…" She trailed off, obviously lost in thought.

"So, Brenna? Can I count on you to keep my secret?"

"What?" Brenna asked, startled back into the moment.

"Can I rely upon you to not share the secret? Until my birthday next month."

"I'll take it to my grave," Brenna pronounced, nodding once. Then she grew abstracted again. "Please excuse me. I have to…be by myself for a moment…"

Heather watched her go, hoping that she hadn't made a huge mistake in trusting the other woman. Clearly, Brenna had something on her mind.

* * * *

Later that day, Heather sat in the large hall, now bright with sunlight from the clerestory windows. She had her paper and ink, and was trying (with great difficulty) to explain the latest developments of her life in a letter to Mrs. Bloomfield. Having spilled her secret to Brenna, it felt easier to write those same facts down on paper, a step she'd avoided thus far in her missives to her friends. But Mrs. Bloomfield was older and more experienced, and she might have good advice. Her former teacher had always said Heather was the most likely of her girls to do something more bold than wise, and Heather was sadly certain she was going to reaffirm all of Mrs. Bloomfield's most dire prophecies in one letter.

Dear Mrs. Bloomfield,

I write to you from Carregness Castle in the northwest of Scotland. To say that I did not anticipate ever being here is an understatement, but it is nonetheless true that I am. What's more, I'm afraid I have got married. The courtship was brief — about one day — but fortunately I suspect the marriage itself will be brief as well. The gentleman I call husband is Niall MacNair, son of the Earl of Carregness. The offer of marriage was a kindness to get me out of a family difficulty, by which I mean my uncle's choice of bridegroom. (Not the other kind of family difficulty! I remember well your advice concerning that issue.)

Life here is as peaceful as one can expect, and though everyone treats me well, I believe that I will soon be back in England, looking for a position to support a modest life as a spinster. For if all goes according to our plan, the marriage will be annulled on my birthday, and I will be a free woman, and Niall will be a free man. I expect some awkwardness regarding my reputation, but as I never intend to listen to gossip or be moved by it, I shall endure.

You no doubt think me

A loud crash interrupted her writing. Dropping the pen, she looked to the double doors at the front of the room, and beheld a most unwelcome sight.

Uncle Cyril had pushed his way into the keep, trailed by two young servants running after.

"He just rode in! Didn't say who he was or anything!" the boy on the left cried to the room in general, clearly distraught that the protocol hadn't been observed.

"I know him," Heather said, rising from the bench.

"Where's my chit?" the intruder bellowed, obviously drunk. His expensive clothing was slightly rumpled, and his hard eyes, like agates, belied the florid cheeks and the rotund figure that could have been easily construed as gentle and even jolly.

Heather was mortified. "Uncle Cyril, what are you doing here?" she asked.

"What do you think, girl? I'm here to take you back. Mr. Webb is not at all pleased that you ran away. He should be arriving tomorrow."

Just then, Brom strode up behind his employer, leering at Heather.

"Mr. Webb is coming here?" she asked, ignoring Brom entirely. "Why?"

"Because you're meant to be his bride!"

"I'm already married!" she shouted back. "As you must know! We informed Brom when he tried to drag me back from the border, ten minutes too late, thank the Lord."

"Gretna Green marriages are a joke," her uncle said.

"They are as legal as anything, sir." That comment came from Ian MacNair, who'd emerged from nowhere and was now approaching the pair of them. "No matter if the fact pleases us or not."

Brenna followed him in an instant later, watching Uncle Cyril with a horrid fascination.

Just then Niall rushed in, probably having been alerted of the invasion by another servant. "What's going on?" he demanded.

"Your wife's uncle has arrived," his brother replied dryly. "Though I don't remember anyone issuing an invitation."

"As if one needs an invitation to enter a barn!" Cyril growled. "That's all this place is. A stone barn, filled with peasants who eat the same slop as the pigs."

"Uncle, please," said Heather.

"Why are you wrapped up in that plaid stuff?" her uncle demanded, glaring at her as though he'd just realized she was there.

"It's not plaid stuff, it's the MacNair tartan," she retorted.

Niall declared, "And she's wearing it because she's a MacNair."

"For now," Heather breathed, so softly only Niall could hear.

Niall wrapped his arm around Heather's shoulders, and she leaned into him, seeking more of that comforting strength. He said, "I see now why you scaled down a tower to get away from the man."

"I'm fine," she assured him. "But I'd rather *he* not be here."

Niall nodded, then turned to her uncle. "So. You're Heather's guardian. The one who hit her so hard that when I met her, she still showed the bruises."

His voice was very calm, but Cyril caught some of the threat there, because he took one step back. Niall continued, "Time for you to go, sir."

"Not until I talk with my niece. That's why I came all

this way."

"If Heather wishes to communicate with you in the future, that's up to her. Not you. She's quite fond of writing letters, and I'm certain she knows where you live."

"She's my ward! I've got business here," he blustered, his drunkenness more evident now.

"You don't," Niall assured him. "Whatever business you may have wanted to use Heather for, it's over. She is no longer your ward. She's my wife."

Cyril turned to the figure at his elbow. "Get her, Brom."

The lackey took a hesitant step forward, perhaps remembering the last time he attempted to seize Heather from Niall and found himself at a distinct disadvantage.

"Ain't got a gun now," he said to Niall. "Nor any weapon."

Niall gave him a pitying look. "I'm in my family castle, surrounded by my people. Who do have weapons."

"I'm only following orders," Brom said. He reached out, intending to grab Heather's shoulder.

"Touch her and I'll rip your arm off," Niall said pleasantly.

Brom froze, his hand out. Then he slowly retracted it.

Heather breathed out. This was the second time Niall had faced off with Brom, and both times he showed no trace of fear, while Brom (a nightmare figure to her) slunk away defeated. She leaned back into Niall, grateful for the solidity he provided.

"Damn coward," Cyril told Brom in disgust.

"Didn't see you try to get her," Brom growled back.

Ian, who was now armed with a dagger that Heather hadn't even noticed he drew, stepped in between the combatants.

"Leave, both of you," he instructed, pointing the blade

meaningfully at the uninvited guests. "Walk out now, or you may not walk out at all."

Her uncle was offended at the threat, but then judged the height of the assorted MacNair men (Robert was standing to one side holding a gun that he'd just happened to aim at Cyril) and their crowd of supporters, glanced at the array of additional weaponry on the walls, and took a step backward.

He glowered at them all, saying "I'm going, I'm going. Barbarians, the lot of you." Then he turned to Heather and gave her a nasty leer. "But don't think this is over, young lady."

Then her uncle turned on his heel and left, Brom stalking behind. Several of the younger men followed, clearly with the aim to ensure that both men got off the property as soon as possible.

When he was finally gone, Heather took a shaky breath. "I never thought he'd keep after me like this! And Mr. Webb coming too? Why? Why can't they leave me alone!"

Niall kept his arms around her, turning her to face him. "You're safe at Carregness, Heather. I won't let him lay a hand on you."

His brother Rob had moved to the window, and was staring down at the road. "They're riding off now. I recognize those horses. They belong to Brodie, the innkeeper."

"Hayes must be renting a room at the Cat & Mouse," Niall said. "Maybe we should have someone keep an eye on him while he's there."

"Good idea. I'll do it," Robert said. "I don't like that man."

"I'm sure it's mutual," Heather said. "As I may have mentioned, my uncle hates the Scots."

"Let's take a little stroll," Niall said then. "You could use some fresh air, yes?"

He meant that she could use some privacy from all the curious or judging spectators, and he was right.

So Heather allowed him to walk her to the little walled garden that looked west to the sea. Niall took in several breaths once they got to the low wall. He sat on the wall and ran his hand through his hair. Heather realized how upset the incident made him.

"Well, as if you needed another reason to avoid shackling yourself to me for eternity!" she said, trying to keep her tone light. "You've finally met my uncle. Cyril is my father's brother and the only example of my family I can point to. Depressing, isn't it?"

"He seems hellbent on keeping hold of you," Niall mused, keeping his gaze on the distant sea. "Why? Are you sure you're not an heiress?"

Heather laughed at the thought. "Mercy, no. I once looked at some papers the bank sent over about my inheritance. It's enough to bring in about a thousand pounds a year. Nothing to sneeze at, to be sure. But not an amount to dazzle, especially as they intended to split the amount — my uncle and Mr. Webb, that is. And I doubt any pin money was going to be allotted to me. No, I think this is all about pride on Uncle Cyril's part. He wants to be in charge at all times. He wants to hand me off to his choice, not mine. Mr. Webb's motivation, on the other hand...." She shuddered.

"He'll never get near you, even after this...arrangement is over," Niall promised.

"When it's over, I won't be here any longer," she reminded him. "And I'm not your responsibility."

Something in his gaze held her fast. Something she couldn't name but her body reacted to, like a magnet to iron. She didn't *want* to leave here, to leave Niall. And perhaps, just perhaps, he didn't want her to leave either?

"Your birthday," he said then, "will be quite an event."

She wasn't certain how he meant it. A triumph for her? A defeat for Uncle Cyril? A sad parting from Carregness? "I'm counting the days," she told him.

"Aye, I expect you are." He gave her a little smile, kissed her lightly, lingeringly on the mouth, and then stood up. "Well, let's get back inside. There will be plenty to discuss. And I can't even guess what my father will say when word of this incident gets to him."

"I'm sorry to be such a nuisance."

"Heather, my darling girl, you are many, many things, but a nuisance isn't one."

When they returned to the main hall, several men had already gathered. Robert was leading the discussion, and it sounded very much like he was planning an invasion of the village.

"Subtly, Rob, subtly," Niall reminded him.

"Oh, I'll be subtle. He won't know I'm there till I stick a knife in his back. He called our house a barn."

Niall squeezed Heather's arm. "Why don't you find Maeve and see what she's up to? I'd like to speak to the men to ensure no one does anything stupid."

"Aye," Heather breathed. She walked to the table where she'd been sitting before, intending to gather her things. The sight of the paper and pen and ink startled her. It had been less than a half hour, but it felt like a day since she'd dropped the pen at the sound of her uncle's arrival. She'd been writing to Mrs. Bloomfield…but where was the letter? Heather looked all around. She peered under the table, then lifted up the cushions on the benches, just in case.

"Lose something, milady?" a housemaid asked.

"I was halfway through a letter before, but now I can't find it."

"The window and doors were wide open. Perhaps it blew into a corner. I'll ask if anyone saw it," the maid offered.

"Thank you. If it's found, just have someone put it in my room. It's not urgent."

Then Maeve hurried over. "Heather, would you mind joining me upstairs? I believe we ought to talk. The presence of your uncle is going to generate many questions."

"Yes, indeed," Heather said. "And we're going to have to make up answers to satisfy."

"So we will. You've got the MacNair clan behind you," Maeve vowed. "That feaertie isn't taking you away."

Chapter 13

NIALL SPENT SOME TIME DISCUSSING the new situation with his brothers and the men of Carregness, and it was decided that Robert and a few others would go into the village and stay there to keep watch on things until Hayes gave up and left...which he hoped would be soon. Ian volunteered to mind the ramparts of Carregness, until Niall pointed out that Hayes wouldn't be coming with an army, but more likely a solicitor.

"In that case, I'll start boiling some pitch," Ian said. "Don't you worry, Niall. We aren't going to let anyone take Heather." He walked off.

Both his brothers had clear opinions on Hayes, and on Heather, Niall realized. She'd certainly found her way into the hearts of everyone in a short time. Including his own. Niall knew he should be more careful with Heather, more distant. But it was getting more difficult every day, and the thought that she'd eventually be leaving Carregness after they revealed the truth made him sadder than he cared to admit.

Niall tried to distract himself from the situation by handling the never-ending tasks that came with being the MacNair in charge of keeping the castle and lands running. Though his father still held the titles and the final authority in anything, Niall had taken over more and more responsibility over the past several months. Looking back, he should have realized that his father giving up control hinted at how ill he'd been feeling, even if Niall himself had been too busy to notice the shift. The MacNair hated allowing anyone but him to make even the tiniest decisions.

With the harvest starting to come in, there was plenty to do. Niall spoke to several tenants who came to report on their progress so far. Crop yields were up, thanks to investments Niall made the previous year. The final shearing looked to be promising as well, and Niall allowed himself a small sigh of relief. It was encouraging. Another year with profits instead of losses, and he might turn the MacNair fortunes around. All was not lost.

Several hours later, Robert came back with an initial report. "Hayes is staying at the Cat & Mouse, just as we thought. He's gone to the church already, I assume to warn Father Ross that he ought to keep his nose out of any marriage questions that come up. His man Brom has been drinking in the taproom since he arrived. I've offered a few small rewards to any workers there who can make our visitors' stay less comfortable, so that may speed things along."

"Let's hope. Any sign of the other man he mentioned? Webb?" Niall didn't want to describe him as Heather's intended husband—he didn't deserve that distinction.

"Not yet, but Brodie mentioned that Hayes told him to expect another guest soon. With our luck, he'll haul along a dozen lawyers as well."

"He can bring a hundred. I'm not letting Heather anywhere near those men."

Rob paused. "Do you think they can win? Legally? I mean, a marriage is a marriage, right?"

Niall wished things were that simple. "I don't know what they can do, or what they're willing to do. All I know is that Heather ran away from them, and that's all I need to know."

Rob nodded once, as if that ended all discussion. "She's a canny girl, and I trust her judgment. I mean, not about *you*, of course. Woman had to be daft to throw herself at you."

"So she's canny *and* daft at the same time?"

"Aye. That describes our Heather very well." Rob headed off, no doubt to think of ways to make Cyril Hayes's stay in Scotland as short as possible.

Our Heather. Oh, things were going to be very awkward when her birthday arrived.

* * * *

For her part, Heather spent the rest of the day with Maeve, overseeing the various chores that Maeve directed in her role as chatelaine. Heather still maintained the fiction that she'd eventually be the lady of the castle and honestly, at some moments, it was exciting to dream of exactly that. After all, not all young ladies got to live in a picturesque castle with a handsome prince...or laird, in this case.

After dinner, Niall walked her up to her room. Heather was charmed by the gesture, especially because she'd been tense ever since her uncle resurfaced. Even though she knew she was safe inside Carregness, she couldn't avoid the feeling that someone was waiting for her around every corner. But when Niall was with her, that feeling receded.

"Thank you for sending my uncle away earlier," she said.

"What else did you think I'd do? That man hit you while you were in his care, and he shouldn't be anywhere near you."

He stopped at her door, and reached out to run his hand along the tartan wrap she now wore every day. "You might not be a MacNair for long, but while you are, you get all we can give."

She got that warm feeling in her belly again. "I'm lucky then," she said.

He smoothed out a few folds of the shawl and smiled at her.

"You look beautiful," he told her, his gaze dropping to her mouth. "After what happened today, I... Can I give you a kiss goodnight?"

"Please! I mean...yes, that would be...acceptable." She'd been dreaming of his kiss.

Just then a pair of maids appeared at the end of the hall, walking toward them. Heather felt distinctly shy about being seen kissing Niall. "Would you, um, mind stepping in?"

"Don't want an audience?" he teased, but very willingly followed her into the room and closed the door.

Heather's stomach felt all fluttery. She felt like that whenever he got close to her.

Niall bent down to offer her a chaste kiss, but the moment his mouth touched her cheek, she turned her head, offering her lips instead.

For a moment, a lightning bolt seemed to arc through her, just from the slide of his lips along hers.

Niall let out a low sound, almost of pain.

"Your mouth," he murmured, sucking on her lower lip between words. "From the first day, I wanted to have your mouth all over me."

Heather gasped, both at the idea of her mouth *all over*

Niall, and the sensation his tugging, pulling, demanding kiss was stirring in her. She inhaled and he left off biting her and plunged his tongue into her mouth, drawing out a moan from her.

"We should stop, shouldn't we?" she asked, even as she kept reaching for him.

"I could be persuaded to continue," he murmured.

"Wait, *what?*"

Niall gave her a funny half-smile that sent butterflies through her stomach. "Well, everyone already thinks I'm the luckiest man alive to have such a bonny bride. To be honest, I'm getting a little jealous of what everyone thinks I've already got."

He captured her face in his hands and again lowered his head to kiss her. Heather was prepared for it this time…oh, no, she wasn't. Not this slow, soft kiss that just went on and on, his lips teasing hers, his fingertips grazing the skin along her jaw and her neck.

Heather's mouth opened up and then the kiss was more than teasing. It was torture. She leaned into Niall, wanting more of the delicious pleasure his kisses created.

"How did you learn to kiss?" she whispered.

"Trial and error. I learned other things too."

He ran his hand down, stroking over her breast then to her stomach, then lower, sliding to her hip, where he cupped his hand and drew her close to him, their clothing doing little to obscure the heat of their bodies.

Heather knew she should object, but part of her yearned for more of this. She liked Niall's hands on her, liked the way he held her and cupped her and slowly massaged her, while murmuring very sweet things about how beautiful and sweet and enticing she was.

A flush of heat between her legs startled her. Why was she suddenly damp there? Did her courses just arrive?

Wasn't it too early for that?

"I can't," she gasped. *I love you too much to do this to you.* Heather choked back the words she almost said. After a moment, she stuttered out, "My life…your life. It's too important to let…emotion get in the way. This can't go on, Niall. Remember our agreement."

His breath came fast, but at the mention of the word *agreement*, his eyes darkened.

"Sorry," he muttered. "I got carried away. You're just…very tempting. If things were different… Good night."

Niall pulled away and left though the connecting door, leaving Heather anxious and unfulfilled on so many levels.

* * * *

Dear Daisy,

I write to you from Carregness…again, yet, still. As I may have mentioned in my previous letter, Uncle Cyril has come here (well, to the village) and claims he is staying until I agree to come home with him. Which of course I will never do! He sends a letter to the castle every day, asking when I will join him on the journey back to Lancashire. I do not answer those notes, though I have kept the ten pound notes (!) he has included with each one. For an attempted bribe, it's very odd.

The only good news is that I've not seen Mr. Webb yet. Perhaps he's decided not to come, which would be a miracle. Uncle Cyril has some other motive for being here, though, and I am not sure what it could be other than kidnapping. Since I have not left the immediate grounds since I saw him, he has had no such opportunity, nor do I intend to give him any. Niall has designated a few men to keep watch on Uncle Cyril, but no one has identified any-one like a solicitor meeting with him. For a man threaten-ing legal action, does that not seem more like legal inac-tion? Perhaps he is too lazy to pursue the matter. He was never a particularly industrious man, not like Papa. So perhaps I should not be surprised. And every day he does nothing brings me closer to my birthday!

Niall and the rest of the family have been very kind throughout the whole ordeal, though I shudder to think what impression they now have of my countrymen. I do hope that someday I can introduce them to better exam-ples...namely you, and Rose and Poppy, and Camellia. They would do wonders for the reputation of that most maligned species, the English wallflower.

Fond regards,

Heather Hayes MacNair

Days had passed. Heather avoided being alone with Niall, embarrassed by her display of lust the other night. Anyone would think she was trying to seduce him. Unfor-tunately, the result of that was that she didn't spend much time with him at all, and she felt rather empty.

Calcutta. Cairo. Budapest. Moscow. Venice. Paris. Porto. She recited the names of some of the cities she wanted to see, tried to imagine the skylines of each as she sailed into port. It was trickier lately.

She rounded a corner of the second story hallway, just where a small alcove was set at the juncture of two pas-sages. There, in the shadows, she saw Brenna embracing Niall. His back was to Heather, so all she saw was Bren-na's arms twined around his neck, and her pale forehead and dark curls visible just above his shoulder. Heather dashed back behind the corner, her heart pounding.

Was that how it was? Heather denied him what he

wanted and his first reaction was to seek out pleasure with another woman? How could Niall *do* what he did to her the other night, when he was also romancing Brenna?

Heather returned to her room and waited until her heart stopped acting like a bird in flight. There had to be an explanation. There just had to be.

About twenty minutes later, she smoothed her hair and her gown, then proceeded to the great hall like nothing had happened. Niall was there, just settling in for breakfast. Brenna was nowhere to be seen.

"Good morning," she said.

"Hello there," he said, looking over at her with a smile that would have charmed her if she hadn't been so annoyed with him. "Just got here now? You're usually up and about earlier than this."

"Oh, I felt lazy. How is Brenna?" she asked guilelessly.

He blinked at the question, giving a very real impression of surprise. "Couldn't tell you. Haven't seen her all day."

The bald-faced lie startled Heather. Was he going to deny everything? Did she even want to confront him about this?

"I'll have to chat with her later then," Heather replied, sitting at her usual place. A maid came up and offered her a bowl of steaming oat porridge with a little assortment of delicious additions. She added currants and poured milk over the top.

If the prospect of Heather and Brenna comparing notes worried Niall, he showed no sign of it. "Perhaps you can both find Maeve and convince her to take a day off from her labors. Did you get everything you needed for your wardrobe? I can arrange for the local seamstress to come here."

"Until my uncle leaves, I can't possibly worry about clothes," she said. The thought distracted her from Niall's previous behavior. "He sent another letter today. I'm not sure what effect he thinks they'll have."

"Sentiment?"

"He has none."

"But you do. He hopes to play on your good nature and get you to think that you owe him something. Loyalty. Pity. Family duty. Whatever." Niall put down his glass. "You don't owe him anything, though. You should burn those letters instead of opening them."

Heather nodded. She'd had the same thought. But then again, each letter had included a ten pound note—Heather assumed that because her uncle was so consumed with wealth that he imagined everyone else was as well. Still, it seemed wasteful to set actual money on fire, so she'd opened them all so far (in fact, she realized, that was probably another goal of including the money in the first place).

Then Niall said, "Listen, I'm glad we have a moment without everyone else begging for attention. I wanted to ask how you're feeling. It's been a while since we, um, talked."

Yes, the last time they'd "talked" they had been behind a closed door doing far more kissing than talking.

"I'm feeling rather hemmed in, to be honest," Heather told him. "I know it's for my protection, but it's difficult."

"I don't want you to feel like a prisoner," he said. "It's been nearly a week since your uncle has arrived, and he's done nothing to threaten you after that first visit. And this Webb person may never appear. Why not go riding? There's little danger so long as you're not alone. Two of the men can follow—"

"Oh, can you not come with me?" Heather asked.

"Unless you're busy. I know you have a lot to occupy your mind." Over the past few weeks, Heather noticed that Niall was constantly meeting with various people, who she learned were tenants and workers all involved in the ongoing harvest. And of course, now she had the cursed image of him kissing Brenna in her head.

"You don't mind?" he asked.

"I think I'd feel better if you were with me. And it's just a ride," she added quickly. How much trouble could she get into while on horseback?

So they went for a ride. The moment Heather was mounted up on Sterling, she felt more free. He was an exceptional horse, far more intelligent than any she'd had before. Niall mounted up on his own horse and they were off.

The hills were gorgeous in the warm, misty afternoon light. Heather rode along the trail, delighted to be outside. She smiled and greeted everyone who happened to cross her path. She even said hello to the sheep cropping the weeds near the path, too happy to hold anything in.

Niall rode nearby, but not so close that she felt herded. He didn't say much, but his mood seemed lighter than it had been in the castle earlier. He'd been working too hard, she thought. And there was some burden on him that he hadn't shared with her, something else weighing him down—whether his feelings for Brenna or a different issue he'd not mentioned yet. She wished she could ask, but didn't want to intrude. She was very conscious of the fact that she wasn't *really* his wife.

Niall directed her to ride up a particular path, sharply inclined along a slope. Sterling practically pranced up, and soon both horses and riders stood on a bald—a patch of bare rock on the mountain that overlooked a huge sweep of lower hills and the distant sea beyond.

"My goodness," Heather breathed. "It's gorgeous."

"One of my favorite spots," Niall agreed, dismounting. He walked over and lifted her down from Sterling. His hands were warm on her waist, his eyes particularly blue, and his smile inviting. Heather took her time stepping away.

She finally turned, drawn by the spectacular beauty of the vista. A person would have to be dead to not be moved by such a scene. The autumn haze settled on the landscape, transforming each range of hills into an almost abstract version of itself, like an artist merely playing with color. The nearest range was green, with spots of orange and yellow. But the farther ridge was deeper and darker, and the one beyond that nearly blue. The ocean glimmered at the back, a silent silver world beyond her reach.

Niall stepped up beside her. "I used to ride up here every few days when I was younger. My mother once took us all here for a picnic. That was the first time I saw it. And after that, I always wanted to come back, because it's such a grand view."

"And because it reminds you of her."

"Aye. She was a good woman."

"You must miss her."

"Everyone misses their mother," he said simply. Then he looked at her with his deceptively gentle gaze. "You must miss your own."

"Every day," Heather admitted. "For a while I hated the sea. I blamed it for taking my parents away. But hating the sea makes no sense. It's not malicious, or good. The sea is just there, part of nature. It's humans who try to make the world like them, full of moods and intent and regret and vengeance and who knows what else."

"Interesting philosophy.."

"Yes, well. I'm a very interesting girl."

He took her hand, drawing her to him. "I know."

He looked like he wanted to kiss her again, and Heather definitely wanted to kiss him. Which was a problem. Hadn't she just been annoyed and offended by seeing him with Brenna? Or was she dreaming that? Could she trust her own eyes anymore?

"I suppose we should go back," she whispered, tilting her head up.

"That would be the smartest decision," he agreed, running a figure along her jaw, sending waves of anticipation down her body.

Suddenly, she heard hoofbeats coming up from behind. Then she heard Niall swear under his breath, and looked over her shoulder.

A trio of riders had come up, and now blocked the path back. Uncle Cyril, Brom…and Mr. Webb.

Chapter 14

NIALL CURSED HIMSELF FOR NOT bringing along a few reinforcements. But things had been quiet, and he'd been so damn excited to spend a little time with Heather without everyone breathing down his neck. However, even if he didn't have men with him, he did have weapons. He reached for the horse's saddlebag, where the pistol was.

"That other man is Mr. Webb," Heather whispered to Niall. "Lord, I was hoping he'd decide the journey wasn't worth it."

Hayes edged his horse ahead of the other two men. "If it isn't my darling niece."

"Steady," Niall murmured, slowly retrieving the gun. "He can't do a thing to you."

"I know," Heather replied, her eyes locked on her uncle. "But trust me, he'll find a way to be awful."

Cyril said, "On a ride with your husband? Putting on a show for the locals?"

Heather raised her chin, looking much calmer than Niall knew she was. "Oh, Uncle, I ride well, but I don't think anyone would stop their day to watch me."

"Shut your mouth, girl. You know what I mean. I mean you appearing in public with MacNair, acting as if you're happy to be here."

"I'm happier here than I ever was at home," Heather said. "At least, since you made it your home, too. Why are you still here, Uncle? I am not ever going anywhere with you. Or *him*."

Heather regarded the third man with complete disgust.

Niall examined the newcomer and had to agree with her assessment. Narrow-bodied and pig-faced, he gave off an air of meanness, as if looking for a reason to snap at anybody.

"You are Mr. Webb, I presume," Niall said.

"And you're the skirt-wearing scrub who stole my bride."

Rude.

"She stole herself, sir, after deciding that she wanted no part in a marriage to you. Which is understandable. You've got to be nearly forty years her senior."

"So? Her uncle approved the union. His approval is all that I need."

"I beg to differ. Her uncle has no more say in her life or her business than a fly in Egypt. For Heather is now my wife, body and soul."

"Soul, perhaps." Webb shrugged, not at all interested in Heather's soul. "But body? You've not taken her yet, and you can't if you're going to annul."

Heather gasped.

Niall squeezed her hand. "Don't say anything, darling. Let me handle this."

"But how could they know—" she whispered.

It was a very good question, but not one he could ponder at the moment. He needed to get these men off their backs so he could get Heather safely home. Niall hadn't yet revealed the pistol he carried, and hoped he wouldn't have to.

He stepped ahead of Heather, using his body to shield

her from Webb's view. He did not like the way the man looked at her, as if she were a piece of meat in a butcher's shop.

"I don't know what you're implying, sir, and in fact it doesn't matter in the slightest because whatever Heather does do with her marriage or her life, I assure you that you will not be a part of any of it."

"The law will side with her family," Webb said. "You are no better than a thief."

"I am much better than a thief," Niall replied coolly. "And you'd better mind your words."

Webb edged back, momentarily aware that he'd blundered. After all, he was speaking to a man who would eventually have an earldom (Hayes must have given him all the latest developments).

But Webb was too angry to modify his tone, and he said, "What *was* the purpose of this marriage? A beard to hide your true proclivities?" He sneered as he spoke.

"If that were the case, surely I'd keep her around to preserve the fiction." Niall just shook his head in exasperation. Even if he did prefer men, what did that have to do with marriage? The upper classes usually undertook marriage for financial or social reasons, or simply to secure an heir. Love and passion happened elsewhere, whether it was a kept mistress, multiple affairs, or a forbidden relationship with the same sex. "But as it happens, I am quite taken with my wife, and I will not give her up, not to anyone."

He chose that moment to subtly display the pistol at his side, keeping it out of Heather's sight.

Hayes noticed it, and the muscles of his neck and back seemed to shrink. He didn't want to make this an actual battle. Not here.

"I have appealed to your decorum, if you have any,"

he told Niall. "I remain Heather's guardian for now, and I have grave doubts about the validity of your so-called marriage. You can expect a visit from my solicitors very soon. Brom, let's go. Webb, come along."

"We're just going to leave her here with this ape?" Webb whined.

"Yes, we are," Hayes snapped. "Remember, we have other plans for her."

The trio rode off, Webb practically dragged along by Brom, who'd moved close enough to take the reins from Webb if he had to. Niall didn't let his finger off the trigger of the pistol until they were out of range.

The moment they'd gone, Heather let out a sound that was half-scream, half-sob. It tore at Niall's insides.

He stashed the gun in the saddlebag and then pulled her to him. Heather's hands lay flat against his chest, and he could hear her breathing and trying not to cry.

"It's fine, Heather. Just empty threats."

"He knows we plan to annul! How could he *know* that?" Heather asked, fury in her tone.

"Did you tell anyone?"

Heather went silent, then said, in quite a different tone, "I told Brenna."

"Brenna? Whatever for?"

"I don't know. We were talking one day, and she seemed so upset about me being there, and I wanted to reassure her that I never meant to hurt her or take her place...and she said she'd never tell..."

"Brenna would keep her word," Niall said. "Trust me, I know her."

Heather pulled back, surveying him with narrowed eyes. "So Brenna can do no wrong?"

"I dinnae say that," he protested.

"Was this her revenge for me stealing you out from

under her nose? I bet she is still in love with you!"

"Brenna was never in love with me, nor I with her," Niall insisted. "And I don't believe she would have confided in Hayes, of all people. She'd as likely spit in his eye."

"But how else could he have found out?" Heather frowned. "It's not as if I was posting an announcement in every newspaper…" She trailed off.

"What is it?"

"Paper," she murmured. "The day Uncle Cyril barged into Carregness, I was in the great hall, writing a letter to Mrs. Bloomfield, asking her advice. I did explain the situation to her, so she'd know how to counsel me…and when he left, I couldn't find the letter! At the time, I thought it had blown away or got tossed in the fire. But what if my uncle, or perhaps Brom, had snatched it up?"

"How would either have known what you were writing?" he asked.

"They wouldn't have, but it's the kind of thing either one would do, just out of spite. And when they read it afterwards, they realized it contained just what they needed to know!"

"They can't prove anything with such a letter. You said you never finished writing it, and therefore you never signed it."

"But my handwriting is known to Uncle Cyril. Ugh! What will we do now?"

Niall soothed her, saying, "Nothing has changed. You'll stay here till your birthday, and then we annul. There's nothing he can do about it."

Heather looked worried, gnawing her lower lip. "You don't know him. He's devious."

"He can be the devil himself for all I care. You're safe at Carregness. Speaking of which, let me get you back up on Sterling. We're riding home, now."

Moments later, they were back on the trail home. Heather was troubled and quiet, which made Niall uneasy. He didn't like to see her worry.

But when Heather spoke, it was not on the exact subject he expected. She asked, "What did he mean when he said *beard*? That didn't make sense to me."

Oh, Lord. How sheltered had her upbringing been? Was he about to shock her? Well, no help for it, because he wasn't going to lie and pretend it meant something else. "He was implying that I preferred men to women, and was only marrying a woman to maintain appearances."

"Oh." Heather considered the idea. "Do people do that? Get married for that reason, I mean. I know about the other part."

"Certainly people marry for strategic reasons, and have done for centuries. Society doesn't allow for any expression of love outside a very narrow channel. And marriages in particular are designed to hold the structure of society in place. If two titled men became a couple, it would be difficult to beget an heir," he said dryly.

"They could adopt," Heather replied promptly. "It might even improve things, for heirs could be selected for their good sense and kindness, rather than simply being born first. We could get rid of a lot of simpletons in the House of Lords that way."

Niall bit his lip, but a laugh broke through anyway. "I'd like to live in your world, Heather. It sounds much more logical than this one."

"Perhaps when I start traveling, I'll find that world," Heather said. "Or start it."

"When you start traveling." Niall's smile wavered. "Of course. I expect you'll discover whole new civilizations."

He didn't speak for the rest of the journey back.

* * * *

When they returned to Carregness, Maeve was sitting in the great hall, obviously anticipating them.

"Niall, Father wants to speak with you. He's been waiting."

"He can wait a bit longer. I'm hungry."

"He's got one of his men watching out the window for you. Trust me, it will go easier on us all if you go up now."

"Perhaps he's not feeling well," Heather added, with what Niall thought was much too charitable a tone. "Go and speak to him. Maeve and I will have some food prepared for when you're done."

"Aye," he agreed, giving in. He proceeded up the stairs to his father's chambers.

Even before he reached the door, his father heard him. "Niall, get in here, boy!"

Niall entered, surveying the scene. His father sat at the large oak table he used for both work and meals, but he wasn't alone. Wiggins, the solicitor that his father had used his whole life, sat nearby. A servant hovered by the window.

"Angus, pour some ale and then close the door on your way out. I must talk to my son."

Niall sat in the chair pulled up to the opposite side of the table, accepting the ale offered to him. But he said nothing until the servant left, and the door shut firmly behind him.

"I assume this is about Heather," Niall said. "And I'm not going to discuss why I should choose Brenna instead."

"Forget Brenna," his father said, waving his hand. "We have something more important to discuss."

The older man's eyes gleamed, and there was color in his cheeks. He looked five years younger, at least.

"Are you…happy?" Niall asked, flummoxed.

"Happy, he asks," MacNair said, nudging the solicitor. "Well he might ask. Yes, I'm happy. You've snatched victory from the jaws of defeat. You have, in spite of all your inborn stupidity, managed to do one thing well."

"What's that?" he asked, growing nervous. Praise from his father had always been rare, and never ended well.

"Your little wife. That one whose uncle is trying to pry her back. Heather Hayes."

"Oh, *that* wife." Niall indulged in sarcasm, because his father never cared for subtlety.

"Yes, that one. You need to keep her."

He looked at his father, swallowed, and then asked, "Why the about-face? You hate Heather."

"Of course I hate her. She's English and a conniving little bitch. But she's going to be useful." He nodded to Wiggins. "Tell him."

Wiggins straightened up, ruffled some papers in front of him, and said, "Upon the arrival of Heather MacNair, nee Heather Hayes, at Carregness, and the news that you had married her along the way, your father very sensibly dispatched agents to investigate the woman's name and background."

Niall sighed. He should have guessed. "And what did your meddling uncover?"

"The particulars of the story she told are true, as far as they go. Her parents did die at sea, and her uncle did take over her wardship and moved to live with her at the family estate in Lancashire."

"Remarkable. You've discovered that the woman did not lie." Niall looked out the window, and put his ale down on the table. He moved to get up. "If there's nothing else, Father…"

"Stay right there, Niall," MacNair ordered. "Wiggins is not finished with his report."

"Then finish it, by all means."

Wiggins said, "Your wife is an only child, with no other relatives in the family line with any standing to contest the terms of the will. Thus, she is to inherit all of her father's possessions, including the property, the business interests of his firm, and the moveable wealth of the family."

"So what does that mean in practical terms?" Niall asked, not liking the way his father and Wiggins seemed to anticipate this recitation.

"In practical terms, ten thousand a year. Approximately."

Niall didn't quite understand. "What?"

"Ten thousand a year!" his father shouted.

"Approximately," Wiggins added.

"No, that can't be right. Heather told me she expected to receive only about a thousand each year."

"She lied to you."

Niall frowned. Why would she lie about that? One answer suggested itself immediately—she concealed the extent of her wealth so that Niall wouldn't try to marry her for her money. But if that were the case, why would she agree to marry him *at all*? If Heather wanted to protect her wealth, remaining a spinster was the way to do it.

True, there'd been mitigating circumstances, in the form of Brom snapping at their heels on the road to Scotland. But even now, Niall had to admit that the hasty marriage was a stupidly romantic notion. He could have easily just had Tavish keep driving and bribed the blacksmith to hide them while Brom continued to follow the coach.

Huh, Niall thought. *That plan would have been much simpler.*

"Boy, are you listening?" MacNair growled.

"No, Father. Were you saying anything worth hearing?"

"Don't be smart, boy. If you care for the MacNair name, you'll shut your mouth and hear what I tell you next."

Niall spread his hands in a gesture to indicate that he wouldn't interrupt.

"This man, Cyril Hayes. I've sent a man into town to talk to him. He's got it in his head that the marriage hasn't been consummated, and thus might be annulled."

Yes, that had been exactly the plan.

"Now it's nonsense, of course. That girl must have been on her back the first chance she got with you. Nevertheless, you cannot let that English gowk take what's ours. Heather must remain a MacNair. And you'll do that by getting her with child, so that no one can dissolve the union."

"What."

"You heard me, boy. What could be simpler? Or is she swelling already?"

"If she is, it would be an actual, Biblical miracle."

MacNair gaped at him, uncomprehending. "My God, is it true? You've *not* bedded her?"

"We only went through the wedding ceremony to convince her uncle that she was out of his reach. We hoped to annul the marriage ourselves once Heather attained her majority." Ah, how long ago and innocent that seemed.

His father began to cough violently into his handkerchief. "Damn fool boy. That sassenach's money is the key to saving this family! You have a duty!"

"I made a promise to Heather. And it involves not doing that…duty, as you say. We entered into the marriage knowing that it was meant to last no more than six weeks. I'm not going to violate Heather's faith in me."

"Damn. Fool. Boy. Go find her and end this charade. You married her, you claimed her, now fuck her."

Niall stood up, towering over the other two. "Father, I'll only say this once. I hate you, and even if she *begged* me, I wouldn't do it. Just to annoy you."

He left, his father screaming and coughing behind him.

* * * *

Niall rushed to the upper room where Maeve and Heather were taking tea. The two women were both lounging in front of the fireplace, drinking strong tea and eating scones slathered with jam.

Heather looked over her shoulder when Niall walked in, smiling at him. "That didn't take long! Won't you join us? There's a bread and beef sandwich for you on the tray."

"Your favorite," Maeve added.

"We have a problem," Niall announced.

"What is it?"

"Your inheritance."

"What about it?"

"It's ten thousand a year," Niall said.

Heather looked at him as if he'd gone mad. "Excuse me?"

"According to Wiggins, the solicitor who's smugly perched in the laird's room upstairs, your annual income will be approximately ten thousand."

"*Ten*?" she gasped out. "That's impossible."

"If true, it explains why your uncle had been so eager to split your income with Mr. Webb," Niall pointed out.

"Ten thousand," Maeve echoed, sounding appalled. "That's a fortune."

Heather said, still shaking her head, "This solicitor you mentioned, is he still here? Let's meet with him—not in your father's room. I have questions for him."

Wiggins was sent for, and a short while later sat with the trio of Niall, Heather, and Maeve. He looked just as pallid, yet composed, as before.

"Good afternoon, Mrs. MacNair. What can I do for you?"

"You can explain why you believe I'm worth ten times more than I believe I'm worth," Heather said sharply. "My uncle told me what I should expect a number of times, and I overheard him discussing financial matters with the man he wanted me to marry, mentioning a split of money that would have given both men five hundred per year. So where is this extra amount coming from?"

"Mrs. MacNair," Wiggins said, "It may come as a surprise to you, but men are not always truthful. If your uncle told you you were worth much less, it was for reasons of his own."

Heather bit her lip, her expression stormy. "That does sound like him."

Wiggins slid a few papers toward her. "A statement from an official at your family's bank in London. It confirms the holdings and the expected annual payout."

Heather picked up the paper and read the figures. Though she was outwardly still composed, Niall could sense the turmoil she was going through, and wished he could stop it. His brief speculation that Heather was playing some game seemed stupid now. She was obviously distressed by the revelation.

"But at my house, a few years ago, I saw a document with the amount…" Heather trailed off.

"What is it?" Niall asked gently.

"I was recalling the moment. I glimpsed the papers on my uncle's desk, and I was curious, because he never shared such things with me. The only document I saw had *1000* written on it…*but* it had been partly covered by another page. A page that must have hidden that last crucial digit," Heather said.

She used the papers in her hands to hide her face from the others. "If only I'd had a few more seconds. I would have known and everything might be different now."

Niall felt a wave of discomfiting heat in his body. What she meant was that she wouldn't be here at Carregness, tangled up with him.

"So Heather really is worth ten thousand a year," Niall said glumly.

Wiggins nodded at him. "Yes, sir. And the money is entirely yours, since the marriage was entered into without any special legal understanding, and nothing entailed. She is *femina covert*, legally an extension of the husband. You control her wealth and worth."

"What? *He* controls it?" Heather looked at Niall, horror written across her face. She bolted out of her chair.

"Heather, wait. We can discuss this."

"There is nothing to discuss," Wiggins interposed. "A wife is the property of her husband, and all she owned is now owned by him."

Heather took in a shaky breath. She looked at Niall, who'd taken a step toward her with the intention of comforting her. But she didn't want anything from him. She glared at him with tears in her eyes. Then she whirled around and fled the room.

Chapter 15

HEATHER RAN TO HER BED chamber and locked her door the moment she got there. Then she stared at the connecting door to Niall's room. Though it was already locked (and Niall had given her the key to keep, to ensure that she had complete control over when the door could be opened), she suddenly felt like a cornered animal. How could she trust anyone after they learned how much money she was worth? How could she trust Niall in particular, when all he had to do to get her money was to refuse the annulment?

She slid the heavy chest from the foot of her bed to block the door. It wasn't perfect, but it was better than before.

Just as she stepped back, panting from the effort of pushing the weight alone, she heard a knock.

"Heather? Can we talk?"

"No!" she shouted back. "What is there to talk about?"

"I can think of about ten thousand things!" he snapped back. "If we're going to keep you free of your uncle, I need to know a lot more about him. With a prize that big, he won't give up easily. I assumed he'd lurk about for a few days and go back home to sulk. But this is much more serious now."

"And once he's gone, then what? You'll take charge and keep me as a wife so you get my money?"

There was dead silence from the other side of the door. Heather bit her lip, wishing she hadn't said that. But it was too late. She had plainly stated her worst fear, and got nothing from Niall to allay it.

After a tortuously long time, Niall's voice came through, low and angry. "Is that what you think of me?"

"I don't know what to think of you! I'm not some little bird you rescued out of the kindness of your heart anymore. Now I'm an easy way to riches. *And* what of Brenna?"

"What of her?" He sounded genuinely confused.

"I saw you kissing her!"

"You *what*? I've not kissed Brenna since we were thirteen years old, and that was at Christmas!"

"I know what I saw."

"Darling, I swear to you that's impossible."

"So now you're calling me delusional."

"No, I'm saying there must be another explanation."

"Or perhaps you want one woman for money and another for pleasure. Which makes you very common indeed!"

Niall was quiet for another long moment. When he spoke again, it was only to say, "I'll let you be."

She heard his footsteps fading, and wished she could call him back. She hadn't meant to snap at him like that, she was just so dreadfully upset.

Heather flung herself on her bed, staring up at the plastered ceiling. She thought back to the years as her uncle's ward. He'd deliberately fostered a belief that they were not wealthy. All the times he'd used a lack of funds as an excuse to not allow her to purchase fabric for a new gown, or visit a friend, or even request the cook serve beef more than once a week. Had he been siphoning off her income already, even before enacting his plan to marry her off and steal the rest? And the whole time, Heather accepted it like a meek little lamb. She'd always prided herself on her independent nature, her desire to know and learn and see the world. But in the end, she was revealed to be as weak and naive as any girl, unable to direct her own fate. Heather rolled onto her side, clutched a pillow to her chest, and cried.

A few hours later, she woke from a troubled sleep, unrested and unhappy. She sat up in bed. It was now past sunset, and the room was full of shadows. She got up and went to light a candle on the desk.

In the warm glow of the candlelight, she looked around the room that had become a cell of her own choosing. She noticed a white square near the hallway door—someone had slid something through the gap. She walked over to pick it up, and found a folded note from Maeve.

Heather —

I know you are terribly upset, and you need some time to yourself. But when you are ready, you will find us all happy to see you and here to help you.

—Maeve

P.S. Niall says that he's posted a man to watch your window every hour of the day and night, so don't attempt to make another rope out of dresses and leave that way.

Heather didn't know whether to laugh or cry. Was her whole past now fodder for the MacNairs to mock? Though Maeve wasn't mocking, she was simply informing Heather that a dramatic escape would not work this time. In fact, the note was very sweet of Maeve. But Heather was definitely not ready to come out and face the family, possibly ever. So here she would remain.

Her stomach gurgled slightly. She'd had only a scone for tea, and it must be near time for supper. Sitting down on the chair near the little fireplace, she contemplated the stack of logs near the hearth, which Susan or one of the other maids had refilled that morning. At least she wouldn't freeze. The fire had been laid as well, so all Heather had to do was hold the candle to the kindling.

When the flames caught and leapt merrily, she stood up and started pacing the room. What had she got herself into? Was there now any chance for her to lead an independent life? It wasn't that she disliked Niall—quite the opposite. But to be attached to a man for life just because she got a *little* bit married to him…it wasn't fair.

Looking out the window, she surveyed the landscape, which was rapidly growing dusky. The sky still held light —a purply, pinkish glow—but the trees turned to charcoal sketches and the hills mere rounded lines. She couldn't see anyone on watch in the buildings or on the walls within her view. But she didn't doubt they were there. Niall wouldn't bluff about such a thing.

She turned to the room again. There were worse places to be trapped. It was well-furnished, cheerful, and just for her. A stack of books on one corner of her desk would provide plenty of diversion, though Heather chafed at any confinement, and she already wanted to be outside, among the trees and lakes. No, she was certainly too restless to read at the moment.

There was the ink and paper. She moved to the desk, intending to write to her friends. The revelation about her inheritance was an important development, and they should know the predicament Heather was now in.

Dear Poppy,

I write to you from Carregness again. This time however, my door is locked (I locked it). We have just received information that my inheritance is far larger than I ever anticipated. Worse, it was actually Niall's father who commissioned the agent to get the information, so Niall is aware of my worth too. How does this change the plan to annul? I cannot say at this moment, but I presume he'll be unlikely to leave ten thousand a year on the table when he has to do virtually nothing to gain the rights to it. Thus, I have confined myself in my room until I can decide what to do to preserve my freedom (a notion that seems ludicrous considering that I am writing about freedom in a locked room).

I must confess that my mood is bleak, though that may be in part due to the lack of supper. WHY must the world be so vexing? Write to me of better things. Give me a report of Miss Mist — the watercolor you sent earlier this summer depicted a fluffball of a kitten, and she must be twice that size by now. And have you heard from Mr. de la Guerra at all? According to Rose, the gentleman was quite dazzled by you, which is to be expected. I pray that any romance in your life is less complicated than what I am enduring now.

Yours,

Heather Hayes MacNair Hayes

She folded, addressed, and sealed the letter. Then she slid it under the door, hoping that it would be posted and not merely tossed into the dustbin (where she now assumed most of her letters had ended up while she was under her uncle's care at Hayes House). Then Heather selected the most interesting book in her collection and tried to read.

She kept losing her place, unable to get through more

than a sentence without staring off into space, fretting about what her uncle was up to, or how Niall was feeling at that very moment. Was he plotting to break the door down? Was he disgusted with her? Was he eating? If he was eating, why wasn't he bringing any food to his wife?

"Because you bolted yourself inside a room and refused to talk to him, you ninny," she told herself.

Fair enough, she admitted, also to herself. But that didn't change the fact that she somehow expected Niall to appear—she'd gotten quite used to him appearing, especially when she was in dire situations.

"He's not going to rescue you this time," she muttered. "It's not in his interest."

Part of Heather wondered if this conversation with herself was the first sign of madness due to her confinement. Another part of Heather countered that she'd been confined for less than a day, and therefore any madness had to have been there already. (A third part of Heather wondered if she'd left any bread in the room, just by chance.) When all the parts of Heather finally pulled the covers over her head, she doubted she'd get a wink of sleep.

* * * *

Morning light filled the room when she woke up to a knocking at the door.

Maeve called out, "Heather? Here's a letter for you. It just arrived. And Susan made some especially flat shortbread, to fit under the door."

At the scraping sound, Heather looked to see a small plate slide into view, followed by a folded letter.

She pounced on the plate first, devouring the cream-colored, deliciously fragrant shortbread in moments. The buttery crumb would have gone perfectly with tea, but alas, she had none.

After eating every last bite, she picked up the letter. It was from Daisy. Heather broke the seal (that of a lion, to reflect her new title as the Duchess of Lyon) and unfolded the thick paper.

Dear Heather —

In light of your most recent news about being married, the duke and I have arranged for some assistance to come to you, in the form of a solicitor. Mr. Kemble, who you met at my wedding, has agreed to travel to Carregness as soon as possible. I only hope that he arrives in time to solve the issue of your irregular wedding and clarify your standing so that your uncle can make no more mischief.

Keep me apprised of the situation. I am not above using my position as a battering ram, and I will do whatever I can to help.

— Daisy

Heather checked the date Daisy had scrawled in the corner. Over a week ago, so Kemble might appear any day. She remembered the man well. Though he was not a particularly striking figure, she had been impressed by his calm manner and the fact that he'd helped Daisy through a very difficult spot before her marriage to the duke.

If he could work the same sort of magic for Heather, perhaps there was a way out of this mess. A quick annulment was the only birthday present she wanted.

And after her outburst toward Niall, he probably couldn't wait to get rid of her.

Chapter 16

To say that relations between Heather and Niall were unhappy was an understatement, and he was miserable because of it. The moment she'd realized that she was tethered to him by a golden chain, Heather had rushed to her bedchamber and locked both doors, not allowing anyone to even lay eyes on her. (Niall took the sensible precaution of posting one man to keep watch on Heather's window from a spot on the outer wall. He honestly didn't know how much fabric Heather might be shredding in an effort to perform another rope ladder escape, but he sure as hell wasn't going to be responsible for her falling and breaking her neck in the attempt.)

After that first exchange, Heather wouldn't even answer anybody calling to her through the door.

"Give her a few hours," Maeve had advised.

Well, he had. He gave her all night. But the next morning, the door was still locked and Heather was still inside.

So Niall tried again. Then Ian, then Maeve, then the little maid Susan.

"Please, ma'am, won't you open the door enough to let me give you a tray?" Susan begged. "It's good hearty fare. Apart from the shortbread, you've not eaten since tea yesterday, milady!"

Nothing. Not even the promise of neeps and tatties could lure Heather from her isolation.

"I don't know what to do," Maeve confessed to her brothers.

"It's easy. We get an ax and chop the door down," Ian grunted. "Don't know why you've not done that already, Niall."

"Just a hunch, but I thought Heather wouldn't look kindly on someone who literally wrecked her room along with her life."

"Bah, women love being chased and told what to do," Robert said. "They just pretend otherwise."

Maeve gave him a disgusted look. "Where's that ax, Ian? I've got another use for it. Rob's head is still attached to his neck."

He grinned. "I'm just kidding, Maevey-doll. You're too easy to tease."

"Oh, indeed? Well, here's something that's no tease. Get downstairs and out to the stables to help the boys turn that sick horse! Tis your job today."

"Ah, hell." Robert stomped off.

Finally, the MacNair himself stalked down, determined to deal with the sassenach. The family was still gathered around the door, along with several servants—the locked door held a certain fascination for everyone.

MacNair banged on her door with his metal-tipped walking stick, telling Heather that she was being a eejit, and as far as he was concerned, she could stay in that room for the rest of her life. It would merely make spending her money easier.

Heather responded to *that*. Not in words…she quietly dumped the contents of her chamber pot under the door, creating a pungent puddle that soaked MacNair's shoes and stockings before he'd realized what happened.

The old man shrieked, cursed her a hundred ways, and ordered anyone and everyone to tear the door down so he could get at the bitch.

Niall stepped up to his father (avoiding the puddle). "You will do no such thing, sir. Why don't you go back to your own chambers…and find a new pair of shoes?"

Behind him, Ian snorted with laughter.

The old man left, escorted by Maeve. Susan had already called for hot water, soap, and rags to be brought up to clean up the mess. While the little maid was working Niall went into his own room and knocked at the connecting door.

"He's gone, Heather. Off to change his shoes." Niall couldn't help but chuckle.

Silence from the other side, but he could hear her moving about the room. He continued, "You'll have to open up sometime, you know. You have no food in there, nor anything to drink, which will make your last trick with the chamber pot hard to duplicate."

"Must you?" Heather said from the other side, sounding quite horrified that he brought up the delicate matter of bodily fluids, never mind that she'd just used some as a defensive weapon.

"Speaking of that, Susan is tidying up. And my father's shoes will likely be fine after a thorough soaking. So no harm done. You can unlock the door at any time."

"I'm not letting you anywhere near me, Niall Mac-Nair! Oh, and tell Susan I'm sorry, please."

Niall sighed and walked away. Heather was going to take some time to calm down. He ought to strangle Wiggins, for being the bearer of bad news.

How could ten thousand be bad news? Niall wanted to laugh at the absurdity of everyone reacting to the news of

Heather's wealth with such distress. Wouldn't most people swoon with joy if they learned they were so rich? And yet for Heather, it brought nothing good. It only meant that she was more trapped than before, with men chasing her for her money. And apparently she now counted Niall among them.

Thus it was actually something of a relief when Niall got a message from Cyril Hayes, asking for a meeting at the Cat & Mouse. Niall decided to go even before getting to the end of the note. He wanted to know more about this man, to understand how far he'd go to achieve his aim.

Later that day, Niall walked into the inn. Ian offered to come along, but Niall wanted a private conversation. He did, however, suggest that Ian go as far as the taproom, just in case Hayes was planning something violent. Ian agreed to that idea quickly, no doubt because it meant sitting back and sipping at least one ale in the middle of the day.

Ian headed directly for a table, greeting the barmaid loudly on the way. Brodie caught Niall's glance and nodded his head toward a private dining room off to the side. Niall moved that way, accepting the whisky Brodie slid across the counter. He'd need it.

The private room held a single table with six chairs. Two were occupied. Cyril sat on one end, already half-drunk. Brom sat at the other, forcing Niall to choose a chair between them.

"Where is Webb?" he asked, surprised at the absence of the third man.

"Never mind him," Hayes growled. "I'm Heather's guardian, so I'm the only one you have business with."

Niall sensed evasion in Hayes's words—did he not trust Webb? Or were the two men perhaps not in total agreement about Heather's future? It was interesting, so he filed the thought away for later.

Niall grabbed a chair and hauled it away from the table toward the fireplace. He angled it so the others were all looking at him, and he had his back to the wall so Mr. Webb couldn't sneak up behind him. Then he sat down, crossing his ankle over his knee in a deliberately casual pose, and took a long sip of whisky.

"Well, I'm here," he said at last. "Speak your piece."

"We got off on the wrong foot," Cyril said, taking a drink of his ale. "I want to come to an arrangement."

Niall raised an eyebrow. He wasn't expecting that. "Go on."

"Heather is a very excitable girl. No doubt you've realized by now that she's quite pig-headed and rarely listens to anyone's advice."

"She is very independent," Niall allowed. He didn't mention that she'd actually barricaded herself in her room at the moment, which would just bolster the other man's point.

"It's my understanding that you were previously expected to wed another, a Miss McGlashen, and that such a union is strategic. This matter with Heather shouldn't disrupt your plans. I appreciate a man who has a strategy."

"While it's true that my father wished me to marry Brenna McGlashen, the fact is that I've married Heather."

"But the marriage can still be undone," Cyril pressed. "Let's work together to speed this annulment. Your father is an earl, whose opinion surely carries weight. And I can testify to Heather's erratic behavior and her weak mind. Between us, we can get the marriage annulled or declared invalid very quickly. I'll take charge of Heather once more, and you don't have to be bothered with her."

"Very generous of you, sir," Niall said dryly. "But court proceedings are expensive."

"I am happy to defray the costs," Cyril assured him.

"Out of your income? Or Heather's?"

The man paused, suddenly wary. "What do you mean?"

"I know how much she's worth. First thing my father did when he heard about the marriage."

Hate flashed across Cyril's face, just for a moment. Then he tried to hide it behind an amiable smile. "Ah, do you. I admit I concealed some details from her. For her own sake, of course. Women are frivolous, silly creatures. If she knew the exact details of her inheritance, she'd likely fritter it away on gowns and jewels and trips to Paris, or wherever she's taken it into her head to go."

"She mentioned Peking and Cairo, among other cities."

"There! You see the problem in a nutshell. What business does a young girl have in such places? She belongs at home."

"Carregness is her home now," Niall said softly.

Hayes didn't like that, but he tried once more. "Nonsense, sir. So you married her. You don't need to *stay* married to her. Let's make a deal. I'll see that you get half her income for three years, provided that the marriage is annulled. Then you can marry this Brenna McGlashen and get control of the lands your family so wants. Is that not the best of both worlds? Must I remind you that marriage to Heather brings you no benefits of land in Scotland, and that is where you need it. The McGlashen land borders yours. Why would you let a prize like that slip through your fingers?"

Hayes was doing his level best to get Niall to ignore the annual ten thousand pounds, wasn't he? Niall thought. But aloud, he just said, "You must have spoken to all the right people, Mr. Hayes. You are very familiar with the situation."

"What else can I do up here?" the man said, rather sourly. "I have plans for my girl. You disrupted them, but we can both work together and get what we want out of this fiasco. Compromise is the soul of civilized society. What do you say?"

Niall drained the last drops of his whisky. "I'd say that you've forgotten one thing."

Hayes leaned forward, anticipating the beginning of a bargaining session. "Oh? What's that?"

"We both want Heather. But I've got her. So I don't need to make any compromises at all."

He stood up and walked out. He gestured to Ian, who hastily finished the ale he'd been drinking and got up to follow Niall out.

"That didn't take long," he noted. "What did he want to talk about?"

"He wanted to buy Heather back, for about fifteen thousand pounds."

Ian's eyes narrowed. "Did he mistake us for Americans? We don't buy and sell people around here."

"Needless to say, we did not come to an agreement." Niall said, as they reached their horses and mounted up. "When we get back to Carregness, your job will be to seal the buildings and grounds. We've posted guards, but we could do more to keep people out."

"Aye, I'll take care of it," his brother promised. "Though as long as Heather has locked herself in her room, I'd say no one will get to her."

"She can't stay in there forever," Niall muttered, frowning as he recalled Heather's words from the day before. If she wasn't going to even talk to him face-to-face, how could he know he was doing the right thing by keeping her in the castle?

Ian chuckled. "What's the matter with you?"

"Nothing."

"Liar. You look as if you're about to fall on your sword. What can be bothering you so? Possibly a wee English wife? Bonny lass like that should be no problem at all. You just take her to bed and keep her there till she sees things your way."

"Can't exactly do that when she's locked herself away."

"Does she not know there's another key?" Ian asked.

"Of course not!" Niall had deliberately avoided telling her that a master ring resided in the MacNair's chambers, partly because that ring was never used (he couldn't remember the last time he'd even seen it), but mostly to give Heather more confidence in staying in the room adjacent to his. "And if I did use the master key, she'd take it as a betrayal. Not to mention that she hates the sight of me."

"She doesn't hate you."

"She does. And I explicitly promised *not* to take her to bed when this whole thing began."

"Niall, I can't tell if you want to be married or not. Your Heather is a charming little lass, and she's got a good head on her shoulders, and she's a heiress to boot. Yet you're tiptoeing around her like she's a catamount you're afraid to wake up."

"Easy for you to say. You don't have a stake in what happens."

"Of course I do!" Ian said. "You being married off makes everything simpler for the rest of us. We know where we stand, and what to expect in the future."

"What does that mean? You always know where you stand with me."

"I just meant...we can make our own plans," Ian

amended, looking away. "I want you to be happy, Niall. If Heather makes you happy, fight to keep her. If she doesn't, let her go. But this in-between is torture."

"Don't I know it."

When they returned home, Ian left him, already working on the task of improving their defenses.

Niall went upstairs, entered his own bed chamber, approached the connecting door, and took a deep breath before he knocked. "Heather? Are you in there?"

Stupid question. Well, considering that she sometimes left rooms by the window, perhaps not.

"I'm here," she replied.

"Can we talk…not through a layer of oak?"

There was a long silence, and then—magic!—the sound of a key in the lock.

Heather opened the door, regarding him with a wary expression. Her blonde hair fell in loose waves about her shoulders and she wore the blue dress he especially liked.

"You look nice," he said, like an idiot.

"I had a lot of time to brush my hair," she replied wryly. Then she said, "I'm sorry for what I said yesterday. And for behaving like a brat. I'm *not* sorry about your father's shoes," she added. "But I'm sorry about all the rest of it."

"You had a shock. It was understandable."

"That's very kind of you to say. But I am aware that it was not a shining example of maturity."

"Are you hungry?"

"Yes."

"Let's eat, then."

Niall requested some food be brought up to his room, guessing that Heather wasn't quite ready for the great hall. The kitchen must have been waiting for the moment, because the meal that arrived was enough for six people, not just two. Dish after dish was set on the table near the window, and Susan carried in several plates of sweets and a large tea service.

Heather thanked each and every servant who entered, and they all beamed at her. It was as if she'd been gone on a year-long journey, not just hiding in her room.

Once they were alone again, Niall brought up the most important subject. "I spoke to your uncle."

Her eyes widened. "When?"

"Earlier today. He tried to get me to work with him to annul the marriage through any means possible. He even suggested that he would have you declared insane."

"He wouldn't!"

"I'm sure he'd try. Unfortunately, if he finds a sympathetic audience, he might not have to do much work to convince them. The story of you escaping out a window barely dressed would be enough for some."

"That was a perfectly sound action taken as a result of being in an intolerable situation!"

"Or, it's an act of an unstable girl who won't listen to her guardian."

Heather frowned. "What did you say to him?"

"I told him I wasn't interested in any deal. But he's up to something."

"He always is."

"He offered a large portion of your income as a bribe. Half for three years."

"Just to get me back? And after my birthday, so I wouldn't need a guardian any longer."

"If you're declared unfit, he'd likely continue as your guardian. Which means he'd have access to your income at that point."

She banged her fork against the table. "Oooh, that makes me mad. Angry mad! Not *mad* mad!"

"I understood," he said with a smile. "But Heather, there's also the other issue. Although I refused to go along with the plan of having you declared insane, he's got another angle he can take."

"What's that?"

He looked at her in exasperation. "The fact that the marriage has never been consummated."

Heather swallowed, blushing furiously. "But he doesn't know that for sure! After finding that letter, he can guess. But we could have…you know…since then."

"If he pursues this course, he'll ask for a doctor's examination. You *are* a virgin, Heather."

She looked trapped, and furious about it. "But… what can we do?"

"We can out-wait him. He probably has to go to London to work with the various attorneys to get all the specifics in place. The law works slowly, so he'll try to expedite things."

"Using my own money, no doubt."

"If he can access it. Oh, by the way, yesterday I sent word to your bank, informing them of your marriage to me, and requesting that only you or I can access your funds. I hope that will help, or at least muddy the waters long enough to get you to your birthday."

"So that's my last hope? That I reach my twenty-first birthday virginal and sane?"

"You're doing well so far."

She shot him a skeptical look. "Am I?"

"Aye. Just a little while more, Heather." He smiled at her, hoping it looked reassuring. But in his heart, he had just one wild notion.

After Heather was no longer married to him, he was going to propose to her…again.

* * * *

The next day, Niall was in a much better mood, and he couldn't wait to share the reason with Heather. When he found her in the garden, he took Heather by the hand. "Come with me. There's something very important I've got to show you."

"What is it?" she asked, a little suspiciously.

"Just trust me. If I'm right, we've got to hurry."

"Very well." Heather allowed him to lead her back inside, then through several rooms and hallways. Niall refused to answer any questions until he reached a small room with heavy brocade curtains along one side. He put a finger to his lips, then leaned to whisper in her ear, "I've been thinking about what you said to me. About Brenna."

Heather blushed beet red. "And?"

"I think I know what's going on." He leaned to the curtain and very cautiously pulled a little fabric aside to look into to another small chamber. On the other side, he saw a couple in a passionate embrace, their voices low and eager.

Niall leaned back, then gestured for Heather to look.

She peeked past the curtains, and saw what he'd seen a moment earlier: Brenna embracing Ian.

When the truth registered, Heather clapped her hand over her mouth in surprise.

"Well?" he murmured.

"*Oh*," she whispered.

"Convinced of my innocence, love?"

"Yes! But what are they sneaking around for?"

"Let's find out."

With that, Niall pushed the curtain aside and stepped out. "Good evening," he said to the couple.

Brenna yelped in fear and jumped away from Ian.

"Niall, what are you doing!"

"Why are ye hiding behind curtains like Polonius after a banquet?" his brother added belligerently.

Niall ignored that jibe. "Ian, are you taking advantage of Brenna?"

"No!" Brenna gasped, putting herself between the brothers. "You don't understand!"

"Looks quite clear to me," he said, hiding his smile. "My heartless brother knew that you were devastated when I came home with a bride, so he played on your sadness and offered you comfort..."

Brenna held up a hand. "One moment, Niall!" She sounded quite indignant. "I was *not* devastated, not even a little bit. I never loved you."

"She's always loved *me*," Ian said quickly. "For years."

"My God, what terrible taste, Brenna." Niall shook his head, then turned to Heather. "Do *you* see anything in him?"

"Any redeeming qualities are offset by his Mac-Nairishness, I must say," Heather replied, keeping her face blank as well. "Perhaps they deserve each other."

Brenna did not appreciate their humor. She crossed her arms as she glared at Niall. "I can't marry Ian, because our fathers are so fixed on me marrying you!"

"Well, that's no longer going to happen," Niall said flatly. "The old men are just put out that their silly plan has come to naught. But Ian is still a MacNair, and you're still a McGlashen. Such a marriage is just as good for the families."

Ian shook his head. "For our father, yes, he can be talked around now that Heather's rich. But apparently Brenna's father aspires for her to be a countess."

"He'll have to be satisfied with her being a MacNair."

Niall put a hand on his brother's shoulder. "I'll get it ironed out. Brenna, you may as well start planning your wedding. We'll have to make it a grand one, to make up for the fact that you'll be stuck with Ian at the end of it."

"You promise?" Brenna asked.

"What? That it'll be grand, or you'll be stuck with Ian?"

"Both."

"Aye, Brenna. It's a promise."

"Then I'd best start planning." She now looked like a cat with cream. "Ian, come with me."

She walked away, Ian at her heels like a faithful puppy.

"*Well*," Heather said after they'd gone. She didn't add anything else.

"You really thought he was me?"

"You're practically twins from the back! And it was quite dark when I saw them together."

"You were jealous," he realized, all at once.

"I was not! Just…confused. You kissing me one moment, then seeming to be kissing Brenna the next. It's not proper."

"As if I haven't got enough on my mind. Romancing two women at once, on top of everything else."

"Well, you were engaged to her. I think it's a very understandable…misunderstanding."

"You're adorable when you're trying not to be wrong."

"I'm not going to discuss this further, Niall MacNair," Heather said, turning her nose up and beginning to walk away.

He reached out and spun her about. "Oh, I think we will, lass. You all but accused me of cheating on you, and we're not even actually married."

"But everyone thinks we are," she pointed out. "So you can understand why I want you to act like a real husband."

"Thought I was." He pulled her closer, fully intending to kiss her on her cute nose.

However, the moment he had Heather in his arms, she ceased to be adorable, and simply became too dangerous to be around. She stared up at him, her eyelashes fluttering. Her mouth was open and incredibly tempting. He could show her that there was only one woman in Carregness occupying his thoughts.

She inhaled, her chest swelling.

Niall released her before he could do any real damage.

"Sorry," he muttered. "I've got to go. Got to speak to…someone…about the thing…" He practically ran out of there, leaving Heather even more confused than before.

* * * *

It took Niall a long time to get to sleep that night, and halfway through, a light blazed in his face, and a hand grabbed his shoulder roughly.

"Niall, you need to get up and come with me." The voice was familiar. "Niall! Wake up! Now."

He blinked, seeing his sister standing at his bedside with a candlestick in her hand and a grave expression on her face. "Maeve? What is it?"

"It's Father."

Niall dressed hurriedly and walked the frigid, dim halls to his father's bedchamber. Maeve's candle cast a wobbling yellow glow against the stone walls, making everything feel strange and unreal.

In the bedchamber, all was quiet. A grey-haired servant sat on a wooden stool near the MacNair's bed, his attitude very calm.

"My lord," he said, standing up to offer the stool to Niall. "I found him like this about a half-hour ago. I always check on him in the middle of the night, to see that the room is warm enough and that he has something to drink. He's often wakeful at night, coughing. But tonight he wasn't making a sound…"

"Thank you, Angus." Niall sat down, feeling numb as he took in the sight before him.

An old man lying in his bed. That was all. No terrifying figure, no caustic words or sly looks. That was over. Because his father was dead.

The consumption must have finally done its work, stealing his breath until he could breathe no more, his lungs bloody and ruined in the wake of the disease. The old man died alone, coughing up his last and perhaps begging for mercy…but there was no one around to hear him, because he'd driven everyone away.

The MacNair finally lay silent, his face relaxing into death, finally, *finally* giving up the constant sneer of dissatisfaction he wore during his life.

"He's gone," Maeve said softly.

Someone reached out to put a hand on Niall's shoulder. "But the MacNair is still here. Whatever you need, MacNair. Tell us and it'll be done."

It was Ian. Niall hadn't even realized his brother had entered the room. But he heard his words and sensed the shift in them, putting Niall in his place as the head of the whole clan. Not just a brother any more, but the Earl of Carregness, and much more importantly, the laird of the MacNair.

Niall wasn't ready for this.

The door opened again and Rob hurried in, half-dressed but alert, his gaze immediately going to the figure on the bed.

"How is he?"

"Beyond all of us," Maeve reported, her tone equally disbelieving and relieved.

Rob exhaled, a huge sigh that seemed to come from his soul. "Thank God," he said. Then he looked to Niall, and straightened up. "What do you want us to do, my lord?"

My lord. How fast it happened, his siblings seeing him differently. Niall couldn't blame them, but he didn't want to be a lord now. He wanted to be himself, with his family.

"I want you all to sit with me," he said abruptly. "Sit up with him till dawn. Then we'll tell the world. But for now, it's us."

"Aye," Maeve nodded firmly. She lit a few more candles, while Ian and Robert pulled more chairs near the bed. The older servant discreetly left the room.

Niall felt the presence of his siblings near him. They occasionally spoke—once, Maeve mentioned that she'd send word to Fionnuala so she could attend the funeral, and Ian suggested that they just put their father's corpse in a boat on the shore and set it alight, the way the Vikings used to do. But for the most part, they sat there quietly, absorbing the truth of the old MacNair's death.

Niall's thoughts were chaotic, hopping from past to present to future. He wondered if he could send someone to rouse Heather, so he could have her near. But it was cold and dark and late…and it would be cruel to wake her at this point, simply for his own comfort. Death was not supposed to be comfortable.

He might have nodded off from time to time, because he was surprised when the shadows in the room faded and the lines became clearer as the dawn crept in. At last,

Maeve stood up.

"I should get to work," she said, her tone practical and unsentimental. "There's so much to do for the funeral."

Ian lumbered to his feet. "Aye, there's messages to be sent, yes? Rob and I will handle that." He looked at Niall. "Stay awhile, brother. We'll see that you're not disturbed."

He shook his head. "I can help too."

"As the MacNair, you'll be busy soon enough," Maeve noted. "Get your thoughts in order now. We'll see things are started."

"Thank you," he said softly, to all of them. In one night, everything changed. What would happen now?

Chapter 17

WHEN HEATHER WOKE, SHE IMMEDIATELY sensed something different in the air—a haste and tension that hadn't been there before. She went downstairs and found servants hurrying to and fro.

"What's happened?" she asked Susan, who was bearing a huge pile of bedsheets.

"The old laird passed during the night," Susan replied.

"Oh, my goodness! Where is Niall?"

"The laird is still at the deathbed," the maid confirmed. "He stayed up all night."

Heather turned around to take the stairs back up. *The laird.* Of course. All the titles and responsibilities came to Niall. She couldn't imagine what he was feeling now.

Oh, no. Did this mean she was now a fake countess? Heather shuddered at the thought.

The upper floor was busy as well, but the closer she got to the laird's chambers, the more muted everything became. People stepped more carefully, voices were hushed.

"He's in there, my lady," one servant whispered, pointing to the open door.

Heather peered in, seeing Niall hunched on a stool near the bed. A figure lay upon it, utterly still.

She came up to Niall softly, making her presence known but also allowing him to ignore her if he didn't want to talk.

He looked over at her, his eye brows lifting in slight surprise—had he forgotten she was even in the castle? Possibly. She said, "Niall, I'm so sorry."

"Ach, he was an arse."

"But he was your father. And with your mother gone before…you must feel lost." She remembered how she felt at the news of losing her own parents—unmoored from reality.

He shrugged, turning back to the corpse. "What I feel doesn't matter. I'm laird now. I have to think of that above all else."

"Of course."

His face had a haggard appearance. She doubted he'd shed a tear for the cantankerous, complicated man he called father. But all the same, the death took a toll, and Niall's usual good humor was buried deep. This was no time for Heather to bring up the touchy topic of their tangled relationship. She put her hand on his shoulder, squeezing gently, wishing that she could say or do something to relieve the burden.

Niall didn't raise his head, but he reached up to grasp her fingers in his. "I hated him," he said quietly. "But I was used to him always being there."

"I barely knew him, but his presence was immense every time I saw or even thought of him. It will take time for everyone to adjust to his being gone."

"I'm the MacNair now," he said then.

Heather knelt to better see his expression. "Pardon me for being an ignorant English woman, but I still don't truly know what that means. It seems…antiquated."

"It *is* antiquated. From the earliest days of our history—Scottish history, I mean—the clans each had a leader, a man who was the center of everything and made the decisions no one else could make, and stood up to the rest of the world to let them all know what it meant to face the weight of the whole clan. It gave us the strength we needed to survive. Any time a MacNair faces trouble, there's someone to go to, to seek justice and get the support needed to fight back.

"And now, that's me."

Heather gave him an encouraging smile. "Then every member of your clan is very lucky. Because you'll do splendidly."

"How do you know that?"

"Well, you dashed to my rescue, didn't you? And I wasn't even a MacNair."

A ghost of a grin crossed his lips. "And look how that turned out."

"It's not over yet." She paused, then said, "*Is* there anything I can do for you? At this moment, I mean? I want to help you if I can."

He looked her in the eyes, and Heather was caught in a swirl of need, a nameless desire for any firm ground to hold on to.

Just then, Maeve entered, bearing a bucket of water and a stack of rags. Heather realized she was there to wash and prepare the body for burial. "Excuse me," Maeve said, putting the bucket down. "But I should not wait longer."

Niall nodded, and stood up. He must have been in that position for a long while, because he almost stumbled when he took his first step. Heather reached out to take his arm.

"Let's go and find some food, shall we?" she suggested. "You'll need it."

She walked with Niall down to the great hall. He spoke very little, but from the way he put his hand on hers, she felt that he was glad she was there.

They sat at the long table, and soon had not just oat porridge but also sausages and thick bread to eat. Heather bit into a buttered slice when a servant approached.

"My lord, my lady," he said. "There's a visitor. A Mr. Kemble, says he came from London."

Heather blinked, having temporarily forgotten that Daisy even instructed him to come. She looked to Niall. "He's the solicitor my friend the Duchess recommended. I expect that you don't want to deal with that matter to-day…"

But Niall pushed the plate away and told the servant to send Kemble in. "Life goes on, and I doubt your uncle will suspend *his* activities for a mourning period."

A man entered the room. He was unprepossessing in all ways: middling height, middling coloring, middling attire.

He bowed to Niall first. "Good afternoon, sir. That is, my lord. I was just informed of the events of last night. May I offer my condolences? I am Jackson Kemble."

Niall nodded. "How do you do? And I don't have to introduce you to Heather, which is good, because I have no idea what her title or address should even be at this point."

"Perhaps we can settle that soon." Kemble gave him a little smile, then turned to her. "I shall address you as Lady MacNair for now, if that's acceptable. For polite-ness, if nothing else."

"It is good to see you again, Mr. Kemble," Heather returned. "I promise that if the title turns out to be incor-rect, no one will blame you. May we offer you breakfast? Or perhaps tea?"

"Tea would be much appreciated, my lady."

Heather nodded to the maid who was standing to the side, and the girl left to fulfill the request.

Niall said, "So you're the man who's going to extract us from our mistakes and save us from ourselves?"

Kemble considered that for a long moment, then said, "No. I'm the man who will tell you the truth."

Niall nodded once. "That's better. Ah, here's tea."

Talk paused while the maid distributed the tea things. Heather poured. Then she took a sip, relishing the strength of the brew. She wasn't sure she'd want to go back to the weak, straw-colored tea she used to get at Hayes House.

Kemble said, "As her grace may have mentioned in her correspondence, I've been a very good friend of her husband the duke for years. Her grace believes most strongly that her friends deserve all she can do for them, and Miss Hayes is a dear friend. So as a favor to them all, I've come here. I've argued before the bar, and studied the law. I'll offer what insight I can into your…situation."

Then Kemble asked a series of questions that Heather was sick to death of by now. But she dutifully recalled the events of her and Niall's hasty drive to Gretna Green, the wedding ceremony, and the subsequent events.

Kemble took a few notes as they spoke, and also mentioned that he'd stopped at Gretna Green himself on the way up.

"Did you speak with the blacksmith?" Niall asked.

"I did, and he remembered you both clearly, and was happy to point out your entry in his book."

"You did that before you even spoke to us? That's dedication," Heather noted. "It was very kind of Daisy to send you to work as my attorney."

Kemble's expression changed. "Well, in fact…"

She frowned. "What is it?"

"I can't be *your* attorney. As a married woman, you can't really have legal representation of your own."

"Excuse me?" Heather put her cup down, the tea suddenly bitter on her tongue.

"To secure any such service requires your husband's permission."

Niall's eyes widened. "Of course I'll give it!"

"No, sir, don't do that," Kemble replied smoothly. "The very act of acknowledging your permission is needed might be taken as more evidence that the marriage is accepted by all parties. So. What I will do is act as Lord MacNair's attorney, which avoids all complications of permissions and what that implies. Since you both seek the same outcome—the dissolution of the marriage after the sixth of October by whatever means we can devise—there is no conflict of interest."

"My God in heaven," Heather gasped. "I really have no rights, do I? Marriage is *awful*."

Niall looked away, then muttered, "Perhaps we'd better continue this discussion in private."

"Oh, please. I wouldn't want to intrude upon a discussion that involves the rest of my life! Do tell me when you've decided my fate." She got up and stomped off… which would have been more satisfying if she had somewhere to stomp off to.

* * * *

A while later, Niall and Kemble sat in a small study on the upper floor (the large audience chamber favored by the old MacNair now closed off for obvious reasons). Niall considered insisting that Heather be present, if only to sit silently in a corner to overhear the discussion. Then he remembered that *Heather* and *silence* rarely fit in the same sentence, and decided he'd simply report the results to her later.

Kemble sat in a large oak carved armchair and pulled out a portfolio, but didn't yet open it. He said, "I will not pretend that this is a simple matter, but where complications exist, it means that opportunities also exist. The law loves specificity, and I believe that any victory we have will come from exploiting the very particular situation we have here."

From those few words, Niall could sense the man's intelligence. Not witty in the way that social climbers are witty, desperate to impress with a bon mot. Kemble's intelligence was slow and steady, built up from observation and careful thought.

"Well, I hope you are not wasting your time. I think that the first question which must be answered is…how married am I?"

Kemble eyebrow raised. "It's not a matter of degree. You either are or you aren't. And since you've both described a wedding ceremony at Gretna Green, which was conducted by a resident who made a record of it…you're married."

"Damn. You're sure there's no way out?"

"As you are no doubt aware, there are points of contention. Even though you married in Scotland, Heather Hayes is English, and her guardian could bring a case against you alleging that his ward is underage as an Englishwoman, even though she is of age if she were Scottish."

"But that doesn't matter, does it?" Niall asked. "The marriage happened on Scottish soil. I could marry a girl from China as long as she was of age."

"That is the counter-argument, and you may be sure that the battle over the outcome would require many attorneys and cost thousands upon thousands of pounds to settle. Not to mention the years of indecision before any conclusion could be reached."

"But what does the law actually say? It must say *something*."

"That's what I'm trying to tell you," Kemble said patiently. "The law is not a single, complete, perfect document. It's a body of cases, its statutes established over time. It's also common law developed over centuries of disputes and resolutions. The law is not absolute, it is interpreted by men…and the final interpretation is not at all certain."

Niall sighed. "So what do you recommend? What are grounds for annulment? There must be something."

"Yes, indeed. Non-consummation—"

"Aha! I knew it!"

Kemble held up a warning hand. "Non-consummation due to impotence, with impotence being proven after husband and wife share a bed for three years with no evidence of intercourse and the wife and husband's public statements that no sexual congress took place."

"Three *years*?" He couldn't imagine sharing a bed with Heather for three *nights* without a significant amount of congress.

"In some cases, a man has been able to prove impotence by demonstrating failure to, ahem, perform. Two reliable male witnesses must corroborate that they observed the attempt. Unsurprisingly, it is not a common defense."

Niall could see why. Only by humiliating himself could a man make himself eligible for the annulment. Virtually every man in the world would prefer to remain married, no matter what difficulties came with it. And how would it look for a *laird* to do so? It would reflect badly on the whole clan.

There had to be another way.

"Was it a *valid* marriage though?" Niall asked. "According to English law, Heather is a minor, and her uncle definitely did not give permission."

"I doubt any court would make much of the lady's so-called minority. Her birthday is weeks away, not years. And she entered into the marriage quite willingly. She was not dragged to the altar. And she continued to stay here in Carregness afterward, suggesting that she is content with the situation."

"I wouldn't go that far. She would prefer not to be shackled to me."

"Is that so?"

"Wasn't it obvious how angry she was earlier? She hates me for tricking her into marriage."

"But it was no trick," Kemble said. "According to both you and Heather, it was an arrangement agreed to by both parties."

"Only because she thought it would last a short time. Even I believed that it could be annulled without much hassle. Or even declared invalid. Is there nothing else?" Niall asked.

"All that is left is divorce. Which is messier, brutally public, and makes it near impossible for either party to marry again."

"Heather may still wish for it."

Kemble looked out the window as he said, "The most common reason for divorce is the wife's adultery. Which would require evidence, usually the testimony of the man who…"

"There is no such man!"

"Not yet. You'd have to arrange it."

Arrange it? "Over my dead body!" Niall snapped.

"If you're dead, no divorce would be necessary."

"Is this what passes for humor among lawyers?"

"Mrs. Kemble laughs at my jokes." The lawyer sat back. "If you ask me, it sounds like you wish to remain married."

"Heather does not," he said, quickly skipping over the painful truth. He did want to keep her. But she didn't want to be kept. "And I won't trap her with me if there's a way out."

"There are ways out. As mentioned before, one of you could die…I don't recommend that. More practically, you could put her aside, give her a house somewhere and pay for her annual expenses while she pretends to be a widow…she wouldn't be the first woman to cover up her past for the sake of a more peaceful future."

Niall shook his head. Maybe if he'd been an ordinary man. But as earl? How could such a fact remain hidden? And he couldn't marry again without risking the charge of bigamy, making any children illegitimate. Again, the clan would never stand for that.

"Not possible," he said.

"Then you must divorce, which as I stated before, will be costly and messy and likely leave both of you far more miserable than the marriage would."

"You can't simply undo it? This femina thingummy—"

"Femina covert?"

"Yes that. It's insane. It demotes Heather from a person to a possession. *My* possession. She can't legally do a single thing without my approval. Do you know how she reacts when someone tells her she's not permitted to do something?"

"It's the traditional legal structure for marriages."

"She is *not* traditional. She hates me for the role I have

in her life now. And I can't live with her hating me."

"Alas, I'm merely an attorney, not a wish-granting fairy."

"So there's nothing to be done?"

"Possibly there's an exception, some case in the past that may give you leverage. It would take time to research the existing law to find it…if it's there to be found."

"Will you?" Niall leaned forward. "Will you do this for us? I have no idea how much the duchess allotted for your work, and I admit that I have very little to spare—less than that, actually."

Kemble held up a hand. "Fear not. I am under strict instructions from the duke himself to do whatever I can. The cost is no obstacle."

"I wish I could say that," Niall muttered. "Well, shall we take this news to my unhappy wife?"

* * * *

Heather pretended to busy herself with other tasks, but she kept one eye on the door from where Niall and the attorney would emerge. She couldn't pin her hopes to the meeting, but part of her very much wished that Mr. Kemble would know some obscure point of law that no one else had thought of, and she could walk away unfettered and able to do whatever she liked without any man telling her the shape of her life to come.

Finally, finally, the two men came into the great hall. Niall immediately walked over to Heather. He didn't look triumphant, but he also didn't seem crushed.

"What did you learn?" she asked anxiously.

"I learned that the law is a many-headed beast," he said. "And that it's a wee bit more difficult to unmarry than I thought. But Mr. Kemble here has graciously agreed to work on the matter, and see if there is any loophole we might slip through."

Heather glanced at the lawyer's face, and noticed the hesitation there.

"It's a long shot, isn't it?" she asked him.

"Yes. But there's always a chance. The law has any number of dark alleys and forgotten corners. I may find something that may be of use to you—or I'll point you to someone else who can."

"That's very kind of you," Heather said warmly, sorry that she'd been so salty before.

"Her grace ordered me to move the earth if it would help you." Kemble gave them both a little bow and excused himself.

Niall took her by the arm and led her to the window. "Do you feel better now? Kemble seems like he knows his business."

"I'm sure he'll do his best, though it may be beyond any mere mortal." Heather sighed, then brightened as a thought struck her. "What if I pretend to die? Uncle Cyril won't harass a corpse."

Niall frowned at that suggestion. "He won't have to. Your fortune would immediately go to either him or me, depending on the court's mood. You'd lose it all, and when you came back to life, you'd be a pauper."

"Blast, I hadn't thought of it like that."

"Heather, you know that you are welcome here, yes? You'll have a home at Carregness. No matter what happens."

She smiled at him, her heart melting a little at the words. Niall and his family were very delightful. It was too bad she and he weren't in love. "I know that, Niall. But we also both know that any place I don't want to be isn't a home. It's a cage."

* * * *

A few days later, Niall and Robert found Heather in the great hall. Niall was smiling. "Ready for a piece of good news? Your uncle has left town."

Heather brightened. "Really? How wonderful!"

Rob nodded. "I was keeping an eye on him. Earlier today, he paid up with Brodie and had all his things packed up and taken down to a coach traveling to London. Whether he'll go all the way is another matter, but at least he's leaving Scotland."

"He may only go as far as Lancaster, to get a private coach back to Hayes House. Did Brom go with him?"

"Aye, and Mr. Webb as well, though he went in his own carriage with his own driver, since that's how he got here."

"That's marvelous," Heather said happily. "They must have given up when they realized that they'd be facing off against the earl himself now."

"Actually," Robert noted, in a slightly amused tone, "it seems that both your uncle and Mr. Webb had been losing very heavily in the local card games. They may have simply run out of money."

Heather realized that her uncle's latest letter had not included the usual ten-pound note. Perhaps Rob was right. Regardless, she was overjoyed to hear that they'd gone. It was as if she'd been under a cloud for weeks, and the wind had just pushed it onward, leaving her to soak in the sun at last. "Bless you, Rob. This is the best news!"

He grinned, and then went on his way, saying he needed some rest after his day of surveillance.

Heather turned to Niall. "I almost feel we should celebrate in some way."

"A feast? Fireworks? Burning in effigy?" He took her

hands in his, his eyes crinkling in the corners as he smiled. "Say your wish and it will be done."

"Well, I was only thinking of a cake," she admitted. "But burning in effigy does have a certain charm. A straw Uncle Cyril would make a jolly fire."

"Then let's do both. Tea and cake out by a bonfire. Could be the start of a new tradition."

She laughed, and was conscious of the strong desire to lean in and kiss him. But then, a strange expression crossed Niall's face. Heather followed his gaze, but saw only a blue-coated man waiting at the far end of the great hall.

"Who is that?" she asked.

"A local man," Niall said shortly. "He's here to speak to me."

"Did he have business with your father? Is he here to offer condolences?"

"I doubt it. Excuse me, Heather. I'll find you later."

Chapter 18

WHEN NIALL SAW THE MONEYLENDER Mr. Ogilvy standing in his hall, he wanted to bolt. But that was not a thing lairds did, so instead Niall told the footman to make Ogilvy wait five minutes before escorting him up to the upper parlor as Niall decided to call it (he still hadn't slept in the room, and didn't think he ever would). Niall went up immediately and attempted to keep himself from grabbing a sword as he'd do if an enemy stormed the keep.

All too soon, the servant opened the door and announced his visitor.

"Yes, come in," Niall said, with admirable calm.

Mr. Ogilvy entered and bowed. "My lord, please accept my deepest sympathies for your loss. And congratulations on your gain."

"The title? It's not much of a gain."

"My lord, I refer to your wife...*are* you married?"

Niall spread his arms in a gesture of defeat. "It's difficult to say at this point."

"Well, in the spirit of courtesy, I will hope that Lady MacNair, Countess of Carregness, is doing well."

"Very kind of you." Niall would have offered the same wish for Ogilvy's wife, except that he knew the man never married...a very intelligent move, he had to admit.

The guest cleared his throat. "My lord, it pains me to bring up so crass a subject while you are in your bereavement, but there is a piece of business we must discuss."

"Go on."

"Two years ago, you borrowed a considerable sum from me, sir. Some eight thousand pounds. And last year, you borrowed another five."

"I used that money for improvement to Carregness and the surrounding properties."

"I am sure that you spent the loan in the wisest and most sensible way, sir. A model I do wish some of my other clients would follow, rather than frittering it away on gambling and vice. However, the manner in which you spend the loan is not my concern. The fact that you pay it back is."

Niall frowned. "When have I even given you cause to doubt my surety? I've paid the interest you so thoughtfully included at every quarter. And I'll pay back the principal, in time."

"'*In time*' is rather vague. You will recall that you agreed that you would repay the loan upon your elevation to the title of Earl of Carregness."

"My father is barely in the ground, and you come to wring money out of me?"

"Believe me, it gives me no pleasure to intrude upon you during your grief."

"Then why did you? Just to remind me? A letter would suffice! I'll pay back the loan. As you say, I am earl now. And I will keep my word. Wait until the harvest is in, and I know the profits made on all the Carregness lands. I will set aside as much as possible to repay what I can of the principal, if the interest is not enough for you!"

"The thing is, I need it a bit sooner than that, sir."

"How soon?"

"Fortnight. All of it."

Niall blinked. "You've got to be joking."

"Alas no. And while I've been generous before in allowing my clients to pay debts back incrementally, I'm afraid that the terms of the debt are very simple. You can refer to the copy of the contract you hold. Should I choose, I can call the whole amount in at any time, as the only limiting term was that you be earl. And that's what I'm doing now."

Niall stood up, paced to the fire. His heart had begun thumping wildly, and his muscles clenched. "I don't have that much on hand. You cannot imagine that I do."

"It is said that the new countess is an heiress to a considerable fortune."

Niall whirled around. "I will not touch my wife's money to repay my own debt!"

Ogilvy raised an eyebrow. "Why ever not?"

"It's complicated, and I do not choose to discuss it with you."

"Fair enough. But I must warn you that if you do not give me the money I am owed, I will take my complaint to the authorities. And if you don't pay me in money, I will take what's mine in land."

Niall set his jaw, appalled at the threat. Taking Carregness from him, when he'd only just assumed true stewardship over it?

Ogilvy bowed once more. "Good day, my lord. Please extend my greetings to Lady MacNair and your family."

He strolled off, leaving Niall alone, poor, and desperate.

* * * *

Later that evening, Niall knocked on the connecting door, his heart hammering in his chest. This was insane. He was going to seduce his own wife for nefarious reasons, and all he could think about was how he'd possibly keep himself under control long enough to actually do it.

Heather opened the door, looking surprised, but smiling.

"It's rather late, my lord. People might get the wrong idea."

Niall didn't respond to the jest. He couldn't. "May I come in?"

Heather moved aside to let him in, then closed the door, her expression changing to worried. She asked, "What's the matter? You look terrible."

"I feel terrible." He sank to the edge of her bed, leaning to put his head in his hands. "I feel...I don't know. Heather, I shouldn't be here. In your room..."

"It's fine. I think we've learned how to behave by now. And if you're upset, I want to know why." She sat next to him, reaching to take one of his hands in her own. God, why was she so bloody sweet?

Niall had to stop thinking so much. He turned and kissed her.

Heather went still for a moment, obviously not expecting it. But then she responded, her hands reaching out to take his shoulders, clearly open to the idea of more.

He loved the feel of her mouth against his, the scent of her breath and her body, and the way she felt in his arms. She was so soft and warm and lovely. He plucked at the few buttons on the back of her gown, distracting her from his intent by opening his mouth and deepening the kiss.

Heather's tongue grazed his and he groaned at how sharply his arousal increased. This was going to be embarrassing.

She continued to kiss him, curious and interested and very trusting. Her hands slipped down to his chest, and he could feel the heat of them through his clothing.

At that moment, he got the last button undone, and tugged at her gown, loosening the top. The damn stays were underneath, blocking access to her breasts. He found the strings and yanked on them.

Heather gasped. "Niall, what are you doing?"

"I want to see you," he muttered. "There's so much of you I've never even got to glimpse." He discarded the stays, leaving only the shift now between him and what he needed. But it was loose, the neckline low and easy to pull down, revealing enough of her breasts to make him want to howl.

Instead, he bent his head and kissed the skin, feeling her heart beat in her ribcage. She was wildly excited, and that urged him on.

He kissed, he licked, he sucked. And all the while, Heather held him close and made little sounds of pleasure and surprise. How could he have not done this before? She was divine.

And he was damned. He stopped, pushing himself away from her, and moving off the bed. Heather sat up, frowning. "What's wrong?"

"Your ring. Can I have it back, please?"

"Now?" Heather held out her hand, examining the sapphire ring as if she'd never seen it before. "Don't you trust me with it?"

"It's not that. It's just…I need it."

"For what?" she asked, puzzled.

"I'm going to sell it."

"But it was your mother's!"

"I need the money."

"Well, if you need…" Heather moved to pull the ring

off her finger, but then went still. Her eyes widened and her jaw dropped slightly. "You need money."

Niall knew that she'd figure it out, but he wished it wasn't now, when he was dying for her. "It's not like that," he protested.

"It's exactly like that," Heather said, her eyes narrow. "Maeve mentioned that man from earlier today was a moneylender. You owe him, don't you? You meant to seduce me just now, to lock me into the marriage once and for all. All this talk of finding a way to annul, asking Kemble to do more research…you were stalling until you found the right moment to do *this*." She gestured to the bed in disgust.

"Heather, please. I didn't do it, did I? I stopped."

"Oh, how *kind* of you." Scrambling to get away from him, Heather moved to the furthest corner of the room. "You refrained from doing the one thing we both agreed to never do."

"If you're so hellbent on acting like you'd prefer a nunnery, then why did you agree to marry me at all?" he asked, unfairly.

"Because I had *no choice*! I was running away from my home. I had no money with me and no way to get money. If you hadn't come by, I would probably have slept outside, or had to *beg* for a room…assuming I survived whatever assault those ruffians planned for me. But you did come by. And you did propose. So I accepted, because it was mad and you seemed sincere, and I had no other options."

She flung the ring at the floor, where it rolled to Niall's feet.

"I should have taken you to a nunnery and dropped you at the door," he said, stooping to pick it up. "At least then you wouldn't be here driving me mad!"

"You seem sane enough to me, coldly calculating each step in your stupid seduction so you can get all my money at last."

"Did that feel cold?" he growled.

"It does now that I know why you did it," she said, slicing into his soul. "Get out."

"This is my home."

"But it's my room. So kindly get the hell out of it."

Niall strode to the connecting door and slammed it shut, the bang of heavy oak reverberating through the whole level.

Behind him, he heard the key scrape in the lock as Heather sealed herself off once more.

Back to this, he told himself. Well, at least he'd know where she was.

* * * *

For her part, Heather fumed for a good long while, too furious to think beyond the next few minutes. How could he do that? How could he just stroll into her room, make her melt with need, and then just casually note that he was doing it for her money?

She glanced at her finger where the ring had been. She'd only worn it for a few weeks, but the spot felt bare and chilled now. She wondered how much he'd get for the ring when he sold it, and if it would be worth giving up the connection to his mother.

Ugh. It wasn't her concern. She was done with Niall MacNair. She was done being the prize. Heather Hayes was meant to be on her own, and tonight was the final, devastating reminder of what could happen when she gave up her own dreams for the sake of someone else's.

She pulled out a sturdy bag that was stored in the

chest at the foot of the bed. Quickly and quietly she packed the few items she could. One gown to change into, a shift, extra stockings and some other essentials. She folded in the banknotes, and shoved the whole bag under the bed until she was ready to use it.

Heather's plan was simple. Act normally until no one was watching, and then leave Carregness forever. It shouldn't be difficult. She knew the stable boys by now, she knew which horses wouldn't be missed, she knew several paths between the castle and the town. By the time Niall realized she was truly gone, it would be too late.

With her goal in mind, Heather went down to the great hall, and when she spied Susan clearing the tables from the late supper, she asked the maid to bring some bread and cheese to her room.

"No hurry," Heather added airily, as if she didn't really care if she got it or not. "Just in case I find myself hungry later this evening. Oh, and perhaps a little shortbread, if there is any. You make it so well."

Susan beamed, and promised a tray would be brought up.

Heather thanked her. In fact, she had no appetite at all. Her stomach was knotted rope after her encounter with Niall. She might never eat again. She intended to pack the food in her bag for the journey tomorrow.

At that moment, she saw Niall enter the great hall at the other end. He noticed her and checked his progress. Heather gave him a frosty look before walking out, her back stiff. She had nothing to say to him. Nevertheless, she could feel his gaze on her, and then realized that she wore the plaid shawl around her shoulders.

Damn it. The very first step in ridding herself of the MacNair influence should be to toss the stupid tartan out the window. But it *was* very warm.

"Lord help me," she muttered as she stalked down the passage and up the staircase. "My nightmares will be in plaid."

Chapter 19

NIALL COULDN'T SLEEP THAT NIGHT. He couldn't even lie down, he was too on edge. So he saddled his horse and rode into the village. It occurred to him that for the price of a few coins, he could find a woman to take the edge off. A straightforward, uncomplicated transaction.

But the moment he thought of that, he knew it wouldn't work. Not for more than a half-hour. He didn't just need a physical release. He needed this whole mess to be done with. And spending the night with a prostitute would change precisely nothing about his situation. Or the fact that the only woman he really wanted was Heather. The one woman he couldn't have.

He kept riding—a stupid, foolhardy thing to do in the nighttime, but then, he was clearly a stupid, foolhardy man. There was a larger town several miles further on, closer to the main roads and therefore a hub of commerce. And where there was commerce, there were lenders.

He knew of a few names, though he'd hoped to never have to visit any more lenders in his life. When he arrived, the business of the first man was locked up tight and totally dark. Niall didn't know where the man's home was, so he went to the next name on his list.

It took him to a narrow but well-kept building on a

side street. The ground floor hosted a seamstress's shop, but he saw lights above and took the rickety side-stairs to the upper door. He knocked, impatient for any response.

He had raised his fist to knock again when the door opened. A huge man stood there, his dull eyes giving Niall a once-over. "What do you want?"

"Is Mr. Halperin in?"

"'S'verra late," the man growled. "I'll see."

The door slammed shut, leaving Niall out in the cold.

A few moments later, the huge man was back. "Follow me," he ordered Niall.

So Niall followed the man through the front room down a short hall, to a small office, where a man stood beside a desk.

"This is him, sir," Niall's guide reported (rather unnecessarily, Niall thought.)

"Mr. Halperin?" he said. "I am Niall MacNair. How do you do."

The gentleman was younger than Niall thought he'd be. Much younger, with a full head of dark hair and the broad frame of a sportsman or an athlete. He did not look like he spent his life in a counting house.

"Actually, it's Lord MacNair now," Niall said, correcting himself. "My father very recently passed away."

"Did he, my lord? May his memory be a blessing."

Niall couldn't stop a grimace. "Hardly, but I appreciate the sentiment."

Halperin's lip quirked, but he just turned to the other man and said, "That will be all, Redford. You should go home now. It's quite late."

"Sure, sir?" the man asked, with a suspicious glance at Niall.

"His lordship will be the soul of courtesy, no doubt."

"Aye, sir." The man lumbered out.

After the door closed, Halperin said, "He was hired to prevent physical threats to me as well as any attempts to steal from the premises. He takes his job very seriously. Please take a seat and tell me why you've come."

"I think it's obvious why I've come. I need money."

Halperin gave him a half-smile. "A common affliction."

Niall offered the basic details of how much he owed and what interest had been paid so far. The other man raised one eyebrow at the amount but otherwise made no comment.

"I was not able to raise a loan from the London bankers I went to. And I refuse to get drawn into any arrangement with the less…reputable lenders."

"Wise, if you enjoy breathing air instead of getting drowned in a river."

"Precisely. And since I will not sell any land, my options are limited. The fact is that another lender—Ogilvy, do you know him?"

Halperin nodded shortly.

"He's recalling a previous loan he made to me, very suddenly."

"You're not the first to tell me so," said Halperin.

Niall paused, taking that news in. "Really?"

"Three others have come to me with a similar tale. For whatever reason, Mr. Ogilvy wants a vast amount of funds available to him. If it's any consolation to you— though I expect it's not—Ogilvy's demand isn't personal."

"Just damned inconvenient. The harvest is still coming in and I need those profits to reinvest. One more year…"

"One more good year," Halperin corrected.

"One more good year, fine. And then the MacNair lands will be well on their way to turning record profits."

"Heartening."

"And I can offer a token of good faith." Niall placed the sapphire ring on the desk. "By itself, the stone is worth a few hundred pounds."

Halperin picked up the ring, surveying it with curiosity but also with professional confidence. "A beautiful piece of jewelry. An heirloom?"

"It belonged to my mother."

"While I appreciate the gesture, I do not hold any items hostage in my business. It is a contract that determines our obligations." He handed the ring back to Niall, who took it with more relief than he wanted to admit.

"Then let's discuss a contract," Niall said. "The sooner I can take care of this, the better."

Halperin sat back in his chair. "Unfortunately, my lord, I will not make you a loan of any amount."

"What?"

"You heard me. I will not loan you any money, for several reasons. The first is that—as you've admitted—no other reputable lenders will make a loan, suggesting that you are a poor investment. They think you'll fail to repay. Why should I think differently?"

Niall couldn't believe what he was hearing. "Sir, I need the money."

"That is undoubtedly true. We all need money." Halperin spread his hands out in a gesture proclaiming *there's nothing new under the sun.* "It is the nature of the world we live in. But you are already in debt too far. You cannot take more on without offering the one thing you say you will not offer: your land. That is a noble stance, in all senses of the word. I would encourage you to hold firm on that."

"I don't understand. You're a moneylender refusing to lend money?"

"In this case, yes."

"But why?"

"Greed is an evil thing, my lord. Let me explain. In my profession, I am succeeding. I am quite comfortable, and will continue to have many clients even if I never lend you a pound. So if I were to make a loan to you now, it would be purely out of greed. A desire to have more and more, no matter how it is acquired. It is one thing to be a good businessman. It is quite another to place one's business above all else. If I were to loan you money knowing that you are in desperate straits and unlikely to be able to repay on the terms I set, then I would be acting unethically to do it. That is why there are laws forbidding minors to sign such contracts, for instance. They lack not just the authority, but the judgment to know what they are entering into."

Niall took a deep breath. "Very nice words. But not of much use to me."

"No, I imagine not. What *would* be of use to you is discovering why Ogilvy wants so much capital," Halperin said, with careful emphasis. "As Lord MacNair, you may be in a position to take some action there."

Niall inhaled. He still hadn't quite come to terms with what his title meant. Could he do something to prevent Ogilvy from demanding all the money at once? "May I ask you a question then, sir?"

"Certainly."

"You mentioned three other people. If you cannot give me their names, can you tell me where they are from, or what they have in common?"

Halperin smiled, reaching for pen and paper. "That is an excellent line of questioning, my lord. And though I can offer you no money, I can indeed give you some information." He wrote a few lines on the page, blotted the ink, and folded the paper carefully. "I regret I cannot do more."

Niall took the paper. "You don't like Ogilvy, do you?"

"Let's just say he does not like me," Halperin replied with a faint, wry smile. "Good night, my lord. And good luck to you."

So Niall returned to Carregness no richer. But at least he had names. He woke his brothers at first light to discuss the matter. Together they'd be able to ferret out what Mr. Ogilvy was up to, and how Niall might use his new-found position to alter things to his own benefit.

Ian was all for chasing down Ogilvy and simply offering him a choice between a slow and steady repayment, or a quick trip off a cliff.

"That's not how it works, ya dolt," Robert said. "Ogilvy has others behind him, and if we were to threaten him, there'd be all kinds of unpleasant consequences."

Niall nodded agreement. "Aye, and anyway, I'm not aiming to evade the loan entirely. I'll pay back the money. I just want to do it on a reasonable schedule."

"Let's go and speak to these others," Rob offered. "And I can ask around to see what Ogilvy's been into lately. Once we find out what he's planning to spend all that money on, you'll know what strings to pull as laird to cool him down."

Chapter 20

Dear Camellia,

I have misplaced the recipe for the lackluster pear tart, so I cannot give it to you. But perhaps we can create a new dessert when I see you in London.

Heather

While Niall was riding back and forth on moonless roads, Heather had also spent a restless night, though she did not leave her room. After penning a quick letter to Camellia with the coded phrase calling for help, she tried to name all the cities she wanted to see: *Paris. Cairo. Niall. New York. Niall.*

Ugh. Every time she closed her eyes, all she could think about was Niall. It was not conducive to sleep. So she plotted her route from the stable, through the gates, to the track, to the village. There, she'd wait for the first coach traveling toward London, and leave the horse with the innkeeper, who'd know to hold it until the MacNairs came looking. And by the time they did look, Heather would be well on her way, living her own life by her own choice, going where she pleased and not looking over her shoulder for pursuers who only cared about her money.

Morning brought a sunny sky and no happiness to Heather, who was tired and hungry. Hunger could be solved, at least. She dressed and hurried downstairs, keeping her eyes and ears open for any hints that Niall suspected her plan. But nothing appeared different at all. There were no more guards about than usual, and everyone just nodded or bowed to her as they always did.

Niall was in the great hall, accompanied by his brothers. Apparently, they'd been there for quite some time, judging by the empty dishes and the scattered cups (some for tea, some for ale).

She said good morning to Ian and Robert and steadfastly ignored Niall—though she noticed he didn't look well-rested. *Good*, she thought. *I hope he didn't sleep either.* She sat at the end of the long table and ate her breakfast with gusto, refusing to even look in Niall's direction.

The day dragged on. She didn't want to leave until the activity in and around the castle slowed. Based on what she'd noticed after a few weeks of living there, mid-afternoon was calmest. The morning chores were all done but the evening ones had not yet started—except for in the kitchen, where work never ended.

To occupy her mind, she offered to help Maeve with a few errands and chores, and truly enjoyed her time doing them. Maeve was a sweet and kind person. Heather would have been delighted to have her for a sister, if things had been different.

She ate a hearty luncheon (having learned the hard way about running away on an empty stomach). Finally, Heather returned to her room and pulled the bag out from under the bed. She concealed it by throwing a blanket on top. If anyone asked, she'd say she spilled some water on it and was taking it outside to dry.

However, no one did ask, and Heather did her best to take the least-populated hallways and stairs in the castle. She threw the blanket over a line with some other laundry, and walked to the stables.

Moments later she was taking Sterling past the gates, casually remarking to the man on guard that it was a lovely morning for a ride. She flicked the reins, encouraging the horse to get out of the gate area as quickly and quietly as possible.

Was it that easy, after all? She glanced behind her, at the towers and roofs and windows of Carregness. She felt a little sad that she couldn't properly say goodbye to Maeve and the others. It was hardly the sort of behavior Mrs. Bloomfield taught her.

But if she'd told anyone she was leaving, Niall would hear and put a stop to it. He was their laird now. They were loyal to him, and Heather was not much more than a stranger. So she focused on the path in front of her, the track that entered a small wood before it wound its way up the ridge.

The path to the village was familiar to the horse, so Heather let her mind wander. But then she instantly relived the moment when Niall admitted that he'd come into the room to seduce her, to seal her fate and take her money. The fact that he stepped back from the brink at the last moment was hardly a relief. If Niall could be tempted to turn on her—after so many times when he'd helped her, staunchly defended her, and steadfastly refused to take the final step that would shackle her to him—then how could she trust *any* man? No, it was time to leave, before anyone else could step in and dictate her path.

With the several ten pound notes Uncle Cyril had included in his nagging letters to her earlier, Heather ought to have enough funds to get to London. There, she'd con sult with her old school friends before she boarded a ship…the one that would take her to all the places she wanted to go. To take her across the world she wanted to see. Heather Hayes, intrepid explorer!

No, she couldn't use that name, not until she was sure her uncle had stopped pursuing her. And Heather MacNair was equally dangerous…she could easily imagine a whole clan of Scottish trackers on her trail. What name could she take, when she didn't even have a home?

Then it came to her—Wildwood Hall. Her school, the source of her greatest friendships and where she learned so much.

"Heather Wildwood," she said out loud, testing the name. "Miss Wildwood."

It would do.

She rode onward, hoping to get to the village well before anyone wondered where she was. The route Sterling took climbed a hill at one point and the trail switched back for a while, so that Heather looked down on the long, narrow valley and loch where Carregness Castle stood. When the place came into view, her heart wrenched unexpectedly. She was only there for a short time, but how the people there had grown into her heart. An image of Niall flashed before her eyes, and Heather suddenly wanted to weep.

Why did it all have to be so complicated? Why couldn't she get his face out of her mind? She didn't even *like* him, after all. And certainly not now, when he'd disappointed her by proving himself to be depressingly human, not the perfect, sweet, funny partner she'd made him into in her own dreams. A man she could fall in love with.

A man she did fall in love with.

"Oh, no you don't," Heather warned herself, far too late.

Because she realized then why Niall's near-betrayal hurt her so much. It was because she had, somewhere over the past few weeks, succumbed to something far worse than losing her virginity. She'd lost her heart.

It was so unfair. She'd fought off the constant attraction, the desire to give in and play the part completely, to experience what it would be like to share herself with Niall…only to completely give over her heart to him without even realizing she'd done it. Ugh, those times he smiled at her and told her some terrible joke. The time he pulled the blanket up to make sure she stayed warm. Those times he'd held her when she was upset.

Each little event added up, assaulting the walls around Heather's heart until they were rubble, like the ancient stone defenses of Carregness.

Leaving was the only way. Heather urged the horse to move; not long after that, she could see the village ahead. She rode in, nodding to the people who greeted her. Some recognized her as Lady MacNair, and others were just polite. Heather couldn't pretend to be anyone else just yet, so she merely returned the pleasantries and hoped no one would ask about the laird.

At the Cat & Mouse, she rode to the side where the stables were. There was no proper courtyard here, and whoever minded the stable likely had other tasks as well, leaving Heather temporarily alone, which suited her well. She dismounted, intending to walk Sterling to the furthest stall. He would be found quickly, of course, but wouldn't be visible from the front.

I could go back, she thought unexpectedly. Right now, I could turn and ride back to Carregness and tell Niall I've been thinking and we could work something out because we're adults and we respect each other and there's no reason to lose our heads over this whole mess.

The idea tugged at her soul. Was it possible to go back? She had acted badly the night before—not just accusing Niall of heartlessness, but also pretending that she was an innocent victim, when the truth was that she *wanted* him to do everything he did. The right act would be to own up to her mistakes and talk to Niall, and perhaps even confess her feelings…though it would only make their relationship more fraught. Running away from her uncle had been a smart move, the only move she could make to maintain her independence. Running away from Niall was different. She was just taking the easy way out now.

She had to go back.

Turning around with the slightly confused horse, Heather walked to the stool near the stable entrance, placed there for solo riders. She'd got one foot on the step when she sensed someone near her.

"Well, if it isn't little Heather."

The voice was familiar…and horrible.

She turned to see Mr. Webb standing there, a gun in his hand.

"What are you doing here?" she got out.

He pointed the gun directly at her head. "I was waiting for you, dear."

Heather wanted to turn again and mount up on Sterling, but the sight of Webb's gun stopped her from making any move whatsoever.

"Surely you don't intend to murder me," she said cautiously.

"Certainly not, dear. But remember that I can shoot you in a lot of spots and still get what I want from you, so really you'll just be hurting yourself."

"Where's Uncle Cyril? He put you up to this."

"Oh, no, he's long gone. Gave up on you. But I

didn't."

"Why?"

He smiled, showing glittering white teeth. "I think you know why. Now come along, Heather. Be a good girl. Walk over here. There's a carriage outside. We're getting into it."

"But Sterling…"

"Leave it. You won't need the horse where we're going."

That avenue of escape cut off, Heather had little choice but to follow Webb's instructions. The ugliness of the gun kept her mind focused. Whatever she did, she could not allow Webb to shoot.

In the carriage, Heather sat on one side, while Webb took the other, facing her and unfortunately not relaxing his grip on the gun at all.

"Please put that away," she said. "It frightens me."

"Does it?" Webb's eyes gleamed, and Heather realized that he liked her scared. "Too bad. You have a history of running away. But you won't try anything now, will you?"

Heather shook her head. He wanted her to be a frightened little mouse, did he? Well she could play along with that until she saw a chance to escape.

If she got a chance to escape.

Chapter 21

AT CARREGNESS, NIALL SPENT NEARLY the whole day chasing after the hints Mr. Halperin had given him. He sent Ian out to speak with several people who either lived near or worked with Ogilvy, hoping to glean some information about what was going on that would cause the man to be so needy for ready cash.

Several times, he nearly went up to Heather's room to beg her forgiveness, but each time he thought of the absolute disgust in her face when she realized what he'd been up to last night, and decided that he did not yet deserve her forgiveness.

But at least she was safe in the castle. That was all that mattered.

Of course Ian and Rob both took note of how frosty Heather had been at breakfast. Fortunately, they didn't start to mock him about it until she finished her meal and got up to leave. He refused to explain what happened, and let them both think it was a mere lovers' quarrel—or a non-lovers' quarrel, to be accurate.

Heather had flitted through the great hall from time to time, evidently helping Maeve with some tasks. Each time, she walked past Niall as if he didn't exist. But after the mid-day meal, he hadn't seen her again, and he was driven to distraction thinking about what she might be doing and why he was such an idiot around her.

Just go and grovel, he thought at one point. *You're not going to get anything done while Heather's mad at you.*

And indeed he wasn't getting much done. Half of what Ian was telling him was going in one ear and out the other.

Bring the ring back to her. Grovel. Would that work? Would *anything* work?

The truth was—and he hated himself for this—Niall was scared to find out.

In the mid-afternoon, he and Ian were discussing what he'd learned earlier, while they waited for Robert to return from his own mission.

Ian was saying, "Sounds to me like Ogilvy wants to buy up all the property along the River Uaine here. But why? Some land speculation? Does he know something about a trade route?"

"Has Brenna ever got mad at you?" Niall asked. "How long did it last?"

"Niall! We're talking about Ogilvy."

"I know that."

"No you don't. You're mooning over your own wife."

"She won't be my wife for long."

Ian sighed, stretching his hands along the table until he lowered his forehead to the surface. He asked (in a somewhat muffled tone), "Have you considered the radical option of…just being married to her? Correct me if I'm wrong, but you *like* the woman."

Oh, God, did he. Not just as a person, though he'd liked her right off. If he hadn't, why would he have ridden across half a county to get her away from pursuit? But it was more than that now. Lust was there too. The memory of her under him in bed nearly unhitched all rational thought. He pulled himself together with an effort. "My feelings have nothing to do with the matter. Heather entered into the agreement with the belief that it was a temporary ruse to get her uncle off her back. I entered into it with that same belief. To change course now would be unfair to her—I'd be no better than a thief."

"Yes, her surprise fortune." Ian lifted his head. "You know, most men would take it as a windfall and not worry about the wife that comes with it."

"Why should I care what most men would do?"

Rob came in then, a strange expression on his face. "Just got back from talking to that one gentleman on Halperin's list. On my way, I saw your wife riding Sterling along the hillside path. She didn't see me. Thought you should know."

"So? I told her she was to use Sterling if she planned to go riding," Niall said, not sure what his brother's point was.

"Don't think that a mere ride is all she's got planned. She also had a rather large carpet bag strapped onto the horse."

Damn it. He should have known. Well, she wouldn't run this time. At least, she wouldn't run far.

He stood up. "Both of you with me. We're going after her."

"See, I knew you liked her," Ian said, smiling in triumph.

"I *just* got back," Rob muttered, though he gamely followed the two to the stables.

The brothers wasted no time getting saddled up and riding out. Niall said little as they moved along the track to town. He was too annoyed—mostly at himself, for not guessing that she'd do this. Was he so terrible that Heather couldn't even come argue with him about things?

Well, considering the previous evening, perhaps he was.

"What if she didn't ride to the village?" Robert asked at one point.

"Where else would she go?" Ian replied, after Niall remained stubbornly silent. "It's not as if she's got kin close by. And she knows little of the area."

"I just worry that we'll miss her," Rob confessed. "The lass is clever, and clever people always think they know what to do, even when they're in over their heads. She could get herself into trouble."

"Don't you think we know that, Robbie!" Niall snapped. He didn't want to think of all the ways Heather could suffer. She could fall from her horse. She could be taken by highwaymen. She could get sick. She could get lost on the road. "We'll find her. She didn't have that much of a lead."

They reached the village. Everything was peaceful, even sleepy. People moved about on their business, but in an unhurried way. No one paid much attention to the trio.

"Let's try the inn first," Niall said. But before they even got to the main doors, Niall reined in.

"Do you see her?" Ian asked.

"I see Sterling." Niall pointed, and headed for the familiar horse, tethered to a post just outside the tavern door of the Cat & Mouse.

Before Niall could dismount, Brodie himself stepped out. "Aye, thought you'd be coming to collect the horse, my lord. Sterling is a fine one. Too fine to lose."

"I'm collecting the horse and the woman. Send her out, will you?" Niall didn't want to go inside, and see Heather among a host of other people. He could barely keep his temper in check as it was.

Brodie raised an eyebrow. "Wish I could, but your

lady isn't here."

"She just rode Sterling into town and then continued on foot?"

"No, my lord. Thought she meant to come in here, for she rode Sterling into the side yard stables. But when I looked out to see what was keeping her, I saw her getting into a coach with a gentleman."

Ian said, "She arranged for a ride? Where was she going?"

"Don't know, sir. As I said, she never set foot inside the building, so I never spoke to her. Thought it was a bit odd, so I posted Sterling out by the street in case someone was looking."

"Describe the gentleman," Robert suggested.

"Oh, you know him, sir. That Englishman who stayed here along with Hayes and his man. Mr. Webb."

* * * *

Heather didn't know how far the carriage had gone since they left the village, and part of her suspected they were going in circles, or perhaps taking a circuitous path, because it seemed like a long time to be on narrow tracks instead of the wide main road that ran north-south.

"Where's my uncle?" she asked, mostly to break the silence.

"Gone to London to parlay with some solicitors, I expect. He still thinks he can get that marriage dissolved, though God knows why he cares."

Heather opened her mouth to say exactly why he cared, but then the words caught in her throat. *He doesn't know!* The size of Heather's inheritance had been kept from Webb, she realized. She almost wanted to laugh. How devious was her uncle? He handed her off to Webb, but he intended to keep the fortune for himself.

"Does he know you intended to kidnap me?" she asked instead.

Webb snorted. "Why do you think we all left that horrible inn in the middle of the morning? Cyril knew the Scots were watching us all. We outsmarted them, and it was damned easy."

"Oh, so it didn't have to do with losing at cards?"

"Who told you that?" he snapped, his eyes narrowing.

"The Scots who were watching you. How much did you lose?"

"Not as much as Cyril," Webb replied.

Webb fell silent for a while, and Heather breathed a sigh of thanks. Perhaps the idiot would give up and let her out of the coach soon. Or simply relax his guard enough that Heather could jump out.

After several moments of tense quiet, broken only by the squeak of the wheels and the sound of horses' hooves, Webb spoke again.

"We're going to London too," he said.

"This isn't the road to London."

"It's the road to the harbor," Webb said, distractedly. "I booked passage on a ship leaving at the tide-turn. We'll be married by the ship's captain along the way, and by the time we arrive, no one can catch up. The captain will offer proof to your family's bank, and I'll withdraw whatever funds you may have on the same day."

"I'll tell the captain I'm already married."

"And I'll tell him you're insane. I'm paying for passage on the ship. Who do you think he'll believe?"

Heather knew all too well that men trusted men over women, especially when paid to do so. "I hate you."

"That's fine."

She lunged for the carriage door, scrabbling for the

latch. A deafening sound blasted out, and the window shattered.

Heather leaned back, pressing herself into the seat, stunned into compliance.

"You shot at me," she whispered. Well, maybe she whispered. Perhaps she shouted. The ringing in her ears made it hard to tell.

Webb pointed the gun toward her. "I shot past you, as a warning. Don't make me shoot again. You'll sit and you'll stay there, like a good girl."

Heather held still, aware that the gun held at least one more bullet. Or more. She didn't know enough about guns to be sure, and she didn't want to find out like this.

The driver took a turn (the unexpected shot hadn't even caused him to slow down), and Heather glimpsed water in the distance.

"Ah, there's the harbor ahead." Webb said. "And by the way, if you say a single word to the captain or the crew, it will be the last word you ever say. After all, a wife should obey her husband, yes?"

"I don't believe that. And anyway, I'll never be your wife."

"You will. I was going to wait until we got on board to teach you your wifely duties. But this carriage may do just as well."

"*What?*" Even as Heather raised her hands to ward him off, Webb lurched toward her, his breath hot and foul against her face. His mouth dragged across her skin, and she wanted to throw up.

Heather twisted to one side. "Get away from me!"

"You need a lesson in manners, girl. Running away on your wedding day, making a fool of me? I'll teach you what respect feels like." He tried to kiss her again.

Heather leaned back and spat in his face.

He slapped her, hard, snapping her head to one side. Stars burst behind her eyes, and she was temporarily stunned.

When she finally got hold of herself again, she scrambled back into the corner of the carriage, prepared to kick and scream and do whatever she had to do.

But Webb wasn't interested in her any more. He was calmly reloading his pistol, taking advantage of her momentary incapacity.

Her cheek stung where he'd struck her, and she cautiously reached up to touch it. Her fingers barely grazed the skin before she winced at the pain.

"A little red," he noted calmly. "No one will notice."

"You're pathetic. No woman will have you, so you're reduced to stealing any bride you can?"

He finished reloading, and smiled. "Not just any bride. You. Since I first laid eyes on you, what was it, five years ago? Six? I knew that I wanted you all to myself. You think I spent so much time at Hayes House just to put up with Cyril? I've heard all his stories a dozen times. But watching you was a treat I couldn't get enough of."

Heather remembered her uncle's insistence on her greeting his guests and playing hostess for them, even at fourteen and fifteen. She'd never liked the role, and now she knew why it was so repellent when Webb was a guest.

The carriage rattled to a halt. Heather looked out to see several ships at anchor.

"Here we are," said Webb, aiming the pistol at her once more. "When the tide turns, we'll begin a honeymoon cruise you'll never forget."

Chapter 22

NIALL'S HEART DROPPED INTO HIS gut at the news of Webb taking Heather. On the face of it, it didn't make sense. Those men had all gone from Scotland days ago, according to Robert's own report. But Brodie wouldn't lie.

"She left with Webb?" Ian asked, in surprise.

"She never would have done that voluntarily," said Niall. "Webb must have coerced her into joining him. Which way did they go?"

Brodie's eyes were wide, and the reality of the situation slowly dawned on him. "You mean she didn't want to get in that carriage?"

"I very much doubt it. Which direction did it take?"

But Brodie just shook his head. "I…I never stayed to look, my lord. I was needed inside, and I didn't think it mattered."

Niall took a deep breath. "So Heather has been kidnapped. And we've got no clue where he took her."

From Brodie's account, it sounded as if the carriage had an hour's head start on them. But even if Webb pushed the driver to hurry, a carriage was unlikely to outpace a determined single rider. And the roads in this area tended to be narrow. There were not many that a carriage could take, and even fewer that it could take at speed.

Rob was the best rider of them all, so he volunteered to take the high road that went south, it being the most likely route that Webb took. He borrowed Ian's pistol, promising that once he caught up to the carriage, he wouldn't let it out of his sight.

"And if he's hurt our sister, I might misplace a few of these bullets in his stupid heid," he swore. Then he signaled the horse and was off.

"Don't worry, he'll overtake any carriage on the highway," Ian told a very worried Niall.

"But what if they're not on the highway?" Niall asked. "There's more than one way in and out of town."

"Then we ask around. Spend ten minutes here, and we may save hours chasing false trails."

The two did so, splitting up to east and west. Niall rode to the edge of the village, stopping at the door of the shoemaker whose business stood at the end of the main street.

When Niall walked in, both the master and his apprentice daughter stopped and looked up from their work.

"Good afternoon, my lord," the man said, giving a respectful little bow. "What might we do for you?"

"Did you happen to see any carriage ride past here about an hour ago?"

The man glanced at his daughter, who shook her head. "Can't say that we have, my lord. Our work keeps our eyes to the bench, not out the window."

"But you ought to ask Gregor, that's the chandler's boy," the daughter added. "He works outside when dipping, and he notices what goes on."

Niall nodded thanks and crossed the street to the chandler's. The workshop door was wide open, and two figures were hanging pairs of dipped tapers to dry and harden. It was the end of the day, and several wooden rods were now supporting the candles made so far. The scent of beeswax and tallow filled the air.

"Who's Gregor?"

"I am, my Lord MacNair," one young man replied warily.

Niall repeated his question about the carriage and was rewarded with a flash of recognition in the other's eyes.

"Oh, aye, the one with the matching chestnuts. Saw it come by just after the church bells rang four. Headed west and turned left at the fork."

"Thank you," Niall said in a rush. He fished out a coin. "Run and find my brother Ian. Tell him I'm going that way, and he's to follow."

Niall couldn't wait for Ian himself. He hurried back to his horse. The left turning was the more used branch, but Niall had a hunch where the carriage was headed.

Riding out of the village, he pushed the horse's pace as much as he dared. When the road forked again, he chose the route to the harbor, praying he was right.

The light was turning golden when Niall reached the harbor. It was nestled in a narrow but deep bay, and the sun had already sunk into the notch between the hills, sending beams skittering over the water, turning the surface into a sea of glittering amber.

Outlined against the stunning backdrop were a few small fishing boats, and one bigger ship with its sails unfurled.

At the far end of the quay was a carriage with two matched chestnuts. Niall galloped onward, squinting to the sun. Yes, on the deck of the ship, there were a number of moving figures, including a woman in a green gown.

Heather.

Once the ship set sail, there was nothing Niall could

do. He had to get on board, now.

Webb spotted him by the time he brought his horse to skidding halt, and was screaming at the crew. "Get moving, you idiots! Don't let him board! You there, take her below!"

A burly sailor took hold of Heather, wrapping an arm around her shoulders, but she promptly bent her head and bit him, causing him to step away, swearing.

"Niall!" she screamed, rushing up to the ship's rail, clearly intending to climb over and jump into the water. But before she could, Webb came up behind her and said something in a low voice.

Heather went very still. What had the numpty said to her?

Then Niall realized what was happening, even though he couldn't see it. Webb had a gun, and was pointing it directly into Heather's lower back.

A couple of the crew were already in the process of hauling the gangplank up, so he couldn't get aboard that way. A normal person would give up. A normal person who hated ships as much as he did would definitely give up.

But Heather was there.

So Niall simply hopped on to the top of the saddle, steadied himself, and *leaped* from the quay to the ship. He caught the port-side railing and hauled himself up onto the deck. He heard Ian shouting encouragement from behind him.

He ignored Webb completely. Standing up, he spotted the captain.

"Sir, I am Lord MacNair, Earl of Carregness. Permission to come aboard?"

"A bit late, but aye, my lord," the captain said, casting a troubled glance around the deck. "What the hell is going on here?"

"First, I'd suggest your crew lower the gangplank again, as the lady will be leaving the ship, and I will be very annoyed if she gets even a toe splashed in the process."

"The tide is turning, my lord. We have to set sail."

"Your plans have changed," Niall said shortly. "Order the gangplank lowered. Now."

"Don't listen to him!" Webb's voice was strident, but he still had enough presence of mind to keep Heather in front of him. "If you do, I will shoot this woman."

* * * *

Heather inhaled, feeling the cold point of the pistol pushing at her back. "He does have *a* gun," she announced, very calmly (considering her position). "He already fired it once toward me in the carriage, and I saw him reload it." She looked to Niall, hoping he'd understand her message: Webb only had one gun, which was loaded. But if it could be wrested or tricked away from him, the danger was over.

Niall nodded slowly. "Mr. Webb, let's talk."

"Nothing to talk about."

"I disagree. And let's not pretend you'll actually fire that gun. What's the point of kidnapping Lady MacNair if you simply shoot her dead?"

"She's not Lady MacNair."

"Yes, I am!" Heather shouted, directly to the captain. Would the man realize he was abetting a criminal if he allowed Webb to sail on his ship?

The captain clearly wasn't pleased by the situation. "Kidnapping is a serious charge," he said, though he didn't seem to know who to believe at this point.

"Aye, it is. If Mr. Webb is innocent, perhaps he'll put away the gun," Niall offered.

The captain nodded, approaching Webb. "Holding any woman at gunpoint is unseemly, sir. Hand it to me."

Webb growled, "If I do that, he'll just take her. *He's* the kidnapper here."

"Oh, please," Heather said, rolling her eyes. "Do you know how stupid you sound?"

"Shut up, woman!" Webb wrenched her arm upward in his anger, which was what Heather was hoping for. She relaxed her limbs in anticipation, and when he met no resistance, the force of his action overbalanced them both (plus, Heather stomped on his foot).

In the few seconds of chaos, Heather spun away from Webb at the same moment Niall *and* two members of the crew rushed him.

The gun was knocked to the deck, sliding to the rail. Heather scrambled after it, and stood up with it in her hands.

She saw Webb in the grip of the two sailors, with Niall towering over him. Content that Webb would do nothing else, she promptly walked to the captain and offered the gun to him "Have you got somewhere secure for this?"

"Aye, miss. Ma'am?…My lady?"

"My lady will do," Heather replied. "Now, will you do me the great favor of lowering that gangplank? I do not wish to sail anywhere today."

The caption nodded, giving a curt order to two men, who leapt to obey. By now, both Ian and Robert (where had he come from?) were waiting to swarm up the moment they could.

"Heather."

She turned to see Niall standing in the middle of the deck.

Giving up any pretense, she rushed into his arms. "Niall. Oh, God, Niall." That was all she said, but the moment she felt his arms around her, she started shaking, her heart beating rapidly within her breast. The terror she'd staved off for so long came rushing up now that the danger was over.

"Did he hurt you?" Niall asked, his voice gruff.

"No."

Then he carefully disengaged, setting her at his side. "Wait here."

He stalked back to Webb. "I should just throw you over the side and let you drown," he said.

"You can't do that!"

"Well, I can. But I won't. Though you're not worth much, I want to keep you around long enough to be punished for kidnapping Heather."

"Heather was promised to me," Webb sputtered. "Me! I would have had her every night, whenever I wanted, and she could never say no."

Like a child pouting about a sweet, he was. Heather listened, more repelled by him with every passing moment.

Niall also recoiled at the rampant lust in the other man's tone. "You're old enough to be her grandfather."

"So? That pretty body, plus five hundred every year, what man could say no?"

"Thousand," Heather corrected automatically.

Webb looked at her in confusion. "What?"

"I'm due to receive ten thousand in income every year, not one thousand. So if you both split it, you'd get five *thousand*." She tipped her head, giving him an almost indulgent smile. "But Uncle Cyril never told you that, did he. I realized that in the carriage, when you never mentioned the size of my inheritance. He let everyone, including me, think I was worth far less."

"Five thousand?" Webb echoed, his mind clearly stuck on that revelation. "Five *thousand?*"

"Aye. Though as we've all made quite clear, I'm already married to another man, so it's a moot point."

"Five thousand."

"Stop saying that over and over," she told him. "You sound like a parrot."

Niall was obviously out of patience, and said, "Enough. Webb, you'll go with my brothers to make a full report to the local magistrate. A written statement, mind. You'll not be backing out of this. And when I pursue charges against Mr. Cyril Hayes, you may hope that your account will give you some leniency regarding your sentence for kidnapping a countess."

Webb's forehead was sweaty and his skin pale. But he had no way out now, so he nodded. Heather suspected he'd cast all the blame he could onto Cyril. And in truth, she didn't much care, so long as both men were punished.

Still, she added, "And you'd better not warn my uncle of this change in fortune. Because if he goes underground or leaves the country, you'll have no one to point a finger at. And he *was* going to cheat you out of thousands of pounds."

Webb nodded again, his lips pursed as he considered his fate. "Let him be surprised," he muttered. "It's his turn."

Niall looked to Ian and Rob. "See that he gets to the magistrate, will you?"

"Oh, he'll get there," Ian said, stepping forward to grab Webb by the arm. "In fact, let's take your fancy carriage."

"Good idea," Rob added, looking to the driver, who had remained scared and silent during the whole exchange. "I'll sit up with you, show you the way."

The driver nodded quickly, accepting that with no qualms. It meant that there would be no last-minute diversion onto another road.

When the carriage rolled out, and the ship captain gave his word that he'd respond to any official request to appear and give testimony, Niall agreed they could go before they missed the tide. The captain lost no time in hollering orders to his chastened crew to get moving and cast off.

Then Niall turned, walking back to Heather. She was shivering slightly, probably from the aftermath of the events rather than any cold. He adjusted the shawl around her shoulders, but said only, "We're going back to Carregness. And there you'll stay."

Chapter 23

THE RIDE BACK TO CARREGNESS was agony. Niall pulled Heather up onto his horse in front of him. It was just like the first day they'd met…except this time, Heather could sense a darkness radiating from Niall. He was furious, and she was the cause.

But she still clung to him. Not just to avoid falling off, but because she didn't have the words for how she felt. The only way she could convey how much she needed to be near him was to…be near him, wrapping her arms around him, getting as close as possible while he rode.

However, there was no softening of his stance along the way. He said nothing to ease her mind, and Heather realized he must be done with her. He'd got her back from Webb as a matter of honor. But there was no hint of tenderness now. She'd lost him.

Shouldn't she want that? Life would be less complicated if there was no emotional connection between them.

At Carregness, Maeve must have been alerted to their arrival, because she stood on the steps of the keep when Niall rode up.

He helped Heather down from the horse, but didn't dismount himself. "Get her cleaned up and fed," he said abruptly, as if she were a lost dog he found on the road.

"Aren't you coming in?" Maeve asked, confused.

"I have other business." Niall wheeled about and rode back out the gate. Heather felt the distance stretching between them, but couldn't call him back.

Maeve was kindness itself, taking Heather upstairs and fussing over her. At Maeve's direction, she took a hot bath and was dressed in a warm wool gown, Maeve getting the whole story of the day's events from Heather in the process. By that time, she'd stopped shivering, though she was still miserable. Maeve insisted she eat something, so Heather tolerated a little broth and tea, mostly to make Maeve stop hovering. All of Heather's protests that she really was fine did very little to convince Maeve that she was, in fact, fine.

Momentarily alone in her room, Heather lay back on the bed and closed her eyes, wondering where she'd be in a week. Not here, probably.

There was a knock at the door.

"No thank you, Maeve!" she called out, not bothering to open her eyes.

The knock came again.

Heather sighed, but got up to open the door. "Really, Maeve, you needn't..." She stopped there. It wasn't Maeve.

Niall stood outside her door, one hand on the frame, his bulk blocking everything else out. Niall, who kept appearing when she needed him most. Niall, who was as trapped as she was in some way. Niall, who she wanted to meet all over again, so she didn't make the same mistakes.

"May I come in?" he asked.

She stepped back to let him move past her. Maybe she could tell him now, tell him all the things in her heart before she lost her nerve.

Then, he closed the door behind him, and Heather's hackles went up. He was going to yell at her.

"Whatever you're about to say, I'm not going to listen to it. I've had quite enough of being berated and belittled—"

Something in his eyes caused her next words to die in her throat. Something haunted. He said, "All I can see is you on the deck of that ship, about to sail away. If I'd been three minutes later, you'd have been gone."

"Well, you got me back," she mumbled, not mentioning that when he arrived at the ship, her heart almost burst.

"But I've never had you, have I?" said Niall, the look in his eyes turning her heart inside out. "It's been an arrangement from the beginning, one I've got all tangled up, but you never did, did you? You just did what you needed to do to keep what freedom you had."

"What? No. Niall, it wasn't like that."

"Wasn't it?"

She reached up and put her hands on his chest, willing him to believe her. "No. It was like this."

Heather tangled her fingers in his hair, bringing him closer. With her teeth, she tugged at his lower lip. For a moment, he didn't react at all, and she wanted to die.

Then, all at once, his arms went around her waist, picking her up effortlessly. He walked her to the bed, laying her back on it. He leaned over her, undoing the buttons at the back and pulling at the wide sash that kept the gown tight to her chest. He tugged the loosened gown away from her body, and Heather inhaled as he watched her, his gaze hot as a branding iron.

"Go on," she whispered, realizing he was waiting for permission.

The stays did not stay around long, ending up in a

corner of the room. Next, he untied the ribbon of her shift, and pulled the top of it down past her shoulders and then lower, revealing her breasts. Heather ducked her head, uncertain how to act when she was literally bared to him like this. He lifted one hand to her cheek, and tilted her head up to catch her gaze.

"What is it?" he asked.

"Just that…I'll be naked soon. I've never been naked with a man, and I've never seen a man naked… How does a person *behave* in this situation?"

He bit back a laugh. "Why behave at all?"

Niall ran his hands over her chest, teasing her relentlessly. Then he bent down and licked the left nipple until it hardened into a pink nub and Heather's eyes slid closed and she moaned softly. She didn't realize he was continuing to pull her shift and gown all the way off until he lifted her from the bed to get the fabric out from under her, and by then she was just happy the tangled clothes were gone.

He stood up and moved away from the bed just long enough to shed his own clothing. Heather stared at the man revealed, her throat going dry. She'd seen part of him unclothed before, but never all of him. And he was by all measures a big man. And her whole body was reacting to the sight of him, clamoring to have him next to her, skin to skin.

"Come here," she said, and was startled by the huskiness in her voice.

Niall's eyes flickered at the command, and a slow smile started at the corner of his mouth. "Say please."

"*Please.*"

He climbed back onto the bed, moving to cover her, bracing himself on elbows and knees so as not to crush her under his weight. Heather touched him, hesitantly at first, running her fingers over his chest and arms, then, with his encouragement, explored more. He guided her downward to his cock, telling her that he wanted her to be familiar with him.

She encircled him with her hand and squeezed lightly, earning a deep moan of pleasure from him.

"That feels good?" she asked.

"Hell, yes," he growled, even as he pulled her hand away. "More of that later, if you decide to indulge me."

"No one ever said this was part of…the consummation process."

"It's a very flexible process." His voice was rich with suppressed laughter.

"Are you making fun of me?"

"Not at all, love. You're so bold at every other time that it's just sweet to see you shy. But there's no shame in not knowing something. I'd love to teach you."

"Then teach me," she begged. "Touch me. I want you to feel all of me."

"I've been waiting for that." He kissed his way across her chest, his hands cupping her breasts until she was pressing herself against him, eager for more. She rubbed one leg against his thigh, and he grabbed it, holding her in place.

He kissed her neck, biting down gently. The bite sent a wave of heat though her, down to her fingers and toes.

"We can be as rough or gentle as you want," he told her. "You'll learn what pleases you, and I'll do whatever you ask."

Heather inhaled, thinking that was a very generous offer.

He kissed her again, deeply. The flat of his hand slipped down to her stomach, and then lower into the curls between her legs, and then into the folds of her body, the fingers delving into the heat that was building and building.

Heather went wild at the contact, both shocked and tantalized by it. Her body was inflamed, and she unconsciously moved her hips in time with his strokes. Why did no one tell her about how marvelous it was to be touched like this?

Niall brought her to a state of distraction with his mouth on hers, and his fingers wreaking havoc between her legs. Heather's breathing quickened to little pants.

"Never run away again," he told her in a low voice.

"Never," she said, arching her back in reaction to his strokes.

He deepened the pressure. "Promise me."

"Oh, oh, Niall. I promise!" Heather whimpered, panting. "Don't keep teasing me, not when I need you so much."

"I'm not teasing you, woman, I'm pleasuring you. Does it not feel good?"

"It feels like I'm going to die of joy."

"Well, don't die yet, love. There's so much more I want to show you."

"But don't stop what you're doing now," she begged.

He moved to kiss her neck and whispered, "Then come for me."

She knew exactly what he meant—having touched herself before—though the idea of such a private pleasure being performed for another was nerve-wracking. "Will you watch?" she asked.

"Unless you want me to close my eyes."

"No," she said impulsively. "You should see. After all, you're why I feel so good."

"Ah, Heather, love." He captured her lower lip and sucked, drawing out the kiss as he continued to toy with her in an ever-faster pattern, until she gave herself up to the wave of bliss and clung to him, her arms twined around his shoulders as she sighed though the lingering aftershocks.

When he withdrew his hand, she felt the moisture that came with it, and asked if that was supposed to happen.

"It's good," he assured her. "The wetter you are, the more I can stretch you now, the less uncomfortable the next part will be."

"Stretching…" she echoed, finally, finally connecting the fact that the place where his fingers had been would shortly be occupied by a much thicker part of him. "How? You're so big."

"Just trust me."

"I do," she promised, kissing him.

He pushed her legs apart even more, and settled himself over her. No more holding back, no more pretending that they didn't want each other. Heather was sick of pretending not to care, when her whole body was aching for him.

"Ready, darling?"

Heather nodded, her eyes wide and locked on him. He eased into her, very slowly, too slowly. She put her hands on his hips and suddenly gripped him tightly, pulling him into her as she gave a little scream of impatience.

"Pain?" he asked, stilling.

"No. I want to *know*," she whispered fiercely. What had all this waiting been *for*?

All at once, he rolled onto his back, carrying Heather with him. She was startled, but then gasped when he thrust inside her, sending her nerves into a cascade of excitement.

"I think you'll like it this way," he said.

"Yes," she agreed in a breathy, eager tone. Looking

down at Niall was a novel and deeply intriguing perspective. She smiled slowly, realizing that she could watch the rise and fall of his chest, and that he was insanely aroused by her, for her.

Despite his obvious need, he moved slowly to prolong the pleasure, to keep them both in this rapturous moment when everything was *right*. She was gorgeously alert, her hips and thighs begging for him to caress and stroke until she was draped across him, molded to him.

He angled his pelvis while he kept hold of her hips, eager to find the pleasure they both needed so badly. Heather writhed over him, her hands flexing and gripping his shoulders as she got closer and closer to her peak.

And then she was there, crying out in startled joy, not expecting the intensity of it, the sensation of coming with a man inside her utterly new. She was totally consumed by the experience.

Niall was moaning her name, and he stiffened as he came within her, holding her hips hard against his, bringing her chest to his own, his big hands spread across her back to hold her to him.

Moments later, he came back to himself, cradling a swooning Heather in his arms as his breathing slowed. He rolled to the side, setting her softly next to him as he finally withdrew.

"Niall," she whispered. She opened her eyes, finding that his face was close to hers, his eyes intent. "How did you wait so long if you knew it would be like that?"

He smiled slightly. "I nearly didn't wait, if you remember." He pulled a few strands of hair that had drifted onto her cheek, then ran his thumb very gently over her swollen, pinked lips. "You're worth the wait, love."

Everything felt newer now, simpler. When Heather tucked herself next to him, fitting her limbs perfectly into the spaces made by his own, it felt so right. Like every-thing should be solved as easily as the puzzle of their bodies.

Some time later, Niall sat up slightly, and ran his fingers over her curves, quite clearly pleased with his work. There was something proprietary in the way he looked at her, which made part of Heather a little annoyed (a part that had been quite absent during their lovemaking).

"So you enjoyed that, beautiful?" he asked, rather smugly.

"I did enjoy it. Which is fortunate." After all, it would be horribly disappointing to give up all her freedom for something that didn't shake her to her core.

"Yes it is fortunate," he said, "because we're going to do that again. Many times."

"As my husband commands," Heather said, a little tartly. *Was* it worth it? Or had her heart finally outrun her mind?

Niall's smile evaporated. "You still think it's like that?"

"Even more so," Heather said, recognizing the truth. "We can't exactly go back now…if we ever could. But isn't that what you wanted?" Niall never pretended he didn't need her money, and she had to respect him for that.

He said nothing, but he slid off the bed, and it took a moment for Heather to realize that he wasn't coming back immediately. When she sat up and looked for him, he was fully dressed.

"Niall? Where are you going?"

He didn't even look at her. "This is your room. I won't bother you any longer. Anyway, I have some things to take care of."

"Wait? We're done?"

"Aye, it does sound as if we're done, doesn't it?" He turned and left the room.

Heather simply sat there, staring at the closed door.

* * * *

Niall was never going to win with Heather. He was never going to convince her that he loved *her*, not her money or anything else that came with it. For a short, precious time, he thought Heather had understood—why else would she finally consent to the single act that would irrevocably bind her to him? He had never been so stirred before when with a woman. It really was different when it was someone you loved.

But she hadn't been that moved, apparently—despite her sweetness during and after sex, like when she said she trusted him. *That* had felt good, almost as good as she felt to him.

It fooled him into thinking all was well, until she just coolly noted that she was stuck with him now. Like a slap in the face, and she didn't even have to raise her hand.

Niall suddenly understood every terrible ballad and poem about unrequited love.

Evening was descending, but he was in no mood for dinner or socializing with anyone. Compelled by something he didn't quite understand, he went to his father's old chambers, and sat in the massive, carved wood chair by the unlit fireplace.

"My lord? Do you require anything?" A servant asked from the door. He must have seen Niall go in, and wondered why.

"Yes. Have the lamps lit, and the fire as well. Then tell Mr. Kemble to meet me here." Niall got up and walked to the window, staring out at the lands of Carregness. He was earl now, wasn't he? He might as well take everything that he was entitled to. That was how the world worked.

When the fire was blazing and lamps around the room made it tolerably bright, another servant ushered Kemble in the door.

"My lord, you wanted to see me? I'm sorry to say that I've not yet found anything of great use when it comes to the arguments for nullifying the marriage."

"Never mind that," Niall said, waving his hand. "Kemble, I need help, and it's help only you can provide."

Niall told the lawyer what he wanted.

Kemble frowned, looking out the window for a very long moment. He tipped his head, obviously going through some sophisticated mental acrobatics.

"If I am understanding the situation correctly, there may be one way to achieve your aim," he said. "Now listen closely."

Chapter 24

IT WAS THE FIRST WEEK of October, and letters arrived in the castle almost as thickly as falling leaves drifted into the courtyard. One arrived on cream paper with the mark of a lion on the seal.

Dear Heather,

This waiting is intolerable. Expect us to arrive at Carregness in time for your birthday. I will expect a full report.

Daisy

The next letter was written on violet-scented paper, with the seal in the shape of a rose in full bloom.

Dearest Heather,

Daisy told us she's coming up to be with you. Therefore, we will do the same. Poppy has consented to be my companion again for the journey, and we hope to get there well before 6 October.

Rose

The third letter had been dashed off on the backside of an old letter, and for a seal it featured old candle wax splattered onto the opening.

Dear Heather,

Rose told me she is going to Carregness, and I begged to go along (it did not take much, since Rose intended to invite me anyway). We ride to your rescue!

Camellia

"Oh, dear. I hope there are enough rooms," Heather muttered, rereading the cavalcade of letters that had arrived over the past few days. Ever since her disastrous night with Niall, Heather almost wished she could run away again. But she couldn't. She made her choice.

She just didn't expect to have her choice thrown in her face the moment after she made it. She wondered how it felt to be left? Well, Niall shutting the door after leaving her that night gave her all the insight she needed.

For her birthday, she decided that all she wanted was a way to toss out her regrets. Instead, it sounded like she was having a party whether she liked it or not. Maeve promised to make a spice cake, having learned that it was Heather's favorite. And there would be an elaborate dinner and music and dancing. *My God, everyone thinks I'm here for good.* Well, not everyone—Niall's brothers and sisters knew it was possible the marriage could still be dissolved, and Heather could quietly leave and hope no one ever asked about her "holiday" in Scotland. But she suspected that Maeve, Ian, and Rob wanted her to stay.

Even Heather wanted to stay…but not if Niall didn't want her there.

At one point, Ian pulled her aside and said, "Heather, m'girl. You're either my near-sister or a near stranger, but all the same I hope we're friends."

"Oh, Ian, of course. You've only been kind to me during this whole fiasco."

"Then as a friend, may I suggest something?"

"Anything." Heather hoped he'd gotten some brilliant insight that would untangle this skein.

"You should talk to Niall."

"Why? What's the point? He doesn't want to talk to me."

"He does. He's just a dolt sometimes and doesn't know how to go about apologizing for his doltishness."

"And what exactly should we talk about?"

He looked at her in exasperation. "The marriage!"

"Ian, my dear heart, that's the only thing we actually agree on. It was a mistake."

"Was it?" he asked, with a surprisingly serious expression compared to his usual jovial air.

"It was for me," she said gently. "Niall gets what he needs out of it, even if he didn't know that at the time. But I need something else."

"What do you need?"

"You wouldn't understand."

"Try me."

Heather shook her head. Men couldn't understand— they didn't give anything up when they married. "It's personal, and not very practical. But it's important to me."

"Aye, well maybe I wouldn't know," Ian conceded. "But I'll tell you this, because he was probably too damn stupid to mention it. When you were taken by Webb, Niall nearly lost his mind. He'd have died to get you back safe."

"Oh, don't say that!"

"It's true. He'd have killed or been killed, whatever he needed to do to save you. And if that's not a good reason why he ought to be your husband, I don't know what is."

He left her pondering that, but she had no time to actually do anything about it. Once Heather's friends began to arrive at Carregness, it seemed no one would ever stop arriving.

First were the Duke and Duchess of Lyon, whose imminent arrival sent Maeve into a fury of cleaning. "We've *never* had a duke stay at Carregness," she whispered to Heather.

"He used to be a soldier," Heather told her. "Believe me, he's slept in worse places. And the duchess has done her own share of sweeping and dusting. She'll not think less of your efforts."

Poppy, Rose, and Camellia arrived the next day, having all traveled up from London together. (Rose's husband Adrian had stayed behind, declaring that a carriage full of giggling schoolgirls would drive him mad, though in fact he realized that the opportunity for his wife to enjoy the company of her friends was a rare thing, and might not happen again for years.)

Ian and Robert flirted with the unmarried female guests shamelessly, and the married ones more shamelessly still. Every night seemed to be a new excuse for a feast, and based on the levels of mirth among the guests, everything was perfect.

However, between Heather and Niall, there was a divide. They were polite to each other (mostly), and didn't avoid each other (mostly). But no one could miss the awkwardness between them. It was an open secret that they were both searching for a way to quietly dissolve the marriage, and that was why Mr. Kemble had gone to Edinburgh to consult with some Scottish solicitors while sending letters to other colleagues in Oxford and London. Thankfully, no one else knew about the consummation, and Heather agreed with Niall that if she showed no sign of pregnancy in the next several weeks, they could safely pretend that nothing had happened. He also apologized, which felt terrible, and promised he'd never touch her again, which felt worse.

With her birthday approaching in a few days, Heather should be happy. Freedom, security, and an independent life lay ahead of her.

She was not happy at all, though she did her best to hide it.

It helped to have her friends with her, and it was easier to distract herself by hearing their stories of all that had gone on in their lives since they'd last been together. Was it Rose's wedding?

Then one afternoon, Niall asked her to meet him in his bedchamber (the old laird's room being given to the duke and duchess for their visit).

Heather stepped in hesitantly, wondering what he wanted. "I'm here."

"Good. Sorry to pull you away from your friends, but we received news of your uncle."

"Oh, no. *Now* what's he up to?" Heather asked, frowning.

"Absolutely nothing. He's dead."

"What?"

"Apparently he was killed while traveling to London. It took several days for the authorities to find out who he was, and then longer to locate you and send word. This notice came via your family solicitors, who forwarded it."

Despite everything, Heather was appalled. "What happened? Was it an attempted robbery? Are highwaymen still a danger on such well-traveled roads?"

"It doesn't say, only that he was killed, probably dying from a stab wound from an unknown assailant."

"But what about Brom? Was he killed too? If he survived, he could tell what he saw."

"Evidently, he's missing. No one has seen him since they were in Carlisle, the last place they spent the night. Brom was very fond of that knife he owned, wasn't he?" Niall asked, not bothering to hide the inference.

"He was loyal to Uncle Cyril," Heather objected.

"Was he? Or was he loyal to a stable position and steady pay? I think he guessed that Cyril's campaign to regain his guardianship of you was doomed. He knew I wouldn't let it happen, even if Cyril wouldn't accept that."

Heather thought her way through it. "So, he finds a quiet spot on the road, waits for a moment when Uncle Cyril's back is turned, and…"

Niall nodded. "He pushes the body to the side of the road, hiding it from view. Then he drives the carriage further, perhaps to an inn where it will be assumed to belong to a guest for a little while. He packs up what money he could find, takes a horse, and vanishes."

"That's awful." Heather shook her head, then said, "But I could picture it."

"Well, whatever the truth is, you'll face no more opposition from your uncle."

Did she face opposition from Niall? Why was it so difficult to just talk to him now? (Aside from the fact that every time she looked at him, she envisioned him naked in bed, coaxing her to bare her whole body and soul to him. It made casual chat awkward.)

"Thank you for telling me," she said. "Have you heard from Kemble?"

"Not yet," he said shortly. "But I would request that you wait until your birthday is over to make any decisions."

"Of course."

"There's no *of course* about you, Heather Hayes."

* * * *

Later in the evening, Heather and her friends (plus Maeve, who got on famously with the Duchess of Lyon) gathered after dinner for tea and sherry.

Gossip was flying around, as usual.

"Didn't you meet a gentleman around the same time?" Camellia was saying to Poppy. "Some friend of Norbury's?"

Poppy sniffed. "Met him, yes. And there the matter ends. For I've not heard from him since Rose's wedding."

"I'm sorry," Heather said impulsively.

"Well, I'm not sorry!" Poppy snapped. "I don't think about Carlos de la Guerra *at all*."

"Oh." Heather reached for Rose's hand and squeezed it lightly. She received a firm squeeze in return, Rose conveying wordlessly that Poppy was lying through her teeth.

Camellia came up to Heather a while later. "Poor Poppy," she said. "I think her heart's a little broken. She had her head turned by that man, and he vanished past the horizon without so much as a farewell."

"He can't be worth much, if he chose to ignore Poppy," Heather said loyally.

"Perhaps Poppy and I can go become old maids together. I'll never meet a man I actually want to marry." Camellia gave her a sidelong look. "Not like Lord Mac-Nair. My goodness, Heather, objecting to him is like objecting to finding buried treasure in your yard."

"It's a little too much like that," Heather noted. "I do not wish to be kept around because it's convenient to dip into my pockets."

"Is that how they describe it in Scotland?" Daisy asked with an innocent look (Daisy read very widely for a lady).

"Daisy!" Heather gasped.

"Oh, don't be a goose. He's obviously head over heels in love with you."

"And you with him," Poppy added.

"I am not! Not…exactly," Heather muttered.

"There's nothing to be ashamed of in loving a good man," Rose said. "And love is a perfectly valid reason for marriage. We are all modern women. We should hold modern values. Like marrying for love. Not money or property or titles."

Daisy conceded, "Though they have their uses too."

"How do you know that I love him?" Heather asked.

Her friends glanced at each other and then laughed out loud.

"Oh, Heather," Poppy gasped through her giggles. "It's the most obvious thing in the world. The way you both tip-toe around each other and then explode because you can't tip-toe forever. The way you talk about him and the way he talks about you…and the way you look at him when his attention is elsewhere."

Heather sighed sadly. "We've had too many harsh words between us. Niall married me in haste, and I think he regrets it. I've been a bit of a pill. Well, more than a bit. I got angry at myself and took it out on him, and he must be ready to wash his hands of me now."

Rose reached out her hands, and Heather took them. "You are being very silly, Heather," she declared. "Fortunately, silliness is curable. You must go to him and tell him the truth of what's in your heart."

"Oh, how simple."

"It is that simple."

Heather wasn't sure that was true. Maybe for Rose, who tended to cut right past social niceties to offer honest thoughts instead (which was fun to observe during a social call and must have been one of the things that enticed Adrian to her). Heather was different. Blunt to a fault, yes. But that wasn't the same as sharing what was in her heart.

And she was stubborn. She hated to be wrong. Was that what was keeping her so miserable? The fact that she'd have to face Niall and admit that she was monumentally wrong? She once assumed that she wanted to be on her own, because she couldn't picture being happy with anyone telling her what to do. But perhaps that idea had come from the years of Uncle Cyril lording it over her, and in particular the last horrible months when he all but reduced her to a product on a green-grocer's shelf: Fresh Young Wife, Cheap!

But since she met Niall, her world had widened. He wasn't like anyone she knew before, and she doubted she could find a better match if she traveled to each continent and searched for years. The truth was that she loved him and wanted to stay with him and be part of his life.

How could she *say* all that in a way that he'd believe her?

* * * *

When she excused herself from the group, saying she wanted an early night, Heather was lying. She wasn't sure she'd ever sleep again. Thoughts seethed in her mind with little rhyme or reason. All she knew was that until she told Niall what she really felt, she'd never have any peace.

She was just passing the door of his bedroom when she heard her name. She looked into the darkness. "Niall?"

Suddenly, he was right there in the doorway. Heather

jumped. "What were you doing sitting in the dark?"

"There's the fire." He looked back into the room. "I guess it is dim in there. I was thinking. I've been thinking for a long time. Can I speak to you?"

"Certainly, for are you not my lawfully wedded husband?"

"That is endlessly up for debate, it seems. Come in for a moment, please."

Heather followed him into the chamber, which was dim, but not actually as gloomy as she first feared. The fire was leaping with orange flames, casting gold light on Niall's face.

He sat down in the chair by the fireplace. He looked tired. Heather saw lines on his face that hadn't been there the day they met.

She moved toward him. "What's the matter? I mean, besides the complete foundering of our marriage and apparently the very notion of marriage in the Isles?"

"Heather, I love you."

She opened her mouth, but nothing emerged. He loved her? Heather inhaled, trying again. "You what?"

"I love you. I know I'm bloody terrible at showing it. But I do love you, and I....want to keep you. I mean, I want to keep this marriage. Make it real."

"Niall," she said.

"Wait, hear me out!" He rushed on, standing back up, towering over her. "I'm not done. I know that you've been betrayed. By me. I didn't mean to, but I did it all the same. What I thought was a lark turned out to be an albatross."

"Ooh, that's a good metaphor."

"Thank you, it just came to me." He paused, then shook his head. "Don't distract me. Heather, I think I've found a way out of this."

Her stomach churned. "You have?"

"It's about the money. Or not the money—the liberty it offers you. As a married woman you're not your own person in the eyes of the law. But by God, you're your own person in my eyes, and you deserve to have what was meant to be yours."

"But…I can't…"

"You can if I arrange it just so. I talked to Mr. Kemble. He thinks it's doable, in a legal sense. He's gone to Edinburgh to make sure it is, and I got a note from him that he believes it can be done."

"That what can be done?"

"I'll settle an annual income on you that is equivalent to all of your inheritance's income. That is, it will all come back to your control—you can either spend it or let it stay with the bank, but it's yours. And yes, as your husband, technically I could change it. But I won't, and Kemble says he can add several provisions that will make it far more difficult for me—or anyone—to alter the terms."

"Mr. Kemble does seem to know the law," Heather allowed.

"Look, it's not ideal. No one can be fully content with a freedom that's granted by others. There's always the risk that it can be revoked. I wish you could cast off all the laws and be the wildflower you are, unencumbered by the rules and the strictures of men. But this is the world we live in, and this is what's in my power to do. Because I love you, and I want you to have what you want. I hope that what you want includes me, but if it's not…I won't be the man who keeps you down."

"Is…is this a plea for female emancipation or a marriage proposal?"

"Why can't it be both?"

"Oh, Niall." Heather reached up and put her arms around his neck, only to find herself swept up in his embrace. "Niall, I do love you."

"Do you love me enough to trust me? To put yourself in my power for a little while?"

"Oh, Niall. You oaf. I've been in your power since we met."

He protested, "That's not true."

"It is. You had me, and you could have done anything you wanted. That first night, when we shared the room at that inn. You stole back your knife from under my pillow."

"You were asleep!"

"I wasn't. But my point isn't that you stole it back. It's that you stole it back so you could shave, since you had no razor. And then you replaced it, because you didn't want to worry me or let me be unarmed for longer than necessary. Niall, you were a man with a weapon, standing over the bed of a defenseless woman. And what did you do? You gave the weapon to the woman. You didn't take advantage when it would have been easy. I couldn't forget that. And I've been in your power since then because I know that about you. That's the only kind of power I'll accept."

And then Heather spilled out all the words she'd been holding in her heart. "Look, the truth is that I'm terrible at admitting I'm wrong. I was certain that what I wanted was a life on my own. I hated living with Uncle Cyril and the way I dealt with my unhappiness was by dreaming of far-off places."

"You have a list of cities you want to see," Niall said.

"I did, but when I think about that list now, it's not as fascinating as it used to be."

"No?" He looked more hopeful.

"I mistook independence for happiness. I thought that anyone or anything that could stop me from doing what I felt I needed to do was unbearable. But that's a very childish way of looking at the world. I…I think I've grown up a little."

Niall ran a finger along her jawline. "You've always seemed quite grown-up to me. I mean, except for the time you locked yourself in your room, or ran away, or spilled out chamber pots on the floor."

"That happened only one time, and it was strategic," she countered.

His lips quirked up into a smile. "I thought it was brilliant. Unexpected. Just like you."

She took a deep breath, looking into the eyes of this man, who so easily offered his protection the moment they met, and then continued at every turn to be the most honest and straightforward man he knew how to be, no matter what obstacle blocked their path. Her next request was the most difficult of her life.

"Niall, will you forgive me?" she whispered, shamefaced at thinking of all she'd put him through.

"Forgive you for what?"

"All the cruel and stupid things I said before. It was easier to blame you than admit to myself that I'd made a mistake."

"Which mistake was that?" He frowned. "Sleeping with me at last?"

"That wasn't a mistake!" she insisted. "I wanted that with all my heart. My mistake was not trusting you after I learned what you stood to gain from me. I just assumed the worst."

"You didn't have much previous experience otherwise," he told her. "Losing your parents, then being betrayed by your uncle…"

"That's no excuse. You've been honorable since the beginning."

"Well, I was also an idiot. I really did think we could marry and unmarry as long as it was just words. It was without doubt the worst solution to your problem."

"I don't know. I think many aspects of it worked out rather well." Heather raised her face to his, kissing him softly. Then she said, before she lost her nerve. "Niall MacNair of Clan MacNair, will you please, please, please keep me as your wife?"

Niall regarded her for a long moment. Then he said gruffly, "Aye, I think I will."

The second consummation was just as moving as the first. Heather discovered several additional ways that Niall could bring her to complete rapture, and when they stretched out together afterward, she twined herself about him so he couldn't escape (though in fact, he showed very little inclination to escape). As she surveyed him after he'd fallen asleep, she smiled to herself, very content with her highlander.

Epilogue

SO, THERE WAS ANOTHER WEDDING after all, which occurred on October the sixth, ensuring that Heather was fully capable of consenting to marry whoever she liked. It took place in a church, what with Niall being the MacNair and the Earl of Carregness now, and too important a man to go skipping off getting married like the common people.

Because everyone was already gathered (indeed, *everyone*, since many MacNairs had come for the funeral of the old laird, and stuck around when they heard about all the rest of it), it seemed prudent that Ian MacNair would marry Brenna McGlashen on the same day.

"Oh, I love a double wedding," Camellia said. "It's so romantic."

"Saves on the cost of food, certainly," Daisy pointed out.

Next to Camellia, the duke and duchess of Lyon sat in the second pew. They were joined by Viscount and Viscountess Norbury (Lord Norbury having been strongly "encouraged" to join the festivities).

Before the wedding, Niall had openly wondered if Heather had also gone to school with a princess or two.

"I'm the princess," she returned. "Remember how you

rescued me from my tower?"

"You rescued yourself, love. I just provided the transportation."

"Much more than that." She kissed him. Heather decided that most conversations with Niall should end with a kiss. It made for very pleasant conversations.

It was arranged that Ian and Brenna should marry first, and the wedding of Niall and Heather would immediately follow. Many people were confused by the fact that Lord MacNair was marrying his wife all over again, but others told them that since it meant a day off and free food and drink, the reasons why were really not all that important, were they?

Never let it be said that the Scots are a foolish people.

Brenna and Ian were beaming as they exchanged vows, and they accepted the well wishes of those in the close pews, but had to wait for the full celebrations until the next event. They took their place in the front pew with the MacNairs, and everyone turned back to see the second bride of the day.

Heather fairly danced down the aisle, unescorted by anyone. She wore a pale blue gown, a woolen tartan of the MacNair colors draped over it and secured with a wide ribbon at the high waistline. Her strawberry blonde hair had been pinned up in a chignon, with a few curls framing her face. A sprig of heather was tucked in among the curls as well. Everyone commented that she looked *almost* Scottish. High praise indeed.

Before the vows, the Viscountess Rosalind sang, choosing a Scottish ballad of enduring love that sounded particularly beautiful in her clear voice. By the last verse, she could have asked the audience for anything and she'd have received it.

Heather and Niall faced each other, with Father Ross

on the step above, reading out the time-honored ritual.

The words were essentially the same as those the blacksmith had read out, but Heather was paying attention this time. She promised to love and honor Niall, and may have mumbled on the part about "obeying." He in turn vowed to take care of her until death, adding under his breath that she'd probably be the death of him.

The priest (a man of discretion) didn't so much as crack a smile, saying only, "I now pronounce you man and wife."

"Very well, it's done now," Niall whispered. "You're married to me forever."

"Thank God," she breathed. "Kiss me, Niall MacNair."

He did, and she decided that forever might be long enough.

ABOUT THE AUTHOR

Elizabeth Cole is a romance writer with a penchant for history. Her stories draw upon her deep affection for the British Isles, action movies, medieval fantasies, and even science fiction. She now lives in a small house in a big city with a cat, a snake, and a rather charming gentleman. When not writing, she is usually curled in a corner reading...or watching costume dramas or things that explode. And yes, she believes in love at first sight.

www.ingramcontent.com/pod-product-compliance
Lightning Source LLC
Chambersburg PA
CBHW020754190726
48285CB00006B/2020